Temptations

Tattoos and Tears
Book 1

By Amiee Louise

This is a work of fiction. Similarities to real people, places, or events are entirely coincidental.

TEMPTATIONS

First edition. September 30, 2025.

ISBN: 978-1968759254

Written by Amiee Louise.

Prologue

Sam - 1 Year Later

To whoever reads this?

First off, know this: all roads lead to the same outcome.

To this very point in time.

I am not a coward, and I most certainly am not a quitter; I'm simply just a man. As I sit here alone in my apartment in the dark and deathly silence with the world at my feet with only the moon, my thoughts, and my thundering heartbeat for company, a lone tear runs down my cheek. I stare frantically at the bottle of vodka and the pile of pills scattered on the floor in front of me, reflecting upon my life so far—my biggest achievements, and my biggest regrets. They all seem to flash before me and then pale into insignificance. Everything is insignificant, void without her in my life. My soulmate, my reason to live. Gone, and it's all my stupid fucking fault; I'm the one to blame. If I hadn't left her alone and unprotected, none of this would have happened. I let it happen—the only woman I have ever truly loved, taken away from me by a cruel twist of fate. No words could describe the depth of feeling I felt for her. My Peyton ... she was my whole world.

As I'm sitting here sobbing like a big fucking pussy boy and knocking back vodka neat from the bottle, the burn of the alcohol soothes the agonising, debilitating ache in my chest as it slides silkily down my throat. My mind starts to swim with thoughts of her, thoughts of the good times we shared together, the soaring highs and the heartbreaking lows, only to be over-ridden by thoughts of how she died. Ever since it happened, it has felt like I have been living my life underwater, struggling hopelessly to reach the surface, all the days blurring into one to create an endless fucking misery. The world carries on around me as if nothing has happened, completely oblivious to my pain. I feel so empty, so hollow and desolate. As if half of my being is missing and I can't function without that vital part.

1

The mixture of emotions barrelling through me make me feel like I'm a teenage girl on the blob, hormones raging and my mood all over the shop. First, I'm happy, smiling and reminiscing about the good times we had, the stupid lame jokes only we would understand. Next, I'm consumed by inconsolable rage, such intense anger, and all I want to do is fucking murder someone. Then, I'm so sad and so miserable it consumes me that I actually want to die and end this car crash I call my life. The only memories I have left of her are the ones I hold in my heart, a collection of photographs, and my memorial tattoo. I can't control the tears; I can't spend longer than half an hour in the studio recording with the band because I can't concentrate long enough to lay down the vocals for even half a song on our new album. I can't sing a single line without breaking down into uncontrollable floods of tears. Today was her memorial, and it was the single hardest thing I have had to do in my whole entire life.

I feel responsible for her death, like somehow all this was my fault. It happened right in front of me on a large screen, and there was nothing I could do to stop it. I felt so helpless, completely fucking useless because there wasn't a single thing I could do to prevent it.

I get this crippling sense of loss every time I think about her. I can't eat, I can't sleep, and I can't close my eyes or dream without replaying the moment she died on an endless loop in my mind. At this point, I am struggling to care about anything, least of all the band and my music career. My career means nothing to me now without her; she became my sole reason to go on stage, my driving force to perform in front of thousands of adoring fans. She saw beneath my stage persona, she saw the real me, on and off stage.

The truth is, I have never really known true love before I met Peyton. You know the kind, the butterflies in your stomach, you can't go to sleep until you have heard her voice, and you can't see anything or anyone else apart from each other. You crave that one person like a drug, and she was my drug of choice. When we were in a room full of people, I only saw her; it was as if we were the only two people in the room.

With Peyton, it was instantaneous. I know it's cliché, but the first time I saw her I wanted her. I knew one-hundred-million percent that she was the girl for me, even though she hated the fact that I was a rock star and she was immune to my charms when we first met.

Touring and being on the road with the band, we don't get to have proper 'normal' relationships like your average twenty-something males. One-night stands, bunk-ups on the tour bus, and blowjobs in dressing rooms is more our style. It keeps the complications of real relationships to a minimum.

I had the ability to switch off my feelings before I met her. It was just mindless sex with the other women, the lust without the love but never with her. Sex without feelings I could cope with, but she opened up feelings in me that I had never experienced before. She showed me how to love and be loved in return.

My head spins as I take a long pull on the bottle of vodka and the sudden realisation hits me like a ten-tonne truck—I can't go on living my life without her in it. I just can't, I can't see my future anymore. My life is pointless and totally fucking meaningless. She was everything, my whole universe.

Frantic pounding begins on the door while muffled voices shout outside, but I ignore them and scramble to my feet. My head feels like it is about to explode; I just want it all to fucking stop. Stumbling to the kitchen, I grab a knife from the chopping block before staggering back into the living room, unable to focus on my surroundings. I collapse onto the floor, hitting my head as I fall. The large bread knife I am holding clatters to the floor and echoes around the room. I reach for the knife and crawl towards the vodka and pills.

My vision is blurry, but I still manage to cut my wrist deep. The pain bites into my consciousness, and I'm relieved to feel something for the first time in weeks. The deep crimson as it flows down my arm brings a flashback to the forefront of my mind and an overwhelming feeling of guilt washes over me like a tidal wave that I wasn't there to help her. She was all alone and I couldn't protect her. I scream hysterically to try to repress the image and hack carelessly at my wrist, watching as the blood drips onto the floor. I grab a handful of pills and down the vodka.

I am so fucking sorry.
Life Sucks. Fuck you, see you bitches on the other side. Peace out.
Sam x

1

Peyton

From an early age, there were three things that were etched into my Peyton Harper DNA, into my very core as a human being. First thing being, celebrate the skin you were born into, which is where my love of tattoos comes from. Every piece of ink on my skin represents a part of my life, every tattoo has a special significant meaning to me, and every single one has a story behind it. I believe that everyone should celebrate the skin they were born with and decorate it with beautiful art. Art galleries have paintings hanging in them; I happened to have my art etched on my body. This is why I got into tattoos.

The first time I picked up a tattoo machine I knew it was what I wanted to do for the rest of my life. I have ink running through my veins. I started from the bottom as an apprentice at the age of eighteen just out of school and worked my way up with pure passion and determination. With hard work, I became a qualified, fully-fledged tattoo artist. It's difficult being a female in an industry which is mainly dominated by males. It is a pet hate of mine that people think that I'm incompetent as a tattoo artist just because I'm a woman.

I work in a tattoo studio in Islington called Saint Sinner Ink, which is owned and managed by Seb Henry. Yes, *the* Seb Henry, celebrity tattoo artist. He has tattooed the likes of Premiership footballers, music stars, rock bands, TV, and movie stars. People come from everywhere just to be tattooed by him. He is a legend in the tattoo industry at thirty-four years old.

He was reluctant to give me a real chance at first until I kept showing up at his shop every day with my portfolio, begging him to look at it. One day, I think he was so fed up with me pestering him, he finally looked, and by the expression on his face, he was instantly impressed. He gave me an apprenticeship that day, taught me the tricks of the trade, and the rest, as they say, is history.

Now, Seb is my brother from another mother, one of my heroes, and one of my closest friends. It is because of him I'm slowly building up a reputation in the tattoo industry as one of the best female artists in the city at just twenty-six years old. Seb is fiercely protective of me, and he has been one of the biggest influences in my life so far. I am eternally grateful to him for giving me an opportunity when no one else would.

Secondly, if you've got it, flaunt it—my mum's wise words.

You see, my beautiful, dizzy, yet sophisticated mother, Sophia Harper—or Sophia Bailey as she was known back then before she married my dad—used to be a pin-up model in the late 1970s, and her face was famous worldwide. Her photograph was used in fashion magazines to advertise world famous brands and on billboards all across the globe. In her heyday, at just a fresh-faced, innocent, nineteen years old, my mum was beautiful—not that she still isn't beautiful. She had legs up to her armpits, quite an ample bosom—which I definitely inherited!—amazing bone structure, and cheekbones to die for. Everyone knew her face; she was a rival to the likes of Twiggy and Jerry Hall. She stood alone on the beauty stakes with her unusual, wide, violet eyes and an air of vulnerability. Which my dad, Max Harper, recognised the day he met her when he was assisting the photographer on a poster campaign. He was instantly attracted to her, and to this day, he still says that every time he looks at her she mesmerises him.

The third and final thing that has been etched into my DNA since I was a child, is that if things sound like they're too good to be true, then they're bullshitting. It was because of the last thing that I met *him*.

Samson Newbolt, a.k.a Sam or Bolt, as his army of fans call him, the lead singer of rock band Rancid Vengeance.

As soon as I laid eyes on him, I knew he was trouble with a capital-T. He was cocky, arrogant, and rude. He was literally everything I despised in a man. Nevertheless, I was drawn to him like a moth to a flame.

I saw underneath the bravado; saw him as a vulnerable, shy, insecure guy who hides behind his stage persona. He was sort of beautiful, and he made leather trousers look sinful; he was the epitome of sex. He oozed sex appeal from every pore in his fine, over six feet of hard-muscled, red-blooded man body. What attracted me to him in the first place were the most gorgeous intricate tattoo designs inked all over his body, but I was kind of indifferent and immune to his charms to begin with. I was determined to make him work if he wanted me as his girlfriend.

He was what music magazines described as 'rock's bad boy', and he was always being photographed falling out of nightclubs with a different woman—sometimes more than one—in the newspapers and gossip columns. He was what my best friend, Ruby, and I described as an 'attention seeking man whore'.

His onstage look was leather trousers with chains and studs, black eyeliner, black, leather-studded cowboy boots, vests, and tight t-shirts to show off his muscles and tattoos. He wears a silver thumb ring on his right thumb and a leather-spiked cuff on his left wrist. The only thing that separates him from his stage persona is his offstage look. Offstage, he wears skinny jeans instead of leather trousers—they do things to his arse that should be illegal in most countries! He also wears black Converse trainers and he alternates from tight fitting dress shirts with the sleeves rolled up to show off his tattoos and rock band t-shirts. In the media, he is as well known for his style and fashion sense as he is for his music.

I had heard of his band, and I was familiar with their cool, guitar-driven, all-out rock anthems because Ruby was a huge fan and played their songs constantly, but I was seemingly unfamiliar with the members. At least, until Seb got a call from their manager, J.D. Apparently, the band was in town, and they all wanted new tattoos. They had heard Seb was the best in the business; the band had seen his work and wanted him to tattoo them.

Cue the rollercoaster that I was about to embark upon.

2

Peyton

"Rubes, please hurry up, babe; I'm going to be so *bloody* late for work."

I share a modern two-bedroom studio flat in Camden Town, overlooking the famous Camden Market, with my best friend, Ruby Logan. She is *the* sweetest, most beautiful, loving girl I have ever met. With long shoulder-length, jet-black hair, flawless olive skin and dark hazel eyes, she has the perfect figure with curves in all the right places, stands at five foot eight, and has legs that seem to go on forever; she could totally be a model. We have known each other since we were five years old and we grew up together. She is like a sister to me, and we have always been close, ever since I can remember. Her family was my family, and my family was her family.

She has an older brother, Remy, who is three years older, and he served in the military. I lost my virginity to Remy at the age of seventeen, and we were close until he joined the army at the age of twenty. He and Ruby were once estranged due to their parents, Pearl and Ray, favouring Remy when they were younger. Previously, this has caused epic arguments, and I have been a shoulder to cry on on many occasions. Remy moved to America six years ago after he lost his leg below the knee due to a roadside bomb. Despite her former estrangement with her brother, she still keeps in contact with him via phone and Zoom and visits him when she can. She is extremely stubborn and refuses to admit when she is wrong.

She is also *the* worst timekeeper and has a very annoying habit of taking at least an hour in the bathroom *every* morning. I have to be up early if I want to get in the bathroom before she starts her daily routine.

Ruby is like clockwork; you can literally set your watch by her. She wakes up to her alarm of 'Dance with the Devil' by Rancid Vengeance and bounces out of bed at six-thirty AM with such enthusiasm for the day ahead before going to the kitchen to switch on the coffee machine. While quietly humming a random tune, she pads across the floor, trying her hardest not to wake me up before my alarm goes off at seven thirty AM. Next, she heads to the bathroom, turns on the shower, and her routine begins.

I love her to death, but she is such a colossal pain in the arse! Especially when we have to be somewhere, whether it's work or a social thing. I very often have to go across the hall to our neighbour, Danny Debonair, who is one of my best friends and the loveliest flamboyant, gay drag queen—also known as Debs on the weekend—just so I can get my morning shower and get to work on time.

"Give me ten minutes, sweetie."

I roll my eyes to myself. *Here we go again.*

"It doesn't matter; I'll go to Danny's. I'm going to be so fucking late."

Irritated, I turn to stomp out of the flat in my pyjamas. I hate lateness with a passion; it is one in a long line of my many pet hates. The bathroom door flings open, and I am slapped in the face with a haze of perfume-filled steam, the remnants of Ruby's morning routine.

"It's all yours, babe."

She blows me a kiss, and she knows I can't stay mad at her for too long. It takes me less than half an hour to shower, get dressed, style my hair, and apply a little make-up ready for the day ahead. The flat is filled with the aroma of freshly-brewed coffee—my favourite smell in the world. I don't have blood running through my veins, I have pure caffeine! I don't function if I don't have my morning coffee fix; it is an essential way to start my day. Ruby leans casually against the doorframe of my bedroom sipping her steaming mug of coffee.

"Do you want to meet for lunch today, babe?"

Ruby works in advertising. Her boss, Isaac Carter, lets her do what she wants, when she wants, and she is paid substantially for it. Mainly because she is fucking him. She takes two-hour lunches and takes full advantage of the company credit card. She calls it 'entertaining clients'. She has him wrapped around her little finger and right where she wants him, usually between her thighs.

"Yeah, why not? I'm not sure what appointments we have today, but I'll call you if anything comes up."

She smiles sweetly.

"You know Seb loves you. I'm sure he'd let you take two-hour lunches if you asked him."

I laugh. God, I love this girl. I admire her ballsy attitude and the fact that she uses her assets to get *exactly* what she wants.

"Seb *so* does not love me, Rubes. He is one of my best friends; that would just be plain weird!"

We both giggle like a pair of schoolchildren.

"Seb and Peyton sitting in a tree, K-I-S-S-I-N-G."

I throw a rolled up pair of socks at her. She is always meddling in my love life; I give her an A+ for persistence. The truth is, I'm happy being single at the moment. I never have any luck with men. Especially after the way my last relationship ended.

My ex-boyfriend of three years, Callum, cheated on me. The worst thing about that was the fact I caught him cheating on me when I let myself into his flat. He was banging her like a shit house door on his kitchen worktop. When I walked in, he didn't stop, he carried on defiantly. She was screaming like a porn star in the throes of passion, and I was screaming, shouting, and throwing things around like a crazy person, but he still didn't stop. That image will be forever burned into my retinas and my consciousness for as long as I live. I've had a couple of one-night stands as a way to get over him—call it blowing off steam—but I find it so hard to trust guys after what he put me through.

I grab my bag, kiss Ruby on the cheek promising to meet her at lunch, and leave for work. My beloved restored and imported, 1967, electric-purple, Chevy Camaro SS is in the garage being repaired, so I have to grin and bear the stuffy, crowded tube journey from Camden Park Road into work. I put my earphones in and connect to my phone, my Spotify playlist instantly coming to life. I'm instantly transported to my own little bubble, which makes the twenty-minute ride more endurable.

When I get to the shop, the familiar calming smell of disinfectant greets me. Seb is there before me as always with my morning pick-me-up; a cup of Starbucks' finest coffee waiting for me at my workstation—my usual: a large espresso macchiato, one sugar, easy on the milk. Seb is six foot six inches tall, well-built and very muscular from his short time in the S.A.S and work as a doorman. He has tattoos on every inch of his body, except for his face, head, and hands. He has dark, intense blue eyes, he has dark hair but always keeps it shaved bald and a crooked smile that makes his harsh features seem softer. He is oddly sexy in a rugged kind of way, and I could possibly fancy him if we weren't as close as friends.

"Mornin', honey bunny!"

Seb always greets me with the same bright and breezy phrase every morning. Even though it is from the film *Pulp Fiction*, it warms my heart that he thinks of me so affectionately.

"Morning, pumpkin!"

We both laugh at the *Pulp Fiction* reference as I take the lid off my cup of coffee.

"How are you today?"

I take a welcome sip of my coffee, and he nods while setting up his workstation.

"Great, babe. In fact, I'm more than great; I'm pretty fan-fucking-tastic, actually!"

His smile is infectious, and I am grinning like a Cheshire cat just watching him. He is so animated and fun to be around. Especially when he gets excited about something.

"Have you heard of the band Rancid Vengeance?"

Yes, I think to myself. *Ruby wakes up to their music* every *single fucking morning. I am beginning to get sick of hearing the same opening guitar riff.* I keep my thoughts to myself as I reply to his question.

"Erm ... yeah. Ruby is obsessed with them, especially the guitarist, Flash."

Seb laughs and rolls his eyes as if to say, *'Why does that not surprise me!'*

"Well, their manager, Johnnie Diamond, called me earlier."

We both smirk at the sheer ridiculousness of the way the name Johnnie Diamond sounds.

"The band wants me to tattoo them. No, actually, correction, they want *us* to tattoo all four of them today."

My eyes widen. Ruby would literally faint at this piece of information, and she would *insist* on showing up at the shop or just make up an excuse to drop by. I nod coolly, trying to take in the fact that we will be tattooing four of the most famous rock gods in the world.

"Are you sure you're up for this, Peyton? Rockers can be *very* demanding, especially world famous ones."

I take a sip of my steaming cup of coffee, take off my leather jacket and my black and white skull scarf, roll up the sleeves of my shirt, and shrug nonchalantly.

"'Course I'm up for it Seb. I can handle a bunch of rock stars; how hard can it be? Bring it on!"

Seb gives me his bright dazzling smile and winks.

"That's my girl," he says enthusiastically, twirling me around and pulling me in for a big bear hug. He smells of musky cologne and pure masculine Seb.

Ruby and my parents always tease that I should get together with Seb because we are perfect for each other. We're always innocently flirting, and we feel so comfortable around each other. However, it would be weird; Seb is like a big brother to me, and I actually love my job, so I want zero awkwardness between us. I certainly do not want to ruin our great friendship and amazing work rapport. He releases me from the embrace, and I let out the breath I didn't know I was holding.

I walk over to my workstation and start to get prepared and set up for the day ahead. The shop is a fairly large and open space, decorated in a simple black and white, with black and white floor tiles throughout. There is a large work area, split into three sections for Seb, Parker, and me. Each station has a leather chair that folds down into a bed, a small desk for drawing up designs, a sterilising machine, and each has a large shelf with various inks and a drawer section which holds spare needles, tubes, grips, tips, machines, and latex gloves. At the front of the shop, there is a reception booth with a large desk, a comfortable, leather office chair, Apple Macbook, printer, and telephone. There is a small waiting area with a small leather sofa and a coffee table in front of it with various tattoo magazines and design books neatly piled up. The walls are adorned with various tattoo designs which customers can choose from and a few large professional photographs of our best work taken by my dad.

"What time are the band getting here?"

Seb looks at his watch.

"Around ten, babe. They've requested for us to cancel and reschedule all of today's appointments, which I've already sorted, so we can focus solely on them. I figured we can split the four between us and do two each, split a morning and afternoon session, seeing as Parker's taking some time out."

Parker Mitchell is the other tattooist in the shop. He is Seb's sister's fiancé and is an amazing tattooist specialising in black and grey and portrait tattoos, and he is really close to Seb. He is a little on the serious side and extremely shy. The minimum conversation I get out of him is a casual nod and "Good morning Peyton." Seb's sister Riley, who has become a very close friend of mine since I started working here, is pregnant—a few months away from giving birth to twins. Parker is on paternity leave and spending as much time with her as possible. There is just Seb and me in the shop for the time being until we can find some temporary cover.

"Are you good with that, babe?"

I nod.

"Yep all good with me, honey, bring it on!"

We smile at each other. His deep blue eyes lock onto mine, and I can sense there is more to come. He talks quickly.

"Are you okay to work through lunch? I'll make it up to you, I promise."

I roll my eyes. He looks at me with the cutest puppy dog eyes, and he knows I can't resist. I sigh loudly, and he smirks. He knows I'll give in in the end.

"Yeah 'course, it better have plenty of chocolate and alcohol involved."

"Dinner and a movie, with all the chocolate you can eat."

My eyes widen. *Was Seb really asking me out on an actual date?*

As if he reads my mind, he says, "Not like a date or anything, just as friends."

We both instantly relax, but the air around us is charged with something more.

"Dinner and a movie sounds awesome as long as I get to pick the movie!"

We both smile at each other.

"Okay, none of that soppy bollocks, though. Chick flicks are banned! I'll even throw in hour-long lunch breaks, and I'll break your station down at the end of the day, so you can get home early for a whole month."

I move across the shop towards him and reach my hand out to him.

"It's a deal, it's a steal, it's the sale of the fucking century!"

We love quoting movies at each other; it is kind of our thing—sad, I know!—*Lock, Stock and Two Smoking Barrels* being both our favourite film. We are cut off by the sudden eruption of screaming girls and camera flashes outside the shop. Seb and I look at each other with our arms folded, eagerly awaiting our famous customers.

"I think it's safe to say the band are here."

3

Peyton

The shop door swings open, and there he is. This Adonis of a man, a tall, muscled, tattooed God. Seb pushes my chin up and whispers, "Pick your jaw up off the floor, babe you're starting to drool!"

He looks in my direction, smirks, and winks. I can feel a flush creep up my neck, and my face feels like it is on fire. I'm not sure if I'm hot, embarrassed, or just burning for *him*. He and five other men walk casually into the shop one by one. There is definitely *way* too much testosterone in the room at this precise moment. Subsequently, the tattooed God's eyes lock onto mine as he takes off his Ray Ban aviator sunglasses, and I can't look away. He is what a Ken doll would look like if there were a rocker version. Chiselled, masculine, and so handsome it's devastating. He has black hair styled into soft spikes, which I am itching to run my hands through, and a beautiful dazzling smile. Which, I don't doubt he uses to get his legion of female fans to drop their knickers for him. He has his stage name, Bolt, tattooed on his knuckles and black and grey skulls on the back of each hand. He has a small tunnel in his right ear, his lip and eyebrow pierced—a definite turn on for me in a man. He smiles the cutest crooked smile that brings out the infamous dimples that Ruby is always talking about. He is toned, lightly tanned, and has the most mesmerizing green eyes which remind me of sparkling emeralds.

"Hey, beautiful."

His voice is husky, and the way he utters those words sounds like honey and drips pure unadulterated primal sex. I instantly feel the heat between my legs. He is wearing the tightest leather trousers that leave nothing to the imagination and a black vest top with a leather waistcoat over the top, which shows off his rippling tattooed muscles. My mind starts to wander, and I begin imagining what his strong arms would feel like wrapped around me while he is on top of me mindlessly fucking my brains out. I quickly snap myself out of that fantasy and regain some sort of composure. I try to convince myself that underneath the image and persona is just another customer I have to tattoo. I must remember to repeat the mantra, *'He's just another customer.'*

"Hi, and I'm not beautiful, I'm Peyton."

As I say those words, I see something flash in his enticing green eyes. I don't know whether it is surprise, disbelief, or pure lust. His bandmates all erupt with laughter, and I extend my hand out to him. He takes it, and as he touches my hand, I feel electricity run through me. Something tells me by the expression on his face that he feels it too and he clears his throat.

"I'm Bolt, but you can call me Sam."

He smiles shyly and reluctantly lets go of my hand, not taking his eyes off me for one second.

"You got owned by a girl, Sammy!"

His bandmates are equally as beautiful as he is. The guitarist that Ruby is so enamoured with extends his hand out to me and plants a gentle kiss on the back of my hand.

"I'm Jax. Any girl that can shoot down our Sammy is definitely the girl of my dreams!"

I laugh at his introduction. He is shorter than Sam by at least a couple of inches; he is lean, tanned and has collar-length, spiky, dirty-blonde hair that sticks out in all directions and looks perfectly mussed. He also has a goatee beard, and as he speaks, I see the light glint on his tongue stud. He is wearing combat shorts, a black Nirvana t-shirt with the infamous yellow symbol on the front, and has full leg, arm and neck tattoos covering his body. He has the cutest, wide, deep-hazel eyes, and he instantly reminds me of a small puppy. *Definitely a Labrador!*

"I'm Peyton,"

Seb comes to stand protectively next to me.

"We should get started, babe; you take Jax and Sam, and I'll take Brody and Lucas, is that all good with you?"

I nod.

"Yep, that's all good with me, Seb. Do you have designs, or do you want me to draw something up?"

Sam casually saunters forward, and Jax rolls his eyes.

"I've got a rough idea, but I think I need a second opinion."

Jax pulls a face behind Sam's back, and I try to hide my smile.

"Okay, that's all good with me. Jax, what about you?"

He nudges Sam out of the way, and Sam grabs him in a playful headlock.

"I'll get her to tattoo *'emergency exit'* on your arse if you're not careful, Jax."

They both laugh.

"Bring it on! It can't be any worse than your lightning bolt."

Jax looks at me and leans in as if to share a secret with me.

"That's where he got his band name from; he lost a bet, and he has a lightning bolt tattooed on his arse!"

He winks cheekily, and I laugh. I instantly sense the love, loyalty, and a strong friendship between the two men standing in front of me. Sam leans closer to me.

"I can show you if you want?" he asks flirtatiously.

"In your dreams, rock star."

All the band members in the shop erupt with laughter again.

"You're wounding my ego, sweetheart."

He smirks, but I sense that it's an alien concept for a woman to turn down Sam.

"If you want to follow me."

Jax and Sam comply and follow me to my workstation. I sit down in my comfortable, buttery, leather chair and spin round to my drawing desk.

"Which one of you wants to go first?"

Sam volunteers fervently, and we go through the ideas he has for his tattoo. As he is speaking, I'm drawing up an idea, but I can sense his eyes on me as my pencil dances across the page. I look up and catch his stare as he looks away. I push the piece of paper with the design on across the table to him.

"Is this what you had in mind? We can make some changes if you're not happy, and I can freehand some parts when the design is in place."

He shifts himself closer to me, and I can feel his breath tickling my cheek. I can smell his Joop aftershave tingling my nostrils. It smells so sweet; I instantly feel full of want and lust for this beautiful man standing beside me.

I turn my cheek and look into his dazzling green eyes. He looks back at me, and a smile spreads across his face.

"No, it's perfect," he whispers, and I'm not sure if he is referring to my design or to something completely different. I nod and smile, suddenly feeling a rush of nerves. I stand up and clumsily stumble. He is instantly at my side and steadying me in his strong arms. His corded muscles undulate as he sets me on my feet.

"Th ... Thanks," I stutter like a complete idiot.

"You're welcome, beautiful."

He smirks, catches Jax's eye, and winks. Jax makes the *'okay'* sign with his fingers and winks back.

What the fuck is wrong with me? I'm never usually like this with men. Well, he is not just an ordinary guy, is he? He is a mega-famous, stupidly-rich, rock god, and it's not every day I get to be in the presence of such a gorgeous man. I clear my throat and don't meet his eyes. *You can do this, Harper, he's just another customer.*

"I'm just going to make a stencil, and we can get started."

I move across the shop towards the thermal copier machine, and I can feel his eyes burning into me. Seb is also at the machine making his stencil.

"Are you okay, babe? I saw the little stumble as you got up. Is someone in love?"

Seb raises his eyebrows and laughs teasingly. I punch him on the arm and frown.

"No, of course not, don't be stupid. He is just like any other client."

Seb nods sceptically.

"Hmm, yeah, of course he is. If he was, you wouldn't be blushing like crazy right now."

My hand automatically goes to my face.

"See, you do like him. I've never seen a guy affect you so much. There's nothing wrong with that, but just be careful, though, honey. Yeah?"

I smile and nod. Seb, bless him, always looking out for me. I must make an effort to be more professional around Sam. If Seb noticed, then obviously his bandmates have spotted it too. Seb brushes my arm reassuringly as he goes back to his station. I put my design on the thermal copier machine and punch in the correct size. I wait for the stencil to come through the machine and take it back to my station, mentally cursing myself for not asking him before I made the stencil where on his body he wants the tattoo. *Really professional, Harper.*

He is in deep conversation with the guy that came in with them. I'm assuming he is the infamous John *'Johnnie Diamond'* Dalton. He is a tall, lean man with a slightly tanned complexion, black hair in an old-fashioned side parting, dark-brown eyes, and black-rimmed glasses. If I were to guess his age, I would put him around late thirties. He and Sam are talking in hushed tones as I approach. There is something in the way Johnnie is looking at Sam that doesn't sit well with me. He has his hand firmly and protectively on Sam's arm. I can't quite put my finger on his strange behaviour and odd body language. However, I dismiss the thought immediately. They stop as I get closer and both turn to smile at me.

"Peyton, let me introduce you. This is our manager."

I nod, and he regards me intently with his beady brown eyes.

"Johnnie Diamond, right?"

He smiles a bright-white, dazzling smile, and it is so white I am almost blinded.

"John or J.D, please, sweetheart. Pleasure to meet you, Peyton. Such a beautiful name for such a beautiful lady," he says in a prominent East London accent. He shakes my hand, and I smile politely.

"Pleased to meet you too, J.D." I look to Sam. "Are you ready?"

He smirks and nods enthusiastically. "I was born ready, babe!"

Why does he see innuendo in everything I say? *Bloody men!* I sit down in my leather chair and set up my tattoo machine. A deep-purple, personalised, Micky Sharpz Iron Hybrid machine with silver tribal patterns and my initials, P.H, on the top encrusted in Swarovski crystals. This was a gift from Seb after finishing my apprenticeship. It is the most thoughtful gift I have ever received, and I haven't used another tattoo machine since. Some people have lucky pants and lucky socks; I have my lucky tattoo machine.

"So, where are we putting this design, Sam?"

He pats his large, muscular, calf muscle. My face suddenly flames at the thought of a gorgeous man like him sitting inches away from me in just his boxers. He senses my embarrassment.

"I have some shorts on the bus to change into. Don't look so worried, babe."

He laughs so hard he clutches his toned stomach, lifting his t-shirt slightly, so I get a glimpse of his defined six-pack and hard-ridged abs. I lick my lips at the sight, and he smirks, knowing he is having an effect on me. *Arrogant bastard.*

"Yo, Bolt, dude, are you making that chick all hot and bothered? I can see her flushing from here!"

Lucas shouts in an American drawl from the waiting area across the shop. I'm glad my embarrassment amuses you, Bolt. I think back to our earlier conversation, "He has lightning bolt tattooed on his arse." I start to fantasize about seeing him naked, and I bite my lip subconsciously at the thought.

"She looks like she is having naughty thoughts about you, mate!"

Brody teases from the tattoo chair, and all the other band members laugh apart from Jax who is giving a look of disapproval to Brody. I sense a mutual feeling of rivalry between the two bandmates.

"Better not disappoint then had I, babe?" Sam winks and gets up. "I'll be right back, I need to change."

He gets up and sprints out of the shop, flanked by his bodyguard. I get the tattoo ink ready into small pots and set them up at my station. I need an emergency pep talk with Ruby.

"I'll be two seconds, Seb."

He salutes as he has already started tattooing Brody. I go into the back of the shop and pull my mobile out of my bag. I have three missed calls from Ruby; I dial her number from my purple Samsung Flip 4 phone. She answers on the second ring.

"Hey, babe. Finally, I've been trying to call you."

I clear my throat. "Hey, Rubes, it's been such a ... hectic start to the morning. I'm sorry, babe."

"Oooh, come on. Spill." She giggles.

"We're tattooing the guys from Rancid Vengeance."

Ruby practically squeals down the phone.

"Oh, my fucking *God*. Why didn't you call me sooner? You know I fucking *love* that band. The guitarist Flash is so bloody hot!" she says dramatically, and I roll my eyes to myself. Ruby gets stupidly excited about random stuff, and she is obsessed with celebrity gossip. I never see her without the latest copy of *OK! Magazine.*

"So, come on, what are they like? Who are you tattooing? I want all the gossip!" she says in a rush, and I pause for a moment. *God,* this girl can be so exasperating at times.

"Peyton, are you still there, babe?"

"Yeah, yeah, I'm here, they're ... really cool. Interesting guys. I'm tattooing Sam and Jax."

She screams again, and I hold the phone away from my ear.

"Fucking hell, Rubes, calm down, I do need my hearing, you know!" I laugh nervously.

"You've got a crush, haven't you?"

I forgot that Ruby could read me like a book. That girl literally knows me better than I know myself sometimes, and she knows what I'm thinking before I even think it. It is actually quite scary at times. I lower my voice.

"Ruby, Sam is seriously, ridiculously, smoking hot; I don't know what the fuck is wrong with me."

I put my hand to my head, and she laughs.

"I know, he is beyond hot. I love his voice, it's amazing, and I could practically orgasm just listening to him."

She sighs dramatically, and I lean heavily against the wall.

"What do I do, Rubes? I'm literally losing my mind around him, and I've tripped over my own feet *and* made a complete tit of myself," I say in a rush, glad to offload to her. She laughs again.

"There's nothing wrong with having a crush, babe. Does he like you, too?"

I let out a breath. "He keeps making innuendo and flirting outrageously. Seriously, I swear, that boy has no shame."

She shrieks, "*Oh, my God,* he *does* like you! You two are going to make seriously beautiful babies! Please, please, can I be a bridesmaid?"

It's my turn to laugh; I knew talking to Ruby would give me the boost I needed.

"Don't get ahead of yourself, babe, he is probably like that with all of the women he meets. Look I can't meet you for lu—"

Before I have finished my sentence, she jumps in. "Fuck that, I'm coming to the shop! I'll be there in ten, love ya."

Before I get a chance to protest, she has hung up. I put my phone away and go back out into the shop. Sam is sitting in the chair with his arms cockily folded behind his head, and he has changed into denim, cut-off shorts. His bare legs are crossed lazily at the ankle. He smiles as I approach from the back room.

"Sorry about that, are you ready?"

He nods, and that familiar smirk crosses his face again. I crouch down on the floor and place the stencil on his leg, careful not to linger too long on his perfect, powerful, tanned, muscular leg. I pat his leg, feeling that all too familiar electricity run through me as I touch him. I peel off the stencil with a trembling hand, and the outline is there for me to follow.

"Do you want to look in the mirror to see if the positioning is good?"

He looks at me. "Positioning looks good from up here, babe," he says suggestively, and our eyes lock. I can sense the sexual energy between us, and I instantly know there would be fireworks in the bedroom. I feel liquid heat between my legs, and my nipples start to harden underneath my vest top. I get to my feet and brush the thoughts aside. I pat the leather bed.

"Could you hop up here for me, please?"

He gets up and leaps enthusiastically onto the bed. He turns on his side, leaning on his elbow, and his long legs stretching out in front of him. "Like this?" he whispers huskily, and I understand what Ruby meant about his voice driving her to orgasm.

He smirks and seems to be getting off on making me squirm under his gaze and his sheer proximity. I put on my black rubber gloves and clip my hair away from my face. , I start the tattoo machine, and begin tattooing him, fully aware of his red-hot gaze on me. This is going to be a very long day.

4

Peyton

I am halfway through outlining Sam's leg, and we are both silent throughout. The awkward silence is broken by the bell on the shop door sounding. In breezes Ruby, her pink, leopard-print, Paul's Boutique handbag on her arm and three of cups of coffee in a Starbucks tray.

"Hey, sweetie."

She comes over to my station, and I finish the line I am tattooing. I stop for a break, pulling off my gloves and setting them down on the table.

"Hey, babe."

She kisses me on the cheek, and I am suddenly filled with the sweet, familiar scent of her Ed Hardy perfume and feel a calm confidence just from her presence. I instantly feel better and perk up; I feel more like myself again.

"I bought you some coffee; I thought you could do with a break."

Seb looks over smiling. I roll my eyes, and he shakes his head. That girl could exasperate any sane person. It's lucky I have known her for so long, even though I wouldn't have her any other way.

"I bought one for you too, Seb."

She puts on her sweetest smile and takes his coffee over to him, her heels clicking across the shop floor. Jax's eyes are fixed on her, and his jaw is practically scraping the floor. He nudges Lucas sitting next to him and whispers something in his ear. Brody shouts from the tattoo chair.

"Think with your brain and not your dick, Jax!"

Clearly, Brody is the joker. She puts Seb's cup down on his desk and struts confidently over to Jax, flicking her hair over her shoulder as she approaches him.

"Hi, I'm Ruby."

She offers her hand to him, and he takes it. She has such a way with the men; no wonder they fall over themselves just to be around her. Across the shop, I have stopped to take a long sip of my second cup of Starbucks espresso macchiato, one sugar, easy on the milk. The warm liquid sliding down my throat gives me the caffeine boost I was craving. Sam swings his long, lean, perfect-muscled legs off the bed and leans down.

"Can I get a sip of that please, darlin'? I'm spitting feathers."

I offer him the cup, and he takes a long sip. There is something strangely intimate and erotic about sharing a cup of coffee with him.

"Thanks, babe." He winks. "Do you fancy coming out with me when you're done? Maybe I could take you to dinner? I can be *very* persuasive."

I pause and bite my lip. *Was Sam, the rock star, really asking me out on a date?* I immediately think he is joking.

"Are you fucking with me?" I lower my voice, and his face turns deadly serious.

"I *never* fuck about when it comes to a beautiful woman."

The way he says those words has me practically panting with want, but I have to get my wayward thoughts in check and think rationally. Could I really see myself dating a rock star, the lead singer, and one-quarter of one of the biggest rock bands in the world? He has sold over twenty million albums worldwide, what have I achieved? An apprenticeship in tattooing and I work for Seb Henry ... Okay, maybe that *is* an achievement in itself. But could I really handle being photographed by the paparazzi, our pictures being splashed all over the papers and gossip columns, intimate details of our relationship for all to see, stories of sordid affairs, exes coming out of the woodwork? *Hell no!*

"Sorry, I don't date arrogant, cocky rockers; it's not my style."

He smiles and nods.

"Wow, playing hard to get. Okay, I can deal with that," he says calmly. He gets back up on the bed. I pull on a fresh set of gloves and continue tattooing him.

"So, how long have you worked here?"

I inwardly sigh. "Are we really going to do this? The small talk, like you're really interested in a girl like me."

He frowns. "Just because you see my life splashed all over the tabloids doesn't mean you get to judge me. I wouldn't have asked if I wasn't genuinely interested. Seriously."

He rolls his eyes and looks genuinely hurt; I suddenly feel bad for shooting him down so quickly.

"I'm sorry, it's just—"

He stops me. "Come out with me, please."

I shake my head. "I'm not going to be subjected to fangirls swooning over you, interrupting us for photos and autographs at every available opportunity."

He smiles that mischievous dazzling smile, and it disarms me momentarily.

"Is that jealousy I sense?"

I roll my eyes. "Why would I be jealous? I hardly know you."

He bites his lip piercing seductively. "Green is a colour that definitely suits you, babe," he says huskily, and I ignore the heat between my legs. I feel unexpectedly exasperated by this man's presence. With him, I appear to have definitely met my match, which seems to trigger off my defence mechanism.

"You seem to have forgotten my name again. You keep calling me babe. It's okay, my name is Peyton. Do you need me to spell it for you? It begins with a P."

I hear sniggers from across the shop.

"Bloody hell, stop busting his balls, babe, and give the guy a chance."

Sam looks across the shop at Ruby.

"It seems you've forgotten her name too, sweetheart."

"Oh, yeah, silly me, my mistake, I'm sorry, *Peyton*." She emphasises my name and narrows her eyes at me. I know she is trying to tell me to rein it in. Sam smirks mischievously and cocks his pierced eyebrow.

"Are you usually like this around other guys, or is it just me?"

I am stunned into silence. I have *definitely* met my match.

"Wow, no wonder you're single. Assuming you *are* single? I mean, God help the guy if he puts up with you, Miss High Maintenance. He must have the patience of a fucking saint," he says sarcastically. I stop tattooing him and forcefully put my machine down on the table, the clattering echoing through the shop. I rip off my gloves, angrily push my chair back, and get to my feet.

"I'm taking a break," I say sharply and storm to the back of the shop. All eyes of the people in the shop are on me.

I need some air. How fucking dare he judge me like that? He doesn't even know me. I know I probably brought it on myself, but what fucking right does he have to speak to me that way? At this moment, I wish that I had taken one of the other band members. I am so bloody angry; I take a few deep breaths, lifting my face to the sky and relishing the cool air on my skin. It instantly calms me. I lower my head, and I sense Sam's presence at my side. He towers over me and leans casually into the doorway.

"Look, I'm really sorry, Peyton; I didn't mean to be such a dick."

I shake my head, infuriated.

"I'm not usually like this around people, women, in particular. I'm complete and utter mush around you. Ever since I set foot in the shop and laid eyes on you ... You do something to me, Peyton, and I've never felt like this before, like *ever*."

I note the sincerity in his voice and look up at him. I instantly feel bad for shooting him down at every opportunity, but I can't resist cheekily bantering back.

"Was that a line?"

I smirk, and he gives me a heart-stopping mischievous grin.

"You caught me! I think it might have been!"

We both laugh, and he brushes my arm. Our eyes lock, and I can't look away.

"Please tell me it's not my imagination. You feel it, too, don't you?"

His hand is still on my arm, and I nod subconsciously. He leans close to me; I can feel his warm breath and light stubble grazing my cheek.

"I'll ruin you, Peyton."

His voice is gravelly and dripping with seductive allure. I look up at him and our eyes lock—I can't look away. My heart starts beating faster, and I bite my lip. I feel bold and empowered just being in this man's presence.

"Maybe I want you to."

He smiles a wickedly devilish smile, and if I'm not mistaken, he growls.

"Is that a challenge?"

He raises a pierced eyebrow, and I laugh. This man definitely has a way with women. At this moment, I would do anything he asked me to.

"Please, come out with me," he whispers huskily. I know I can't look away, and I can't bring myself to say no. I am drawn to him like a moth to a flame.

"Okay, I'll come out with you."

His face lights up, and he tucks a strand of my hair behind my ear. My whole body feels like it's buzzing and tingling all over at his slightest touch.

"I'll see you at seven, then."

I nod, hardly believing that I have actually agreed to go out with him. *Shit. What the fuck have I let myself in for?*

5

Peyton

We stand still outside the shop for a few minutes, and I relish his closeness to me. It oddly comforts me knowing that he is so interested in me. Folding my arms for added warmth, my teeth still chatter from the afternoon chill.

"Are you cold?"

I nod.

"Just a little. Actually, I'm bloody freezing!"

We both laugh, and he silently wraps his strong arms around me, pulling me close to his hard, muscled chest. I feel his warmth as he runs his hands up and down my back; goose bumps instantly break out from his touch.

"There's something between us, Peyton."

As he says those words, I feel a delicious tingle between my legs and feel myself dripping with desire. Pure want, need, and white-hot, unbridled lust. I watch as he looks into my eyes, then drag my gaze to his sensual mouth and plump, full lips. I imagine his mouth on my clit, licking and sucking, driving me to a shuddering, Earth-moving orgasm. I shake myself back to reality and vow to use that fantasy with my vibrator as soon as I get home.

"You feel it too, don't you? I know you do; the way your eyes glaze over when I'm near you tells me everything I need to know," he whispers with his nose in my hair. He has me reduced to a trembling mess, and I can't hold back the facade any longer. *I want him so badly.* I boldly wrap my arms tighter around him and pull him closer to me by the soft hair at the nape of his neck. I press my lips hungrily to his and kiss him passionately. Slowly feeling the contrast of the softness of his lips and the roughness of his stubble. His velvet tongue softly caresses mine as he kisses me as if his life depends on it. When I pull away, we're both breathless with burning, molten desire.

"I'm sorry ... I ..."

Running my fingers across my lips, I wonder if I just dreamed that kiss. My lips feel deliciously bruised—I most definitely didn't imagine it. He clears his throat before he speaks, his clear green eyes blazing.

"Don't be sorry. I'm not."

I look at him, shake my head and hurry back inside, leaving him standing there with a satisfied grin plastered across his handsome face. All eyes turn to me as I walk back into the shop; I must look flustered. A look of concern crosses Seb's face.

"Is everything all right, babe?"

I nod and put on my best fake smile. "Yep, everything's all fine and fabulous, thanks, Seb," I say a little too enthusiastically. Something in the way Seb looks back at me says he doesn't believe that everything is OK. Ruby looks over and frowns as if signalling: *I know something just happened, and you're going to bloody tell me what it is whether I have to drag it out of you, missy!*

Fucking hell, why do I have to be so transparent to those close to me?

Sam walks casually back into the shop with his hands tucked into his pockets, and Jax throws him a knowing look. Sam smirks and shakes his head. He goes back to the leather bed and settles himself back, ready for me to carry on tattooing him. If I'm honest, I don't know if I can go on tattooing him without wanting to rip his clothes off. I bite my lip subconsciously at the thought, and Brody wolf-whistles.

"Oi, oi! Looks like she's having those naughty thoughts again, dude!"

The shop erupts in raucous laughter, and I feel myself burning with embarrassment. I suddenly start to feel faint and unsteady on my feet, the feeling that reminds me I haven't eaten today. Sam leaps down off the bed and is at my elbow within seconds.

"Are you OK, babe?"

A look of concern mars his beautiful yet handsome features. I look into those captivating green eyes of his and nod. He pulls me towards my leather chair and sits me down gently. Crouching in front of me, he caresses my face softly with his calloused hand.

"Are you sure you're OK? You look really pale."

From the corner of my eye, I see Seb jump up from his seat, and within seconds, he is at my side, crouching on the opposite side from Sam.

"Peyton, are you sure you're OK, honey? You don't look too clever."

I nod and smile. "Please, stop fussing, sweetie. I'm fine. I haven't eaten today; I missed breakfast, that's all. I need to finish Sam's tattoo then I'm going to lunch."

Seb shakes his head. "No, you're not, babe. You're going to lunch, and then you're finishing his tattoo. Is that all right with you, mate?"

Sam looks at Seb, and it's clear on Seb's face that it isn't a request. He clears his throat.

"Yeah, sure, man, no worries. The lady needs to eat; I'll even take her to lunch myself."

I get to my feet and nudge them both out of the way, feeling bereft at the loss of contact from Sam's warm hand.

"Hello, guys, I am here, you know. I'm not bloody invisible, I can speak for myself. I'll finish Sam's tattoo, I'll be an hour tops, and then I'm going to lunch with Ruby. Do you want anything bringing back, Seb?"

He nods, and Sam looks dejected at my blatant brush off at his offer to take me for lunch.

"Yeah, one of those southern fried chicken wraps with sweet chilli sauce would be awesome, a Mars bar, and a can of Red Bull, please, babe."

He puts his lips to my forehead and kisses me gently. He and Sam look like they are in some sort of Mexican standoff—a good old-fashioned pissing contest! It is quite amusing to watch, and it takes everything in me to stifle my giggles. Sam hops back up onto the leather bed once more while I put on a fresh pair of rubber gloves, so I can carry on with his tattoo. We spend the next hour in a comfortable silence, the atmosphere between us crackling with sexual energy. The sly glances, the affectionate winks, the knowing smiles. My heart is beating so fast and hard I think everyone in the shop can hear it. Another half an hour passes, and I have finally finished Sam's tattoo. The skull, microphone, guitar, roses, and music notes with the words 'Vengeance Forever' in script lettering around it on Sam's calf is something I'm proud of.

"All finished."

Sam looks down, the look on his face is full of wonder and awe. I can tell by his expression that he is rendered speechless by the design.

"Babe, it's perfect, I love it."

I smile shyly.

"They really weren't lying when they said you were the best female tattooist in the business."

"Thank you."

Seb comes over and inspects my work. "Babe, that's ... bloody amazing."

He brushes my arm; the look of pride and affection in his eyes is there for all to see.

"You should photograph it and use it for the shop portfolio, if Sam doesn't mind. Then you're definitely going to lunch no arguments."

I nod and salute. "Yes, boss!" We both laugh.

After photographing Sam's leg on the shop's Nikon D810 camera, I spray antiseptic on his leg and clean the excess ink off. When I'm rubbing Vaseline on the finished tattoo and wrapping it with cling film, Ruby comes over, sighing dramatically.

"*Finally*, I'm bloody *starving*."

Rolling my eyes, I go to the back of the shop to get my coat and my bag, so we can leave for lunch. As we're leaving, I can't help but notice that Sam can't tear his eyes away from me.

Ruby links my arm, and we walk down the high street to a quaint little bistro called Swingin' Eli's Bistro. This place is a regular haunt and a particular favourite of Ruby's and mine. It is famous for its homemade, authentic, southern American food. The decor is old school swing, with paintings of old swing artists scattered on the walls. We are in there so often we sit at the same table by the window.

The owner, Eli, knows us by name and knows exactly what we're going to order. He is a tall, southern American man in his mid-sixties, with coffee-coloured skin, greying hair, and a wide, infectious smile. When we walk in, he has our drinks ready: a strawberry milkshake for Ruby and a caramel hot chocolate for me.

"Good afternoon, Peyton, Ruby." He nods politely.

Ruby and I take our drinks from the counter and sit down opposite each other at our favourite table. I'm barely in my seat before Ruby practically squeals in my face.

"Oh, my *God*, Peyton, what the fuck is going on with you and Bolt?" I roll my eyes, and she points her finger at me. "Before you think of lying and saying nothing, I call bullshit."

Hanging my head and smiling coyly, I say, "We kissed."

Ruby shrieks, causing the other customers in the shop avert their attention to us.

"Could you please be a little less dramatic, Rubes?"

She laughs. "Sorry, but my life would be so boring without drama, babe. If I'm not having my own drama, I like to live vicariously through yours!" she says dramatically. Her enthusiasm makes me smile.

"Come on then, I want details. Spill, was it a peck or a full-on snog? What was it like? Did he use his tongue? At one point, I actually thought the shop might spontaneously burst into flames with the sexual tension."

I feel myself blushing. "We kissed when I went out to the back of the shop for some air, it was a full on snog, tongues as well, and he asked me to go out with him."

Ruby is about to shriek again, I just know it, so I shake my head and hold my finger up to stop her.

"Please tell me you said, yes."

I nod and bite my lip. "I really like him, Ruby. I know it's mental. I don't usually go for guys like him, and he is a mega-famous, mega-rich rock star. What would he want with a girl like me? I'm sure women throw themselves at his feet on a regular basis. I'm just ... ordinary; he can have any girl he wants."

Ruby rolls her eyes. "There's that fucking self-doubt again. God, I want to kill that bastard Callum for making you feel that way."

Ruby scowls, and I inwardly cringe at the sound of Callum's name.

"Sam wouldn't have kissed you if he didn't like you. From the second I walked into the shop I knew there was something going on with you two. My psychic superpowers told me so!"

We both laugh. I love Ruby so much; I admire her honesty and her ability to read me like a book. The truth is, she is right. Ever since I split with Callum, I have been filled with self-doubt, self-pity, and a sense of worthlessness that I can't seem to shake.

"What are you thinking about, babe?"

Ruby drinks her strawberry milkshake through a straw and flutters her eyelashes. She has an air of innocence about her which she hides behind her tough, feisty persona. Over twenty years of friendship, we have seen the best of each other and the worst of each other.

"Cal and Sam."

Ruby sighs. "That bastard doesn't deserve even an inch of headspace from you. Sam is your future, and quite clearly, you're going to go out with him tonight, fuck his brains out and wash Callum-fucking-Kennedy out of your system for good. He can't keep doing this to you; you've been split up for like—"

I jump in and stop her. "It's been twelve months, three weeks, and six days."

"You're actually keeping count? God, you need to get laid!"

We both laugh, and I take a sip of my hot chocolate. Our food arrives, and my stomach growls in favour. I tuck into my lunch of traditional, Louisiana, fried chicken with a side of coleslaw—it is mouth-wateringly delicious. Ruby digs into her pulled pork sub roll and side salad. After we finish lunch, we sit for a few more minutes.

"Are you going back to work?"

Ruby pulls a face. "Hell no! Not when you have four of *the* hottest rock stars in your shop right now. I was working my womanly charms on Jax!"

I laugh. When it comes to Ruby getting a man's attention, she is relentless, and she doesn't give up until she has snared him in her trap.

"What about Isaac?"

She rolls her eyes dramatically. "He is my married boss who I shag every now and again. When he isn't getting it at home, he is a nightmare to be around. I just ... ease the pressure a little."

Ruby twirls her hair around her finger innocently, and I shake my head.

"Are you sure *he* knows that, babe?"

She nods. "Of course. I know what I'm doing, I've got him right where I want him, and it's staying that way between us. Now Jax is a whole *different* story. Just think, if I get together with him and you get together with Sam, we can double date."

She claps her hands excitedly. I leave twenty pounds on the table to settle our lunch bill and get to my feet. I feel so much better now that I have finally eaten something. I pull on my coat, and Ruby does the same. I collect Seb's order, we leave the bistro and head back to the shop for round two.

6

Peyton

We get back to the shop in less than five minutes, and I go straight to the back. Seb and I decided we were going to make it into a relaxing space for when we needed a break or just a place to chill for five minutes. It has a comfortable black and zebra print sofa that seems to swallow you when you sink into it, a few beanbags scattered on the black carpeted floor, and framed movie posters adorning the walls. Sam is waiting for me, and I jump as I see all six foot four of him standing there.

"*Jesus*, you scared the living shit out of me."

He smirks devilishly. "Sorry, I didn't mean to scare you; I was like a caged animal while you were gone."

His voice is soft, and he has his hands shoved in his pockets in such a boyish way. I smile, take off my jacket, and stow my bag away. He reaches towards me, tucks a loose strand of my hair behind my ear, and strokes my face.

"You're like a drug to me, Peyton. I don't know how to deal with these kinds of ... feelings."

I look up at him and lean into his hand.

"*Fuck*, what are you doing to me?" he curses, and I'm not sure whether it is directed towards himself or me.

"Sam, I really like you, I mean I really, *really* like you, and it's the same for me too."

I feel so conflicted, and when he is looking at me with those intense green eyes, I lose all sense of rational and coherent thought.

"Why do I sense there's a but coming?"

His hand is still on my cheek, and he is regarding me intently.

"Is there something going on between you and Seb, is that it? Is he standing in my way? Do I need to kick his arse?"

My eyes widen, and I dismiss it immediately. "*Jesus Christ!* No, of course not! Seb's my boss, and we're close friends, that's all we've ever been and all we ever will be"

A look of relief washes over his face, and he visibly relaxes.

"You should know it's not like that; I need to get to know you first. I can't just jump in feet first. It's not that simple for me. God, I wish it was."

I sigh. He nods, and something about the way he looks at me knows I'm holding back.

"Then I'll wait, for as long as it takes. We can take it slow, I just *know* I have to have you."

I get a warm feeling inside at the closeness and his sweet words. Every second I am alone with him makes me want him even more. He leans down and kisses me tenderly on the lips. I ache for him, and I know I am falling fast and hard for this man, which usually spells trouble for me, so I pull away at the unwelcome thought. A look of confusion crosses his face.

"What's wrong, babe?" he asks softly, and I shake my head.

"I ... Erm ... I-I can't ... I should get back to ... work," I manage to stutter and go to leave. He grabs my wrist, and his green eyes look into my blue.

"I meant what I said. I have to have you, Peyton. I'm a patient bloke; I'll wait as long as it takes, and I'll take what I can get with you. Give me a chance; please just don't walk away from me."

He subconsciously makes circular movements on the back of my hand, and I instantly get goosebumps from his touch. I sense a presence outside the door, which unnerves me.

"Someone's outside," I whisper.

"Fuck them, they can wait. I really don't know how I'm going to hold out until seven."

We both smile at each other, and I can feel my brain turning to mush every time I'm within touching distance of him.

"I have to get back to work."

He nods but looks disappointed. He leans down, pulls me into his hard chest, kisses me gently on the lips, and strides out of the back room. I hear voices and instantly know that it was J.D who was standing outside the door. There is something about that man that doesn't sit right with me—he is unnerving and creepy. I shake the feeling and go back out into the shop. Ruby looks at me and winks while I take Seb's lunch over to him.

"Here you go, babe."

Seb is sitting at his desk with his hands behind his head.

"Thanks, honey, you're a total star. I'm taking a break. I have some paperwork and stuff to do out back. Will you be OK out here on your own for a while?"

Seb code for: '*Are you going to be OK out here on your own with these unruly rockers?*' I smirk and nod.

"Yeah 'course. I need to make a start on Jax's tattoo anyway."

Seb points with his head. "If you can tear him away from Ruby. That girl is ... extremely fucking challenging." He rolls his eyes and we both laugh. "Give me a shout if you need anything, honey."

Winking, he heads for the back of the shop.

"Jax, you're up," I shout.

Brody laughs. "He is definitely up, darlin'!"

The boys in the shop burst out into raucous laughter. Jax stands up and makes his way over to my workstation, hops up on the leather bed—which has been wiped down, sprayed with anti-bacterial spray and laid out with a fresh paper towel ready for my next client. I also find that my workstation and my tattoo machine have been thoroughly cleaned, sterilized, and wiped down. *God bless you, Seb Henry!*

"OK, so what did you have in mind, Jax?"

He explains to me what tattoo he has in mind, and I make a rough sketch. When I'm finished, I show him the design.

"Something like that?"

He nods and smiles. "Yeah exactly like that, love; it's like you read my mind! You're fucking awesome!" he says, excited. I can't help but laugh at his child-like enthusiasm.

"I can freehand some of the other parts as I go. Where are we putting it?"

He laughs. "Well, I'm kind of short on space but have a wicked space on my upper thigh."

I nod—another awkward place. *Great. What is it with these guys and wanting to purposely embarrass me?* Although I should be used to tattooing awkward and embarrassing body parts by now, it never gets easier. I make a stencil on the thermal copier, and when I get back to my station, Jax has shamelessly removed his combat shorts and is casually sitting on the leather bed in his bright, neon-green boxers. Sam is standing across the shop, arms folded, biting his thumbnail, his thumb ring glinting in the afternoon sunlight. He is visibly trembling, and I sense that he is silently seething at seeing Jax half-naked. From the corner of my eye, I see J.D go towards Sam; he brushes his arm, and Sam snatches his arm away. There is definitely something going on, so I vow to ask Sam later. I place the stencil on Jax's upper thigh, and as my fingers make contact with Jax's skin, I hear Sam growl from across the shop.

"Do you need to look in the mirror to check the positioning?"

He shakes his head. "Looks great from here, love."

His smile is infectious, and I find myself smiling along with him. I set up the needle and put on my black rubber gloves ready for my afternoon tattooing session. I can sense Sam's eyes burning into the back of my head as I line Jax's tattoo of a rocker skeleton playing a flaming guitar with the words 'Vengeance Forever' just like Sam's. I am suddenly interested in the other two band members' tattoos and whether they have the exact same words. Ruby comes over and leans in to check my progress on Jax.

"Nice work, babe."

She smiles, and her eyes lock with his.

"So will you come out with me tonight sweets?" Jax confidently asks Ruby. I hope she follows her own advice and says yes. She deserves to be truly happy with someone and not just a quick fumble with her scumbag married boss. She flashes a flirty smile.

"Yeah. OK, sure."

Jax's face lights up. "Excellent, I'll pick you up at seven thirty?"

She nods coolly, and he hands her his mobile phone.

"Could you put your digits in my phone please, love?"

She takes his phone and quickly types her number into his phone then hands it back to him and smiles.

"OK, I'll see you then. I have to get back to work now, though," she says to both of us. *Ugh, now I need to get home before she does, or I'll be waiting forever for the bathroom!* She will take extra-long being as she is going on a date. I stop tattooing for a second and kiss her on the cheek.

"I'll see you back at the flat, sweetie."

She looks at Jax. "See you at seven thirty, rock star."

She turns and leaves, swinging her hips as she goes, and Jax's eyes follow her as she leaves. Jax adjusts himself in his boxers, and I avert my gaze. Sam is quietly boiling with rage at the other end of the shop still trembling and deep in hushed conversation with J.D.

"Fuck me, that girl makes my dick hard."

I laugh at his shameless comment and pick up my tattoo machine to start again.

Four hours pass quickly before Jax's tattoo is complete.

Looking down at his thigh, he exclaims, "Babe, that is totally awesome work. I love it, you are a total bloody legend."

He hops down off the bed, hugs me, and goes over to the other guys. They seem suitably impressed with what I have designed and tattooed on his leg. They all compare tattoos, and I think our work for today is complete. Seb comes over and puts his arm around my shoulder, pulling me close to him.

"Great work today. You did some amazing tattoos. I'm so proud of you."

His praise warms me inside. Since Callum, my confidence and self-esteem have taken a beating. Seb's words make me feel fulfilled and worthy of my position at the shop. He kisses my forehead, and I see Sam's shoulders tense at Seb's gesture. J.D comes over and stands next to us.

"Thank you so much for cancelling your appointments and fitting the guys in at such short notice. I'll see that you get substantially reimbursed for your losses today."

Even the way he speaks has me on edge. You know that niggling feeling when you instantly take a dislike to someone? I instantly took an intense dislike to J.D, and with him standing so close to me, I feel my skin crawl.

"Seb, could I get a word, please?" J.D looks at me but gestures to Seb.

"Yeah, sure, give me a second, mate. Peyton, do you want to get going? I said I'd break your station down and wipe down for the day."

I brush Seb's arm. "Are you sure? I can stay if you want me to, honey."

He dismisses it. "Don't be silly, babe. Go home. You've done such a fantastic job today you deserve to let your hair down and unwind."

"If you're sure. Thanks, Seb."

I kiss him affectionately on the cheek, go to the back of the shop, and put on my coat. I sense a presence as I bend down to retrieve my bag—I automatically assume it's Sam.

"Couldn't stay away, could you?"

I smile and get to my feet. My smile fades as J.D is standing in front of me.

"Sorry, sweetheart, lover boy Sammy isn't available right now."

He looks smug and pushes his glasses further up his nose.

"What the fuck is your problem? Sam might think the sun shines out of your arse, but I've got your fucking card marked, *J.D.*"

I emphasise his name, and he tightly grips my arm.

"Owww, you're fucking hurting me, get your filthy hands off me."

He leans closer to my face, and I can feel his stale breath on my cheek.

"You see, there are some things that you don't know. Sam is fiercely loyal to me as his close friend and his manager. You fucking stay away from him; he doesn't need groupie whores like you upsetting him. It's blatantly obvious he is smitten with you, so back the fuck off, little girl, or you're going to get yourself seriously hurt."

I struggle against his steel, vice-like grip.

"Get the fuck away from her *now,* John."

I hear Sam's gruff, stern voice from the doorway. Spinning around, I kick J.D square in the balls, catching him off-guard. His eyes are glazed, and he drops to his knees, clutching his crotch, but he doesn't say anything.

"That's for grabbing me, you fucking prick," I spit before rushing to the doorway.

"Are you OK?"

I nod, but I am physically shaken by the incident. Sam brushes my arm, and I flinch. A look of concern washes over his features, and his voice is soothing.

"Hey, it's OK, I'm here I promise. I'm not going to hurt you, and I'm definitely not going to let anyone else hurt you, babe."

His muscular frame towers over me and pulls me into his hard chest for a hug. He tenderly kisses my forehead.

"Go home, Peyton, I'll sort this."

I look up at him for reassurance, and he cups my face in his hands.

"Go. Everything is going to be OK, honey, I promise; you're going to have to trust me." He winks to reassure me. "I'll see you at seven."

He smiles that panty-dropping smile and I reluctantly go back out to the shop, hearing the sound of Sam and J.D arguing.

"See you tomorrow, honey bunny," I tell Seb who is breaking down my station. I stand on my tiptoes and kiss him on the cheek.

"See you tomorrow pumpkin, love ya."

As I walk to Highbury tube station, I am hit with a blast of cold air. I put in my earphones and connect my phone, and for the second time today, I am transported to my own little world ready for my journey home.

7

Peyton

When I get back to the flat, I kick off my shoes, put my bag and coat down, and then call out, "Rubes?"

My voice echoes through the flat, and I'm met with nothing but silence. I am secretly happy that I have beaten her home and don't have to wait an hour to use the bathroom. After I do a little victory dance, I make my way to the bathroom, lock the door, and look in the mirror. Immediately I notice the rosy glow on my cheeks. I am not sure whether it is from the cold or the fact that I have a hot date with an equally hot rock star tonight. I am oddly excited and feel kind of nervous about seeing him again.

I turn on the shower, strip off my clothes, and climb in. I pull the curtain across and switch on my waterproof phone dock, and soon the bathroom is filled with steam and the dulcet tones of Amy Winehouse singing about love being a losing game. Letting the hot water sting my back, I reflect over the day so far. Meeting the members of Rancid Vengeance was the highlight of my day—the prospect of a brand new chapter in my life on the horizon fills me with a renewed purpose and fresh hope.

Then I think of J.D. and the creepy way he was with Sam. He grabbed me and threatened me as if I was a cheap groupie whore. I only met the bloke today, and I already hate him. That is a record even for me; I usually give people the benefit of the doubt, but there is something in the way he acts around Sam that seriously unnerves me. Frankly, it scares the shit out of me, and I vow to ask Sam exactly what is going on when I see him later.

It has been a while since I have been on a date. I haven't really been part of the active dating scene since I split with Callum just over a year ago. This date with Sam is a big deal to me and is my introduction back into dating and the whole romance thing. After I finish my shower, I go into my bedroom and turn my stereo up full blast and instantly recognise the song that is playing. It is a song by Rancid Vengeance called 'Whispers of Hell' on the radio. I start to think that it might be a major sign that this thing with Sam is the real deal. Quickly, I style my hair poker straight and apply natural-looking makeup with a daring splash of red lipstick to finish the look.

I hear the door of the flat slam shut, and I know that Ruby is back.

"Hey, babe."

She breezes in and greets me in her sing-song voice, which lets me know she is in a really good mood. I stand in the doorway of my bedroom with my GHD hair straighteners in my hand.

"You're back early. Are you getting ready for your hot date?" she asks.

"Yeah, Seb offered to break down my workstation for a month if I took a late lunch to tattoo the band."

Ruby matches the smile that's been plastered on my face all day.

"That boy loves you. Men are like buses: you wait a long time for one, and then two show up at once. Actually, that's not strictly true. Seb's been under your nose for what, eight years?"

I roll my eyes and stick my tongue out at her, halting her rather annoying inquisition.

"Anyway, I need your help with something to wear tonight."

Ruby laughs. "Smooth change of subject, babe! I like your style. Yeah, I can give you a hand. Give me a second. I'll get us some wine."

She kicks off her shoes, takes off her coat, and puts her bag down. Then she pads into the kitchen. She returns with a bottle of white wine and two glasses. "What choices have we got? Or do you need to borrow something of mine?"

She sits down on my bed, opens the wine, and pours two large glasses. Hanging by a coat hanger on my wardrobe door is a black, corset dress with a full ruffled tutu skirt and another black, knee-length, tea dress with white skulls on the front.

"Both little black dresses. Love your choice, babe, definitely very you!" She winks as she sips her wine.

"Are you planning on skipping straight to dessert and getting lucky, or playing it cool?"

I sit with a thud on the edge of my bed. I take a large gulp of wine, and the cold liquid instantly warms my insides.

"I'm so fucking nervous, Rubes."

She brushes my arm reassuringly. "It's going to be fine, babe. I know it's been a while, you know, since Cal, but the way you two were today in the shop ... He likes you a lot. Actually, I think he might more than like you, Peyton. He's got that ... look."

She takes another sip of her wine, and I sigh dramatically.

"I really like him, Ruby."

She puts her arm around my shoulder. "You want something that says you're staking your claim on him but definitely something that will guarantee you some hot nasty sex! So, go for the black corset dress and those Iron Fist heels. Wear some sexy underwear, that black lacy bra, and those black French knickers with the ruffles, you'll knock him dead."

She winks and takes a sip of her wine before getting up from the bed.

"Now, I need to go and make myself look beautiful for *my* date!"

She rushes out of my bedroom, and I get dressed. Glancing in my full-length mirror, I have to say, I'm impressed with my reflection. Half an hour passes and a text dings on my phone. There is a text from Sam, and I instantly get butterflies in my stomach at seeing his name on the screen.

Hey Beautiful ☺

I'm outside your flat

See you in a sec

S x

How the hell did he get my address and my phone number? I'm sure I would have remembered giving it to him. Pushing that thought aside, I grab my clutch bag with my phone, keys, purse, lip-gloss and a hairbrush in it.

"Wish me luck," I tell Ruby.

Ruby looks at me and wolf whistles.

"Excuse me, but where's Peyton?"

We both laugh, and I do one final check in the mirror.

"You look stunning, babe. Now, go get him, tiger!" She blows a kiss, and I leave the flat.

I go down the stairs and out into the cool night air. Sam is leaning against a white sleek Porsche Cayenne 4x4 with tinted windows and the number plate BOLT1. He looks breathtakingly beautiful. His black hair is perfectly styled in a spiky fashion. He's wearing black skinny jeans, black Doctor Marten boots, and a white dress shirt that clings to his muscles. However, three buttons are unbuttoned revealing his chest tattoos, and the sleeves are rolled up to show off his full-sleeve tattoos on both arms. He looks up from texting on his phone, and a grin spreads across his face. Honestly, we make quite the pair with my tattoos on full display as well. Stowing his phone in his back pocket, he meets me halfway.

"You look ... *Fuck*. Wow, you look amazing." He clears his throat, and a shy laugh escapes my lips.

"Thanks, you don't look so bad yourself, rock star."

He laughs too and leans down to kiss me softly on the cheek. My body instantly responds, and my blood feels like it is on fire from just his touch.

"Are you ready then? I've got reservations at this Italian restaurant I know near Chelsea."

I nod—Chelsea; *very swanky*. He comes 'round to my side of the car and opens my door, not taking his eyes off of me for a second. I get in the car and feel suddenly lightheaded from the weight and intensity of his gaze. Sam closes my door, goes around to the driver's side, and climbs in beside me, closing his door behind him. He starts the engine and pulls smoothly away from the kerb. He handles the car with careful control and smooth turns of the wheel. I can't help but think there is more to Sam than the public facade he puts on for his fans—a strong man who conducts the press like a seasoned professional, in quiet control of himself and those around him.

Being in such close proximity to this man is so intoxicating. Just being near him is making me want him so badly; I am physically aching to feel his hands on me again. I lean back in my seat and fidget with my bag.

"Am I making you nervous, babe?"

From the passenger seat, I look over and see the smirk on his face.

I dismiss him immediately. "No, 'course not. Is it me, or is it hot in here?"

I fan myself with my hand and take a breath. *God, I think it might be the wine going straight to my head.* He turns on the air conditioning with a smirk still on his face, and I swiftly change the subject.

"How's the tattoo?"

He nods. "Yeah, it's all good. I want to say thank you so much for designing it and tattooing me."

I smile. "You're very welcome, it was ... my pleasure."

God, Peyton, stop being such a dickhead. I clear my throat and try to block out the irritating voice in my head.

Suddenly, the thought occurs to me about him texting me when I quite clearly didn't give out my phone number or my address, for that matter.

Turning to him, I narrow my eyes at him. Before I know what I'm saying, I blurt out, "How did you get my address and mobile number? I'm pretty sure I didn't give it to you."

He chuckles softly. "I'm an extremely rich man, babe; I've got the best security in the business. I can get anything I want, within reason. I can get access to almost any information I require, whenever I want. Plus, you were being ... difficult, so I didn't want to push my luck."

He smirks. *I was being difficult? How fucking dare he call me difficult!*

"I wasn't being difficult! I was ... keeping you on your toes. You automatically assumed because of your status as a famous rock star I would swoon and fall at your feet just like every woman you meet. But when you realised that wouldn't work with me, you reverted to using your charms."

I know I'm being judgmental and a tad unreasonable, but he evokes feelings in me that I can't even begin to comprehend.

With a laugh, he says, "And what would those charms be, Peyton?"

His voice is low and raspy. *Bastard.* He knows exactly what he is doing and the effect he has on me. I feel slick heat between my legs and suddenly hate him for making me want him so badly. It takes every bit of self-control I have not to make him pull the car over, so he can fuck me hard on the bonnet of his car and bring me to a toe-curling orgasm. I bite my lip at the thought and shift in my seat. *Where the fuck is all this coming from?* He cocks his pierced eyebrow as if he can read my mind as he attempts to suppress a devilish smile.

"Is everything all right, babe?"

How does he do that? I nod and clear my throat to rid myself of the thoughts. We spend the remainder of the journey in silence with a thick sexual tension hanging in the compact space of his car. Before I know it, we are pulling up at the kerb and Sam comes 'round to open my door. He gives his car keys to a man at the door that I recognise from the shop earlier. He is a very tall, at least six foot if not taller, gentleman with skin the colour of dark chocolate, around mid-forties, very well built and looks like he could definitely handle himself in a fight. He nods to both Sam and me. There is a group of around ten paparazzi with cameras outside the restaurant, too. Shouting and calling to Sam, their cameras are flashing wildly.

"Bolt, this way, is this your new girlfriend?"

I instantly wonder what it must be like on a day-to-day basis for him with the press and paparazzi following his every move. The man from the door directs them back and away from us. Sam protectively shields me and reaches for my hand as we walk into the restaurant.

Sam leans down to whisper in my ear, "I'm so sorry about that."

His voice is apologetic. I smile sympathetically, and there is a short, dark grey-haired man wearing glasses in a grey suit standing near the entrance of the restaurant, which I now know is called Ricardo's Italia.

"Ricardo, so good to see you, mate. Thanks for fitting us in at such short notice; I really appreciate it."

Ricardo smiles warmly, and Sam shakes his hand. Ricardo gestures for us to take a seat in a secluded booth at the back of the restaurant and assures us that we will not be disturbed. I sit in the dimly-lit booth while Sam sits opposite me. I know beautiful isn't usually a word to describe a man, but in his case, it is the *perfect* word. His face is perfectly sculpted with high cheekbones; his profile is so striking I can definitely see why all the girls would go crazy over him. He catches me staring at him and licks his lips suggestively.

"See something you like, babe?"

He winks, and I feel myself blushing.

"You're actually ... beautiful"

He throws his head back and laughs. I cringe when I realise I actually said that aloud. *Shit, think before you speak, Harper.*

"Thanks, no one has ever described me as beautiful before; it's not a word generally associated with rockers, but I'll take it as a compliment."

I feel myself blush. He reaches across the table and brushes my hair away from my face. It's such an intimate gesture that my skin breaks out in goose bumps.

"Don't hide yourself away from me. You're gorgeous. I don't want you to ever be embarrassed around me." His voice is husky as he says those words;

I feel that familiar slickness between my legs. What is it about this man that has that effect on me? *Get it together, you silly cow.*

"I'm sorry, I'm just really fucking nervous!" I say in a rush, and we both laugh.

"Don't be nervous. I won't bite ... unless you ask me to!"

I put my head down, but he tips my chin up to face him.

"That was a joke, babe."

"I'm so sorry. I haven't been on a date in so long. Men don't usually have this effect on me. You-you do something to me, Sam."

He shifts closer to me and lets out a breath. "Glad I'm not the only one," he whispers while he strokes my face.

"It's just that you're a famous rock star, and I'm just ... an ordinary girl, a tattoo artist from the city. I'm just kind of overwhelmed by you."

He looks me in the eyes. "I overwhelm you?"

I nod shamefully.

"Look, I introduced myself to you as Sam, not Bolt; he's some cocky, egotistical prick I pretend to be on stage. You're seeing the real me, Peyton, straight up, what's in here." He gently places my hand over his heart.

It's in that tender moment that I see Sam for who he really is and not just some unreachable rock star.

"Don't underestimate yourself. I really, *really* like you, what do I have to do to make you see that? I can see pain in those beautiful blue eyes; I want to be the one to take all that pain away."

He is saying all the right words, and I instantly feel like saying, *'Screw dinner, take me home and fuck me right now!'* But I dismiss that thought. He regards me intently, with my hand still gently placed on his warm chest and over his thundering heartbeat.

"Was it an ex that hurt you?"

I am taken aback by his forwardness and pull my hand away from him. He cocks his head and looks at me, waiting for me to answer.

"Do you really want to talk about exes on our first date?"

He nods. "Why the hell not? We've established that our relationship is different... *unconventional.*"

We both laugh. Although, I was unaware that we had a *relationship*. I thought we were just two people getting to know each other? *Presumptuous, much?*

"OK, I split with my ex of three years just over a year ago; he cheated on me with some filthy slut. When I let myself into his flat, he was shamelessly fucking her on the kitchen worktop. Even though I was going crazy, throwing things around the room, shouting and screaming like a banshee, he still carried on shagging her. It shattered me, and it ripped my heart out completely. He is the reason why I haven't dated in... awhile."

The expression on Sam's face changes.

"Where does he live? I want to fucking kill the bloke, and I don't even know him."

I laugh, but I don't meet his intense green gaze. "There's more, I can tell. You're holding back on me."

How does he know that? "There's no getting anything past you, is there?"

He doesn't smile, nor does he take his eyes off of me.

"I've just gotten pretty good at reading people over the years, that's all."

I clear my throat, but I can't bring myself to tell him the rest. My heart is thundering in my chest, but there is something about this man that makes me not want to lie to him and not keep anything from him. I swallow hard to brace myself and try to still my trembling hands.

"I was pregnant with his baby; I had a miscarriage around two weeks before I caught him cheating."

My eyes glaze over, and I swallow back the tennis-ball-shaped lump that has formed in my throat. *Jesus, do not let him see you cry.* Sam clenches his fist so tight his knuckles turn white.

"I'm so sorry, Peyton. To do something like that is abhorrent to me. What a fucking piece of shit. Now I really want to hurt him."

He runs his hand through his hair, and I know he is trying to control his emotions and his temper at hearing what I had to say.

I let out a sigh. "Don't you think this is a bit heavy for a first date?"

He takes my hand and makes small circles on my palm.

"No, not at all, a date is about getting to know someone. The good, the bad, and everything in-between."

I move back a few inches from him, and it is my turn to regard him intently.

"Your turn."

He laughs and nods.

"OK, fair trade, I suppose. Her name was Piper Gibson, it was around nine years ago, and I was only twenty when the band really took off. We'd known each other since school, we were together for five years, I cheated on her, and I hold my hands up to that. I-I was a complete dick back then. I let the fame thing go to my head in the beginning, and I wasn't a nice person to be around. Booze and women jaded me, but I haven't had a serious girlfriend since her. Strictly one-night things, no feelings just stupid meaningless flings. But I don't want that with you; I want you to be the girl that changes all that."

I bite my lip. He brushes his thumb gently across it, so I release it. The waiter comes over and interrupts with a bottle of Dom Pérignon. He starts to pour it into two glasses then he smiles politely.

"Do you need a few more minutes before you order, Mr. Newbolt, madam?"

Sam looks at him and nods. "Yeah, please, mate. That would be great, thanks."

Sam smiles and tucks a twenty in the waiter's top pocket. He nods and walks away.

"So, where were we?"

I smile. "You were being incredibly sweet."

He strokes my face, and I lean into his hand. The waiter comes over and interrupts us again. "Are you ready to order, Mr. Newbolt?"

Sam rolls his eyes, and I laugh.

"Erm. Two chicken, bacon and mushroom Alfredos, hold the parmesan."

The waiter takes down the order and leaves. I look at Sam and cock my perfectly-plucked eyebrow.

"How did you know that's what I'd order?"

Sam laughs. "We're more alike than you realise, sweetheart."

He winks, and we both take a sip of our champagne at the same time, his eyes never leaving mine. The bubbles instantly come alive in my mouth, and I feel myself start to relax around him. I lean back in my seat and regard him intently.

"So, tell me about you, Sam; I hardly know anything about you."

He smirks and takes another sip of his champagne with a cocky look across his handsome face.

"What do you want to know? I'm in a rock band; I'm the lead singer in Rancid Vengeance with three of my best friends. We've been together for ten years. What else is there to know that you haven't already read in the press?"

He shrugs nonchalantly, and I look at him as if I have been slapped in the face. It is as if the incredibly sweet, sensitive and caring Sam from five minutes ago has vanished. He has been replaced with his stage persona Bolt who is cocky, arrogant, and to quote Sam himself, "an egotistical prick". It is as if there are two completely different people inside him.

"What happened to the Sam from five minutes ago?"

He looks down, and his face drops.

"*Shit!* I'm so sorry, I don't know how to do anything else other than sing and perform on stage. I'm kind of in awe of you, and you're so talented and so incredibly beautiful and— Totally fucking amazing. I feel like a bit of a fraud."

"You're definitely not a fraud. I'm nothing special, I just found something I was good at and something I wanted so badly and went for it. We're the same, you and me, we're connected. I felt that connection as soon as our eyes met, Sam, I've never felt that with a guy before."

He puts his glass down on the table and clears his throat.

"Now I feel like a complete twat. I'm no good at dating or wooing women; I don't usually have to. You're the first girl I've chased."

I pause for a moment and contemplate the difference in both of our lifestyles. He is used to getting his own way, people tending to his every need, the press following him around, women falling at his feet—*quite literally*. It is at that precise second that I vow to make him work to get what he wants with me; I'll play him at his own game. I take another sip of my champagne. He mirrors my action and puts his glass down on the table before cocking his head to the side.

"What are you thinking about?"

I smirk. "Nothing. Just this—you and me." I gesture between us.

"There is going to be a you and me then?"

I pause, and he hangs his head.

"Come on, sweetheart, you're killing me. Don't leave me hanging here. I really like you, and I want there to be an us. You're the first girl I've felt truly open and honest with. I feel a magnetic pull towards you, and I can't walk away, I just can't."

He cups my chin and moves his face closer to mine. The mood completely changes between us in the private booth. The atmosphere is filled with an electrifying sexual energy, and I am burning for him. My core is aching for him to be inside me. I feel that familiar heat ignite between my legs, and I gasp for breath as he audaciously slides his hand up my dress. I want to push him away, but I can't, I want him so badly. He caresses my inner thigh with a feather-light touch.

"You want me, Peyton, I can feel the heat radiating from you, and you want this just as much as I do."

He rasps, and I can feel his scent taking over me, the smell of mint mingled with his Joop aftershave filling my nostrils, the feel of his breath on my cheek and the way his fingers feel against my skin, inching closer to the edge of my knickers.

"Tell me you don't want this; tell me you haven't been thinking about having my cock buried deep inside you," he whispers. I let out a soft moan as his fingers gently tease my slick, aching folds. He leans closer to me and kisses me deeply and passionately on the lips. I grip his shirt desperately. He responds by pulling me closer to him, gently tugging on my hair. Suddenly, there is a presence at our table, and the waiter clears his throat.

"Ahem."

Sam pulls away from the kiss, completely unfazed by the presence of the waiter. He removes his hand smoothly from under my dress and reluctantly moves back from me. I am panting with desire and feel my face flush with embarrassment at being caught in such a compromising position. I can't look him in the eye as the waiter sets our meals down on the table.

"Is there anything else I can get for you both, Mr. Newbolt, madam?"

Sam shakes his head. "No, thanks, mate. We're all good. Just one thing, though? Could you make sure we get no more interruptions, please? If we need anything, we'll let you or one of your staff know. Is that OK?"

The waiter looks sheepish. "Erm, yes, Mr. Newbolt. I'll take care of it personally," he stutters.

"Cheers, mate."

The waiter walks away with his eyes cast down on the floor. We both tuck into our meals in a comfortable silence, but I can't keep my eyes off him. The way the muscles in his arm tense as he lifts his fork to his mouth, the way his eyes sparkle as the soft candlelight hits them. He is pure male perfection; this man mesmerizes me, and I have no idea why. I have never been this way around a man before, not even Callum. I feel a connection with him, and he makes me feel safe like no man has before. I think he is right: I can't walk away, either.

8

Peyton

We finish our meals, and both agree to skip dessert. He settles the bill by placing a few notes on the table. He is the perfect gentleman. A warm fuzzy feeling settles in my stomach, and I am not sure whether it is butterflies from just being around him or the effects of the champagne. He escorts me out of the restaurant with his hand at the small of my back and holds open the door for me. His bodyguard is waiting outside the door for us, and he hands Sam the keys to his car.

"Thanks, mate. Sorry I haven't introduced you. Peyton, this is Cole, my security guy, close friend, and occasional chauffeur. Cole, this is Peyton."

He tips his hat and smiles infectiously. I smile back, and we shake hands.

"It's a pleasure to meet you, Peyton."

His voice is a deep baritone and reminds me of a British Barry White. I smirk to myself at the thought.

"Pleased to meet you too, Cole."

He nods and smiles. I instantly like him—for guarding Sam and for being such a gentleman. I am so used to working with men at the shop and being around men in general. I am treated as if I am one of the lads and it is a refreshingly welcome change to be treated like a lady.

"Do you need me to escort the lady home, Sam?"

Sam smiles and shakes his head, not taking his gaze away from mine.

"No thanks, Cole. I'll take her myself."

Sam winks at me, and I look away from him, unable to hide my shyness. Cole raises his eyebrows questioningly and nods.

"Do you need anything else, Sam?"

Sam shakes his head. "No thanks. You go home to Amy and Addison, make sure you give them both a big kiss from me. I'll text you in the morning if I need anything, mate, and tell Addison Uncle Sammy will see her really soon. Enjoy the rest of your night."

Sam pats Cole on the back and winks.

"Goodnight, Sam, Peyton."

He tips his hat to both of us and walks towards his car, which is parked on the opposite side of the road. Sam unlocks his car and opens the passenger-side door for me. I get in and am instantly hit by the warmth and safety of his car. He goes around to the driver's side and gets in beside me. He starts the ignition, pulling away from the kerb and into the sparse night-time traffic. I lean back in my seat and look over at his profile under the street lamps. I am enamoured with this man, and he only walked into my life a matter of hours ago. I need to hold back, be cautious, and not rush into things, but as soon as he is close to me, all my thoughts are completely scattered. I lean my head back in the seat and softly sigh.

"Hey, are you OK, babe? You seem deep in thought."

"Yeah, I'm fine, just thinking about this—us." I gesture around us. "You literally walked into my life just a few hours ago, and you've completely turned my life upside down. In a good way."

He smiles his dazzling smile again. "That's good to know, I feel the same"

Before I know it, we are pulling up outside my flat. He pulls up at the kerb, unclips his seatbelt, and turns to face me.

"So, am I going to see you again?"

I bite my lip, and before I know what I'm saying, I blurt out, "Do you want to come up for a coffee?"

He laughs, and I bite harder on my lip. *God, I have turned into a walking cliché.*

"Yeah, sure, why not?"

I breathe a sigh of relief and open the car door. He gets out, locks the car, and is at my side in seconds. We go into the foyer of the building, up one flight of stairs and I open the door to my place. I kick off my shoes and the door swings shut. Before I turn on the light, he presses me against the wall. He kisses me deeply, his tongue probing my mouth, gently sucking on my bottom lip. He grabs both of my wrists in one of his hands and lifts them above my head, pinning me to the wall, holding me in place. His other hand slides under my dress and strokes my inner thigh as he did in the restaurant. His lips move from my lips down to my neck, planting a trail of frantic kisses down my neck to my collarbone. I instantly feel slickness between my legs—my pussy is throbbing for him. He slides his hand from my inner thigh and finds the edge of my knickers. I am relieved that I decided to wear my sexy underwear tonight and not my magic, flesh-coloured, pants! He pushes my knickers aside and finds my slick folds begging for his fingers to touch me. He slides a finger inside me, and I moan with pleasure.

"*Jesus*, you're fucking soaking, babe. I knew you were wet for me in the restaurant," he whispers huskily. I'm trembling with white-hot desire just from his touch.

"Oh, God, Sam!"

He is lazily sliding his finger in and out of my wet pussy while I whimper.

"*Fuck*, you feel so good."

I feel my knees start to buckle underneath me. He scoops me up into his arms with ease and carries me across the flat.

"Which one's your room?"

I point to my bedroom and giggle as he carries me to the door. I push the door handle down, and he carries me inside. My bedroom is a modest size with a large king-size bed dominating the room, with a black, feather dream catcher hanging above my bed. I have two, black-lacquer bedside tables on either side; the walls are decorated with purple leopard print wallpaper, black carpet and a series of arty tattoo prints that my dad took, pictures of Ruby and me pictures of my family and friends hanging in black frames on the walls. The window has a wind chime hanging in the centre and blackout blinds to block the sun and the prying eyes of our neighbours.

He drops me down onto the bed and collapses on top of me. We are both laughing, completely comfortable in each other's company, and he suddenly stops and gazes at me. He strokes a strand of hair away from my face and kisses the corner of my mouth.

"God, you are the most beautiful creature I have ever seen. I can't believe my luck. When I walked into the shop today, I thought I was just going to be tattooed and go about my life as normal afterwards. I didn't plan on meeting the woman of my dreams."

Blushing, I manage, "You're amazing."

He kisses me gently on the tip of my nose and sits up. I get up from the bed, suddenly feeling completely overwhelmed by the whole situation.

"Erm, I'll be right back. Don't go anywhere."

He laughs. "As if I would."

I pad across the floor to the bathroom and shut the door. I lean my head against the door and feel unexpectedly besieged by the way Sam is making me feel. I never have sex on a first date, and I *never* bring men back to our flat. He is making me break all my rules, but it feels so ... right. I move over to the sink and look at my reflection in the mirror. My face is flushed; my blue eyes are wide and glossy.

"Get it together, Peyton, there's a gorgeous man waiting back there for you."

I give myself a pep talk, take a deep breath, and drag a brush through my mussed hair. I open the bathroom door and stand in the doorway of my bedroom silently observing him. He looks so at home and gorgeous. He is in my room waiting for me, and I suddenly feel like I can't do this. I just *can't*. I really like him, but our lives are poles apart. Our personalities are so similar, but our lives couldn't be more different.

I give myself a mental shake, *you deserve this man, Peyton, you've waited so long for a man like Sam, and he is not Callum. Stop being so bloody pathetic and get your shit together*. I take a breath, about to step back into the bedroom, and I watch as he runs his hand over my faux animal print journal. My private journal full of my thoughts and memories. He picks it up from my bedside table, and two photos fall out and onto the floor. A picture of Callum and me and our first scan picture. He bends down to the pick them up, and I feel a sense of overwhelming panic rise in my throat. As soon as he picks them up, I know he is going to make an excuse and walk out. I gasp and put my hand to my mouth to stifle my shock as he examines the photos. His eyes become hard, and he growls as he looks at the picture in front of him. He looks up and seems startled to see me standing in the doorway.

"I'm-I'm sorry. I was just—"

I hold my finger up, and I start to feel bile rise up in my throat. I feel like I am going to throw up. My instincts kick in, and before I know what I am saying, I am telling him to leave.

"Go," I manage to whisper, and he looks puzzled.

"Peyton, babe, please."

I shake my head, my eyes brimming with tears. I will *not* cry in front of him. He does not need to see me like this. The aftermath of what Callum did to me— I will *not* put him through that.

"Sam, just go," I say, louder this time through clenched teeth. "Please, just go."

He moves closer to me, and I back away.

"Peyton, it's just me, please," he says, pleadingly, and by the look in his eyes, he doesn't want to walk away. He doesn't want to leave me here like this, but I am fiercely determined. I don't want him to see me this way; I *can't* let him see me like this.

"Sam, please just get the fuck out!" I scream and the flat door slams. I hear Ruby's heels clicking across the floor.

"Peyton? Is everything all right, babe? Has he hurt you?"

I pause, and Ruby grabs Sam's shirt.

"If you've fucking hurt her, I swear to the baby Jesus I will make sure you won't *ever* pro-create," she snaps. Ruby is fiercely protective of me. She looks from him to me at this very fucked up situation unfolding in front of her.

"Rubes, please, he hasn't hurt me, I just want him to go. Please make him leave," I plead, and she loosens her grip on his shirt.

"You heard her; you need to leave now, Sam."

He holds his hands up in defeat.

"OK, I'm going, but we need to sort this out. This isn't over, babe. I'll call you tomorrow, or I'll come to the shop."

I shake my head. "Don't call me, and please don't come to the shop. I've got nothing more to say. I don't want to see you again."

He hangs his head.

"Fine, have it your way, I'll go."

He looks me straight in the eyes, silently begging me not to do this. However, I have no choice. He moves closer to me, and I go to back away. He tenderly takes my wrist and pulls me into his hard chest. I take his scent in for the last time, and he leans down.

"Please, don't do this, Peyton," he whispers in my ear, and his warm breath tickles my cheek. He brushes my hair from my face, and he kisses me so gently on the lips I want to cry. It takes everything I have not to break down in front of him. The truth is, for the first time in a long time, I feel whole and safe. I pull away knowing this will be the last time I will see him. My eyes glaze over at the thought, and before I have hold of my emotions, a tear rolls down my cheek. He wipes it away with the pad of his thumb. I can see it in his eyes that this is hurting him too and he shakes his head dejectedly.

"Goodbye, Peyton."

He kisses my forehead, walks out of my flat, and out of my life. I hear the door close, and as soon as it closes, I break down on the floor in floods of tears—I can't stop them from falling. Ruby sinks to her knees beside me and rubs my back. Silently comforting me, knowing that I'll open up and tell her what happened when I'm ready. I sob hard into her chest, and just knowing that she is there for me is enough to make the tears subside.

"Babe, do you want to tell me what the fuck happened?"

I look up at her with a pained look in my eyes; she nods in understanding and tucks a strand of my hair behind my ear, instantly reminding me of Sam and the same tender gesture. It has me in tears as I think of him and what I have thrown away.

"I fucked up, Rubes," I sob.

"Shhh, it's going to be OK, babe, I promise."

I sob well into the night, and I'm so exhausted as the tears subside, I fall into a deep dreamless sleep.

9

Peyton

The next morning, I wake way before my alarm goes off, and the events of last night immediately rush to the forefront of my mind. I automatically feel embarrassed and humiliated at the way I acted in front of Sam. I pull back the duvet and get out of bed. I am up so early that I can't hear the sound of Ruby's morning routine. I decide to go for a morning run to clear my head. Changing quickly into my jogging bottoms, a t-shirt, my hoodie, and jamming my feet into my trusty Reebok trainers, I check my phone as I pull my hair up into a messy ponytail. I have one text message from Sam, and my heart leaps as I see his name on my phone.

I'm so sorry

Please call me I have to know you're OK

S xx

I toss my phone on the sofa not wanting to be reminded of him. I put my earphones in and go out of the front door. Walking out into the street, the fresh air mixed with the beat of my iPod is a welcome distraction from the melee in my head. I start with a gentle jog around the block, and as soon as I hit my stride, I am pounding the pavement through Regent's Park. The city seems so quiet at this early hour, and it is strangely calming. I run for what seems like an age before stopping near a bench to catch my breath. I bend to stretch my legs out.

"Looks like we both had the same idea this morning, babe."

I look up to see Seb's smiling face jogging towards me. He looks fresh for first thing in the morning, wearing long black shorts—highlighting his muscular, tattooed legs—a black sports jacket, a grey vest underneath and black Nike trainers. I am happy to see a friendly face. As soon as he stops inches away from me, I feel the overwhelming urge to blurt out what happened and break down in front of him. I take a breath of fresh morning air to quell the tears.

"Yeah, I couldn't sleep; I needed the distraction, to be honest."

I plaster a fake grin on my face, and he laughs.

"Last night ... exhausting then?"

I laugh and cock my eyebrow at Seb's attempt at subtlety. *You're about as subtle as a sledgehammer, Henry!*

"Nothing happened, shockingly enough."

Seb looks concerned, and he brushes my arm.

"Do you want to go for a coffee and talk about it, babe? Starbucks my shout?"

As tempting as his invitation is, I know that if Seb finds out about what happened, he would want to go and rip Sam's head clean off his shoulders. I don't want to have to break up a fight between the men in my life.

"No thanks, I'll see you at work in an hour or so."

Seb nods, and by the way he looks at me, I know he understands—he knows not to push me when I'm in one of my moods.

"As long as you're sure you're OK, babe. You know I worry about you. You mean the world to me, and you're like my baby sister."

We both smile. I'm grateful for his compassionate words, and that he feels so strongly towards me.

"I'm fine, honey; we'll chat properly when I get to the shop, I promise."

"See you later, darlin'."

With those words, he resumes his run, and I resume mine. I run for half an hour more and then make the twenty-five-minute journey back to the flat. Ruby is just emerging from her shower in her bathrobe as I let myself back into the flat.

"Morning, babe, how are you feeling this morning?"

I take a long pull on my bottle of water before I answer with a nod.

"Yeah, I feel so fucking humiliated, and my ego feels like it has done ten rounds with Mike Tyson. Other than that, I'm peachy fucking creamy."

Ruby looks at me sympathetically.

"I've fallen so hard for him, Rubes. He's everything that Callum isn't. He's ... amazing, and I've gone and fucked it up royally."

She comes towards me and hugs me tightly. "If it's meant to be, he'll be the one chasing you by the end of the day. Listen to Aunty Ruby! I'm always right!"

I can't help but laugh. "Shut up, you tart!"

I mimic a Cockney accent, and she throws a towel at me. I go into the bathroom for my morning shower. Half an hour later, I am showered and dressed, with my hair straightened and my make-up done.

"Meet me for lunch?"

Ruby asks me the same question every day, knowing that I always meet her for lunch, so I roll my eyes.

"Yep, I'll text you when I know my appointments."

We both leave the flat at the same time; she kisses me on the cheek and hugs me before bouncing down the stairwell in an unusually good mood.

"Love ya."

I follow her at a leisurely pace, knowing that she probably got lucky with Jax last night. I brave the tube ride to the shop, crossing my fingers that my car will be repaired by tomorrow, so I don't have to endure public transport for another day. I get to the shop in record time, and Seb is there as always with my usual cup of Starbucks coffee waiting for me.

"Mornin', honey bunny." He winks.

"Morning, pumpkin."

I go into the back of the shop, and there is a huge bunch of pink and purple orchids on the counter.

Popping my head around the doorway, I tease Seb, "Who are the flowers for? Who's the lucky lady?"

"Nothing to do with me, babe, came about half an hour ago. My guess is he's got a *lot* of making up to do."

He cocks his eyebrow questioningly. I go to the counter and look at the card.

Peyton,

I'm so sorry about last night. I fucked up, please forgive me? Just so you know it changes nothing between us, I'm still crazy for you. Everyone is entitled to a past, and we all have secrets. We have a gig tonight, and I have put your name on the guest list, the info is on the back. Please say you'll come? It starts at 7, call me.

All my love

S x

What Sam said in the note brings the familiar butterflies from last night fluttering in my stomach. *Could this really work between us? Me and Sam the rock star? Could he really handle my past and my hang-ups about trusting the opposite sex?* I am suddenly more than willing to try to give it a go—the note brings my feelings flooding to the surface. I have fallen head over heels for this man. They say that love at first sight doesn't exist but my faith in men has been restored, and it's all thanks to him. Not that I plan to tell him anytime soon because of the fear of scaring him away. I bounce out into the shop, and Seb looks at me as if I have gone crazy.

"I take it the flowers are a good sign then, babe?"

I nod. "Yep, the world is a beautiful place, Seb."

I do my victory dance, and my mood is infectious as Seb gets up from his seat. He picks me up and spins me around.

"I'm happy for you, babe."

When he sets me down, I pick up my coffee and take a long sip, welcoming the hot liquid as it slides down my throat.

"So, what appointments do we have today?"

He sits down at his desk and pulls out the appointment book.

"No famous rock stars today, I'm afraid!"

We both laugh.

"Your first appointment is in half an hour, I've already set your station up for you, babe, just a small one apparently, so the girl said on the phone, and you've got three this afternoon."

I nod and smile, grateful for Seb's thoughtfulness. I put my coffee down on the reception desk.

"Give me a second, babe."

Seb salutes. "No rush, honey."

I go into the back of the shop, pull my phone out of my bag, and dial Sam's number. He answers on the third ring.

"Hello?"

I pause. "Hey, Sam, it's—"

Before I have said my name, he jumps in.

"Peyton. I take it that you got my flowers then?" His voice is husky and sounds like he has just woken up.

"They're lovely, thank you so much, you didn't have to."

I hear the smile in his voice when he replies, "I wanted to make it up to you, babe."

I smile to myself and suddenly feel like I'm a teenager all over again.

"Thank you. I'm so sorry about what happened last night."

It's his turn to pause; he breathes audibly into the phone.

"Don't apologise, it's OK, really. We'll talk more tonight, I promise. Are you coming to the gig?"

I nod to myself and instantly scold myself for nodding, knowing he can't see me.

"Yeah, I'll be there."

"That's great. Your name is on the guest list, just tell security at the door. Text me when you're there, I'll come and find you."

I smile so wide I feel my jaw starting to ache.

"I'll look forward to it."

"Me too, babe. I want to make up for last night so badly, maybe we can finish what we started."

He says those words so seductively, I immediately feel desire dripping between my legs. The effect this man has on me is uncontrollable and exciting all at the same time. For the first time in a long time, I finally feel alive.

"Sounds ... awesome."

He laughs.

"Look, Sam, I've got an appointment in twenty minutes, so I should go, but I'll definitely see you at the gig tonight."

"Yep, see you at seven, babe."

"Bye, Sam."

I press the end call button by swiping my finger across the screen. I quickly fire across a text to Ruby with my appointments, put my phone away, go back out into the shop, and prepare for the day ahead.

***

My morning of tattooing goes by quickly, and before I know it, the door to the shop is opening. Ruby struts in, her heels clicking across the floor.

"Hey, Seb. Hey, babe," she says in her familiar singsong voice. I am just wiping down my station after my relatively short and small tattoo session—a small pair of angel wings on the back of a girls neck.

"Are you ready for lunch? I'm bloody starving. Isaac has been in a meeting in the city since nine this morning and isn't due to finish until well after three, so we've got time to catch up."

I laugh.

"Taking advantage of the bosses' kind nature again? You'll have that promotion in no time!" I joke. She laughs and raises her eyebrows.

"Sooner than you think, honey."

She winks, and I know what she is referring to. I roll my eyes.

"I have to be back here by one thirty, babe. My next appointment."

It's Ruby's turn to roll her eyes, and she salutes. "Yes ma'am!"

I slap her playfully on her arm and skip into the back of the shop. I wash my hands in the sink, dry them on a towel, then grab my bag and coat before heading back out into the shop.

"I'm going to lunch, Seb."

He nods. "Grab me something, please, babe? The usual?"

I nod. "Yep, no problem, see you in a bit."

Ruby and I walk the five-minute journey to Swingin' Eli's. Eli is behind the counter with his familiar smile, our drink order ready, and writes down our regular order. We go to our usual table and sit down opposite each other.

"So, are you going to tell me what the fuck happened between you and Sam last night?"

Typical Ruby, straight for the gossip jugular. I hang my head.

"I fucked up, babe, totally. We had dinner, and we started talking exes."

She shakes her head disapprovingly as she is sucking her strawberry milkshake through a straw.

"First date rule, Peyton: *never* talk about exes. Have I taught you nothing?" she says dramatically.

Sighing, I say, "I know, he was the one who brought it up, and then he's asking who hurt me because he could see 'pain behind my eyes.'"

"Oh, *please*!"

"I told him about Cal and the baby—it kind of all just came tumbling out. He was telling me about his ex, and then things started to ... get a little heated in the middle of the restaurant."

Ruby almost chokes on her milkshake. "Fucking hell, Peyton! In public? Hi-five!"

"It just kind of happened, but we got interrupted by the waiter."

She laughs hysterically. "*Oh my God!* How embarrassing!"

My face heats at the memory. "I know, I was fucking mortified! Anyway, we skipped dessert and went back to ours. There's something about him, Rubes, and he is making me break all my rules. Before we've even got inside the flat he is pinning me to the wall, and things are getting heated between us. Then he carried me to my room, and we collapsed on the bed."

Ruby is across the table leaning on her hands, listening intently and eagerly waiting for me to finish the story.

"Did you fuck him?"

Now it's my turn to almost choke. "No! I fucking panicked and ran to the bathroom. I needed a minute."

She rolls her eyes again. "*You needed a minute?* Wow, fucking hell, Peyton, you had the perfect opportunity to screw him; he was practically sprawled out naked on your bed waiting for you to rock his world."

Way to make me feel bad, Ruby, thanks!

"I know, I just panicked, and by the time I got myself together, he's in my room picking up my journal and the picture of Callum and me falls out along with our scan picture."

Her mouth drops open. "Why the fuck have you even still got those? I thought you burnt it all?"

I shake my head. "I don't know! He picked them up from the floor, and before I know what I'm doing I'm telling him to leave!"

Ruby tuts. "Oh, my fucking *God*. Are you completely insane?"

I nod. "Apparently so. I screwed up so badly, Rubes. I'm telling him to leave, and he's point blank refusing, begging me to talk to him and that's when you walked in."

She leans back in her chair. "Have you heard from him since?"

I smile shyly. "Yeah, he sent me flowers this morning and wrote me a note."

I pass the card across the table to her, and she reads it then breaks out into a grin.

"Aww, he is definitely still interested then. Are you going to go to the gig?"

I nod and swiftly change the subject. "So, what happened with you and Jax? How did the date go?"

It's her turn to be coy. As she goes to answer, our lunch arrives. We tuck in straight away, and my rumbling stomach reminds me how hungry I actually am.

"He took me for dinner; I sucked him off under the table in the restaurant and fucked him in a toilet cubicle."

I cough loudly and almost choke on a mouthful of food. "Ruby!"

She giggles. "I wasn't going to be just another groupie whore, babe; I fucked him first before he could fuck me over. Plain and simple, play him at his own game, and he's been constantly calling me this morning, leaving messages practically begging to see me again."

I laugh. Ruby has taken to dating like men do—she got it from an episode of *Sex and the City.* It usually works, and they always, without fail, call her practically pleading to see her again. Sounds like it has worked yet again with Jax.

"Are you going to see him again?"

She smiles coyly. "Hell yeah, I'm coming to the gig tonight, we can be each other's wing woman!"

I laugh at her *Top Gun* reference. She winks, and my shoulders visibly relax knowing I'll have some moral support at the gig later. We carry on gossiping over lunch, settle the bill, and head back to work soon after we finish. I get back to the shop and the afternoon tattoo session flies by in an endless flow of ink. Before I know it, I'm looking up at the clock, and it's time to go home.

"Good job today, babe, you make me so proud to have you working with me. We make an awesome team."

Seb's words warm me inside, and I hug him tenderly. "Thanks, Seb."

I smile, and he pulls away first.

"Go home, you silly tart. I'll break your station down!"

We both laugh. I skip to the back, and my phone is ringing.

"Hello?"

I scream down the phone, and I am jumping around at the news. Seb comes running to the back.

"Peyton, are you OK?"

I nod.

"Yep, my car is fixed, no more tube rides."

I do a little victory dance. Seb visibly relaxes and smiles at my childish excitement.

"Thank fuck. I thought something was wrong. You nearly gave me a bloody heart attack, you silly tart!"

"Sorry, babe, I'm just so excited to get her back, it's been a long time coming."

Seb rolls his eyes, but he doesn't say what he thinks because he knows that I will punch him. He thinks that my car is a shit heap, but she is my pride and joy. I took a mechanics class, watched many videos on YouTube, and bought a pile of books on restoring old American muscle cars. My dad got her imported from the States as a present to cheer me up, and I immediately set to work my 1967 Chevy Camaro SS. It was my first restoration project—after I split with Callum I needed something to take my mind off what happened, so I turned to fixing her up. I completely rebuilt the engine, had it resprayed, restored the upholstery, installed a kick-ass sound system, and changed all the wheels. It took a long time, but I managed it with a little help from my brother, Dexter, and my dad. But a month ago, she broke down on my way to work, and she has been in the garage ever since. My dad paid for her to be fixed, and I'm *finally* going to be reunited with my pride and joy.

"I'm going to pick her up now!"

Seb smiles. "See you tomorrow, sweetie. Be careful and have fun."

He kisses me on the forehead before I leave the shop. An hour later, I am back at the flat with my beloved car parked in the underground garage. Even though I took a little longer to get back home, I am back before Ruby, which is unusual. I dump my stuff and go into the bathroom, shower in record time, and by the time the flat door slams shut, I am doing my make-up in my full-length bedroom mirror.

"Hey, babe." She sounds fed-up. I smile as Ruby leans in my bedroom doorway.

"Hey."

"God, Isaac is such a prick; he kept me after hours and sounded me out in front of everyone. I was so fucking embarrassed I wanted to punch him."

Her voice is so full of anger I instantly stop what I am doing.

"Are you sure you're OK, sweetie? You know you don't have to put up with him treating you that way, put in a harassment complaint."

She shakes her head. "I can't. He's a powerful man; he'll make sure I never work in advertising again."

I roll my eyes and keep my opinion to myself before she bites my head off. Instead, I carry on with applying my make-up. She walks away knowing that I'm right. I opt for a pair of leather shorts, a black *Guns N' Roses* vest top, fishnet tights, and black patent Doctor Martens. I team my outfit with a pair of black feather earrings and a candy skull necklace. My tattoos are on show, and as I look in the mirror, I am happy with my outfit choice. Ruby comes to the door with a glass of wine in her hand.

"I think I'm going to stay in tonight, babe."

I find her choice to stay in very unusual. Ruby loves the male attention, especially the rock star variety and she loves a gig. I thought she would be chomping at the bit to go to a Rancid Vengeance gig.

"Are you sure everything's OK?"

She nods and smiles, but her smile doesn't reach her eyes. I instantly know that something is wrong.

"Rubes, talk to me."

Her eyes glaze over as if she wants to say more, but she swallows a large gulp of wine.

"It's nothing, honey. Honestly, please don't worry about me, just go and enjoy your date."

She smiles, and I hesitantly grab my bag.

"I don't want to leave you this way, babe."

She narrows her eyes at me. "Just go now, or I'll drag you out of the door myself!"

We both laugh.

"Give him one for me!" she says with a wink.

I kiss her on the cheek and reluctantly hug her goodbye. In the underground garage, I unlock my car and get in. It is good to be back behind the wheel. I start the engine, and she roars to life straight away. I crank up the stereo for my daily dose of rock, opting to listen to a Rancid Vengeance album called *Carpe Nocturne* that I downloaded and drive the thirty-five-minute journey to my date. All too soon, I am pulling into the car park, getting out, and going to the stage door of the o2 arena in London. I go to the front of the queue, and a bunch of girls are giving me dirty looks and whispering to each other. The large burly security guard looks me up and down.

"Let me guess. You're here to see one of the guys? Nice try, sweetheart."

I frown, and he rolls his eyes as if he has heard that so many times before. I clear my throat.

"Actually, I'm here to see Sam, my name's on the guest list if you wouldn't mind checking, please?"

I flutter my eyelashes and put on my sweetest voice.

"Name, please?"

He looks bored, and I look up at his large frame.

"Peyton Harper."

He checks his clipboard and clears his throat.

He smiles warmly and nods. "Apologies, darlin', these girls will do anything to meet the guys, but Sam's expecting you."

"Thank you."

He lets me through the door, and the other girls at the door are left dumbstruck as I wander through the brightly lit corridor. There is a hustle and bustle of roadies setting up and carrying equipment down the wide corridor. I text Sam quickly.

I'm here, wandering the corridors looking for you

P x

Suddenly, I collide with a tall, lean figure. I look up, and my smile fades as I see who I have bumped into. J.D, of all people. His all-too-bright white smile is creepy and reminds me all over again why I instantly took a dislike to him. In fact, I think I hate him.

"Ahh, Peyton, my love, how *nice* to see you."

As he emphasises the word nice, I know he is being sarcastic, and he is less than thrilled to see me. But guess what, *buddy,* the feeling is mutual.

"I heard all about your shenanigans with lover boy last night, my darling, in great depth. I told him you're no good for him, but he seems to think he's fallen for you. I've warned him it will end in tears, but I'm pretty sure those tears won't be his by the time I've finished, sweetheart."

He grabs my arm.

"I've told you before you don't fucking scare me, J.D. What the hell is wrong with you? What is your fucking problem?"

He leans in close, and I can smell the scent of his too-strong Hugo Boss aftershave mixed with alcohol. He is about to say something else when someone clears their throat behind him.

"John, I've told you to leave her alone," Sam says sternly, and I snatch my arm away from J.D's grip.

I turn to look at Sam, and he is looking especially sexy tonight. He is wearing tight, black-leather trousers that emphasise his impressive package, black cowboy boots, and a tight, black, Rancid Vengeance vest defining his muscled and tattooed arms. His hair is a messy spiky style, and he is wearing black eyeliner. Sam puts his hand at the small of my back, and before he leads me down the corridor, J.D leans into my ear and whispers so only I can hear him.

"Just remember this; Sam won't always come to your rescue, sweetheart."

He winks, and Sam leads me off down the corridor. He opens the door to the dressing room which is empty and unusually tidy and definitely not what I would expect from four male rock stars—I was expecting beer and groupies. "Where are the other guys?"

Before he answers, he backs me against the wall and claims my lips with his. He pulls away and looks deep into my eyes.

"I've wanted to do that all day," he whispers in a voice that instantly makes me bite my lip. "It's taken all my willpower not to just show up at the shop. I can't seem to stay away from you, you're like an addiction."

I reach up and stroke his freshly-shaven face.

"I'm so sorry about last night, Sam. I truly am."

He pulls away and pulls a chair out from the dressing room table. When he sits down, I sit down on the sofa opposite him, and our eyes lock. It is taking all my strength not to sink down to my knees and take his length in my mouth. He smirks.

"Having those naughty thoughts again, babe?"

I laugh. "You have no fucking idea."

"Oh, I think I do. I've been having the same thoughts all fucking day, and I haven't been able to concentrate on anything else."

Without much thought, I bite my lip.

"Don't bite your lip, please, or I will take you right now on this floor and we can't because we need to talk, and I need to be on stage in an hour," he rasps, and we both laugh.

"So ... what happened last night? I wanted you to talk to me, but you were pretty God damn adamant you wanted me to leave."

I pause and swallow back the lump that's forming in my throat.

"It's complicated. Fuck, *I'm* complicated."

He shakes his head. "That's not an answer, Peyton. I need to understand what's going on in your head. I have fallen so hard for you. I want you so fucking bad it physically hurts. I couldn't sleep last night because I was terrified that I'd lost the only good thing to happen in my life in a really long time."

Shaking my head, I tell him, "I've fallen hard for you too, Sam, really fucking hard. I can't deal with how strong my feelings are in such a short space of time. My feelings for you consume me." Taking a deep breath, I let it out with a sigh. "Callum hurt me so badly he had me convinced that no other man would want to be with me, that I was somehow damaged goods. After we split, all I did for the first few weeks was cry and blame myself, then Ruby practically dragged me out of the flat and convinced me I needed to move on. So I moved on, or should I say moved *under* another man, or numerous men, just to get him out of my system. How fucked up does that make me?" I laugh bitterly at the thought. "I turned into everything I despise and vowed I'd never be. It took a long time for me to come to terms with that and the fact that I'd probably never be that blissfully happy ever again and then you walked into the shop."

He smiles and moves to the sofa next to me. He subconsciously strokes my arm willing me to continue.

"You walked into the shop and into my life. It was like my whole world was in HD again."

We both laugh before I begin to speak.

"I know it sounds cheesy, but as soon as I saw you, I knew."

He strokes my face, and I lean into his hand.

"Fuck," he curses.

"When I saw those photos last night, I didn't blame you; I wanted you to sit down with me and talk it out. I definitely didn't want you to kick me out—*fuck*. Do you know what I did after I left? I called Jax, and we went to the nearest bar and got absolutely shit-faced. I ended up blurting *everything* out to him."

I nod.

"I blurted out everything to him, and he understood. I was a mess after I left, an absolute mess and he talked me down. It took a lot of fucking vodka to convince me not to call you or just turn up on your doorstep. He confiscated my phone and took me back to the hotel where we're staying, put me to bed, and then went off with some groupie from the hotel bar!"

We both laugh. However, I look at him puzzled.

"Wait, Ruby said that she had sex with Jax in the restaurant toilet."

Sam's eyes widen, and he is about to say something when the door swings open. The other three band member's walk in all dressed in their stage attire.

"Did she? I think that might be news to Jax, babe."

Jax looks at me with a smile. "Hey, Peyton!"

Jax slumps heavily down on the sofa next to me, and I know that our conversation is over.

"What's news to me, dude?"

"That you shagged Ruby in the restaurant toilet."

Jax laughs hysterically.

"Did I? Wow, that must have really escaped my attention. No, she got a phone call, and she started acting weird. Then she just left abruptly. I've been calling her all fucking day, but she won't answer my calls or my texts."

I frown. It isn't like Ruby to lie to me. She is usually so honest, and we tell each other everything. *Why would she lie? What could possibly be so bad that she feels the need to keep it to herself?*

"I'm sure she has a logical explanation." I try to stand up for her.

"She sucked me off under the table in the restaurant. *Jesus,* that girl could suck start a leaf blower! We were in the toilet about to fuck, but she got the call, and before I could protest she ran off like someone had lit a fire under her cute little arse." Jax smiles and shakes his head at the same time. "Fucking women!"

He rolls his eyes, and a tall, slim woman walks in with Latino features. Long waves of caramel-coloured hair flow around her face and shoulders like a halo; she has dark brown eyes and the most amazing cheekbones I have ever seen. She smiles brightly as she sees me.

"This must be the famous Peyton I've been hearing about all day," she says in accented English. Sam stands up and pulls me to my feet.

"Peyton, this is Blu, she is our make-up artist and stylist," he introduces her fondly. I smile, and she air kisses me on both cheeks. *Very European.*

"I'm so happy to meet you, Peyton; Sam's told me all about you."

I nod and raise my eyebrows at Sam.

"All good, I hope?"

She laughs. "Of course all good, my darling. He hasn't stopped talking about you all day."

Sam pushes her playfully. "All right, babe, I've got a reputation to keep up, you know!"

She laughs and flicks her hair over her shoulder. A sure fire sign of flirting, automatically making me think that she and Sam have a romantic history. I dismiss the thought and suddenly feel out of place in a room full of rock stars and their entourage. Sam grabs my hand and gives it a reassuring squeeze.

"Come on; let me give you the backstage tour," he says excitedly and leads me out of the dressing room.

Brody shouts from sitting on top of the dressing table, "Wa-hey! We all know what our Sammy's backstage tour consists of!"

All the guys shout and cheer as we leave.

"I'm really sorry about that, please just ignore them."

I smile and can't help but worry about Ruby. I vow to call her as soon as the gig is over. Two men are in the corridor carrying a drum set between them. One is bald, one has long black hair, and they both wear a Rancid Vengeance vest.

"Peyton, these two are our roadies, Donovan and Caleb."

They both put the drum sets down with ease and grin.

"Pleased to meet you, Peyton, I'm Donovan." The man with the long black hair reaches for my hand and shakes it.

"I'm Caleb."

Caleb shakes my hand, and Donovan shoves him out of the way. They playfully grab and shove each other. Sam rolls his eyes.

"Don't worry, they're always like that, they're brothers."

I nod and smile. I am overwhelmed at meeting new people and being thrust into the world of Rancid Vengeance.

10

Peyton

The backstage area of the venue is bustling with people wandering around, and I am in awe of the way Sam handles himself around the people close to him. His bandmates and the people who work for him. He seems so confident and so at ease with the idea of fame. He handles the female and press attention like a second nature, as if it is all he knows.

When we get to the side of the stage, all I see is a sea of people chanting, "Vengeance, Vengeance, Vengeance."

I look up at him and smile. He pulls me into him, and I feel his erection digging into my thigh.

"That's what you do to me, baby; I have no idea how I'm going to get through the show with a raging stonk on!"

When our mutual laughter dies down, he leans down, and his lips claim mine as his. Every time he kisses me, it's as if he needs me to breathe. I hear a noise and pull away from him. I look over his shoulder, startled.

"What was that?"

Sam smiles and strokes my face.

"You worry too much, babe. Just relax, I've got you," he whispers and reassures me. He brushes his finger across my bottom lip tenderly. "I'll never let anyone hurt you, Peyton, I promise."

He gazes into my eyes and leans down to kiss me passionately on the lips. His tongue slowly caressing mine and claiming me as his—his one and only. I reach down and stroke his growing erection through his tight jeans.

He thrusts his pelvis against me and whispers against my lips, "Baby, please not here, I want it to be more than just a knee trembler in a dark corner. It's not about just sex with you. You're not like the others, you're special."

I smile mischievously and carry on stroking him, his erection bulging through the material of his tight trousers.

"Something about you makes me feel bold and invincible."

He smiles and gently moves my hand from his crotch. To soothe the rejection, he lifts my hand to his lips and plants a kiss on the back.

"You're all I'm going to be thinking about when I'm up on that stage, counting down the minutes and the seconds until I can be inside you," he whispers in his familiar husky voice, and I feel the ache between my legs. I'm not sure whether I am in the presence of Sam or Bolt. I feel his phone vibrate against my thigh.

"Shit."

I laugh, and he pulls his phone out of his pocket.

"Babe, I need to go, J.D's called an emergency pre-show meeting." He rolls his eyes and smiles. A young woman passes us in the corridor and Sam whistles.

"Hey, Willow, would you mind looking after Peyton for me please?"

She smiles warmly, and I instantly like her.

"Yeah, sure, bro, no problem, but it's going to cost ya!"

He laughs and pulls her in for a big bear hug.

"Cheeky! Thanks, sis, I owe you."

Pulling away from Willow, he winks at me and whispers, "Keep thinking those thoughts."

He kisses me on lips before he runs off down the corridor leaving me with Willow. She is average height, slim with black hair short on the one side and long on the other. She has Sam's green eyes and a warm smile. She is wearing a tight red t-shirt that says 'I'm with the band' on the front, denim skirt, and knee-high Doc Martens—a girl after my own heart.

She offers me her hand. "I'm Willow, Sam's little sister."

"Peyton"

We smile at each other infectiously.

"So, are you Sam's new girlfriend?" she asks, and I nod.

A nervous laugh bubbles up from somewhere deep inside of me. "Yeah, I guess I am."

"Great! Come on, we can go and watch the show together," she says brightly, linking her arm with mine and dragging me down the corridor. We both flash our backstage passes to the waiting security guard, get into the concert venue, and wade through the crowd and to the front row at the side of the stage.

"So, how long have you and Sam been together?"

I pause. "We only met yesterday."

She nods inquisitively. "OK, where did you meet?"

"At the tattoo shop where I work, I'm a tattoo artist."

Her face lights up. "Oh, my God, that's so cool."

"Thanks, I think so. I work at Saint Sinner Ink."

Her eyes widen. "Oh, my fucking *God*. You work for Seb Henry? I love that guy, that tattoo show he did was amazing."

I can't help but laugh. Seb did a reality tattoo show on one of the cable channels a few years ago. It got the shop a lot of publicity, recognition for his work, and a lot of custom for the shop. Because of that, the shop is booked up months in advance, and we work by appointment only. Seb is quite the celebrity in his own right.

"I'll tell him you're a fan and get him to sign something for you. I'm sure you'll make his day." I smile, and her mouth drops open.

"Really? Wow, that would be so awesome!" she says excitedly, and I instantly like her. Her inquisitiveness and childlike excitement makes me feel on a high. After the support band, The Devil's Henchmen, the lights go down, and a drumbeat fills the arena. The stage is in darkness and Sam's husky singing voice comes through the speakers. Ruby was right; I could definitely orgasm by just listening to him sing. His voice is like honey filling my ears and the crowd singing the lyrics back to him. Jax's guitar riffs accompany Sam's voice and Lucas' pounding drum beat. He steps out of the darkness, and the lights on stage come up. He is standing on the stage with the microphone in his hand and his eyes closed. I am in awe of his stage presence; he looks almost God-like. He comes out to the front of the stage and looks out into the crowd. A genuine wide grin comes across his face.

"How are we doing tonight, London?"

The crowd goes wild, and he goes back to singing *Unspoken Conversations*, a song I have heard Ruby singing in the shower countless times. His voice melts me inside. It is at that moment that I think that he is so passionate about his music and he is so enigmatic, full of energy and charisma when he is on stage performing. Yet, when we're alone, he is so full of self-doubt and a need to be reassured. It is like being in a relationship with two completely different people—Sam and Bolt. I'm starting to doubt whether I can actually do this at all. My self-doubt starts to creep in, and every part of me is telling me to run screaming for the hills in the opposite direction, the sane part, anyway. The other part, the part that craves all-consuming love and affection is driving me forward. I look up, and his eyes lock with mine. He crouches down on the edge of the stage and sings his lyrics to me. It is as if it is just him and me in the room, my own personal serenade. Soon, the song finishes, and Sam puts his microphone on the stand.

"How the fuck are we doing tonight then, London? It's so good to be back home. We're Rancid Vengeance, and tonight we're going to fucking rock this place to the ground!"

He looks so comfortable up on the stage. Performing must be like second nature to him—he is a true showman.

"Let me see those fucking hands in the air. I need to hear you *scream* for me, London!"

The crowd goes wild—cheering, screaming, and stomping their feet.

"Give me a bit of 'Lullaby', boys. Let's rock this shit!"

Jax's solo guitar riff on his custom Schechter black guitar with electric blue stars fills the venue; I can understand why his stage name is Flash with the way his fingers effortlessly dance up and down the fretboard. It is fascinating to watch. I'm hooked and can't tear my eyes away from the stage. Next to me, Willow is singing the lyrics at the top of her voice, and her excitement is infectious. I am bouncing up and down to the beat and cheering along with her.

After the gig finishes with a light show and expensive pyrotechnics, Willow is whisking me backstage. She runs down the corridor, and I follow her. I see Sam, and he even looks sexy covered in sweat. His face lights up as he sees me. Taking off his earpiece, he hands it to a passing stagehand. He has a black towel with the band's skull logo stitched on it around his neck, and with it, he wipes the sweat from his face and takes a long pull on the bottle of water he is holding. He comes towards me and scoops me up in his arms.

"Hey, babe."

I smile and shriek as he lifts me off the floor. He smells so good—even if he is covered in sweat—of his signature Joop aftershave, mint, and the scent of pure Sam Newbolt.

"You were amazing."

"Glad you liked it. Look, we've got to do some press interviews and some meet and greets with some competition winners before I can leave, but you're more than welcome to hang around and wait, babe."

I smile and whisper in his ear, "I'll go home and wait for you, babe. I'll be the naked one in my bed!" I wink seductively and bite his ear. He growls from deep within his throat.

"You horny little bitch!"

We both laugh, and he sets me down on the floor.

"I'll be as quick as I can. I promise."

He kisses me on the lips and Willow shoves him.

"Oh, *please!* Put her down!"

She rolls her eyes dramatically, and we all laugh.

"I'll see you later then, gorgeous?" I wink, and he smiles that sexy, signature grin.

"Later," he mouths, and a man talking into a headset is whisking him off down the corridor.

"I'm going to head home, Willow."

She nods. "OK, it was really nice to meet you, Peyton. I don't usually like Sam's choice of girlfriends, but I like you. We could be friends, and we should meet up for lunch or something soon? I can fill you in on all the dirt about my big brother!"

I laugh, flattered by her words. "Yeah, that would be really great."

She claps her hands excitedly. "Can I get your number?"

I recite my mobile number to her, and she punches it into her phone. She holds it up to her ear, and my phone vibrates in my pocket.

"There, now you have my number too. No excuses not to call or text me!" I save her number and store it in my phone. She throws her arms around me and hugs me, promising to meet up soon.

"It was so nice to have met you, Willow."

She pulls away and skips off down the corridor. I go off in the opposite direction and head out of the venue. The cool air on my face is a welcome contrast from the stuffy heat inside the venue. I walk to my car, unlock it, and drive home.

Half an hour later, after stopping off to grab something to eat, I open the door to the flat, and Ruby is on the sofa crying. My face is full of concern as I drop my bag at the door and rush over to her.

"Hey, Rubes, what's wrong?"

I throw my arms around her and comfort her. She sobs harder.

"Hey, come on, I'm sure it's not that bad. Broken nails and spilt wine definitely do not warrant tears!" I try to joke, but she doesn't laugh. "Rubes, talk to me."

I run my hand up her back. She looks up at me with wide, sad, and scared eyes.

"I-I-I'm pregnant, Peyton," she chokes out. I am stunned into silence by her admission, so I rub her back—it's the only thing I can do.

"Before you even ask, I'm getting rid of it. I can't have a baby, Peyton. I can't, I just fucking can't," she sobs. "Don't you dare judge me, babe. Please. I couldn't stand it if you did."

Forcing her to look at me, I lock my eyes with hers. "I'd never judge you, Ruby. I love you, you silly tart!"

She laughs through her tears. "Isaac-fucking-Carter. Of all the men in the world, it had to be him. We've always been careful, and I don't understand how it could have happened." She shakes her head.

"You're not thinking straight at the moment, babe. Please don't rush into something you might regret."

She looks at me as if she wants to strangle me. "Can you really imagine me with a fucking *baby*, Peyton? Come on. I'm selfish, and I love my lie-in's. Me getting up to feed a screaming brat in the middle the night ... It's not going to happen, my mind's made up." Her voice is filled with determination, and I pause.

"Does Isaac know?"

She laughs sarcastically. "Of course he doesn't fucking know. He would frog march me straight to the abortion clinic himself. He has made it clear that I'm nothing more to him than just a fling. He is married already, he is not going to leave his wife of twenty years, and he is definitely not going to be proposing marriage when he finds out he is going to be a daddy. This isn't the movies, babe; girls like me don't get the happy ever after."

She sighs and bursts into tears again. I hold her in my arms and comfort her. I hate seeing my best friend in a state like this over a man. It's not just a man, though. This time, she is pregnant. My best friend is *pregnant*—a word I would never associate with Ruby. She has always said she never wanted kids, ever. Period. I have to be there for her like she was there for me when I was in pieces over Callum, and she was there when I lost our baby. I owe her. She is my best friend, she is like a sister to me, and she has been there when no one else was. As I'm rubbing her back and comforting her, I vow I'll stand by her and be there for her, as best friends should be.

11

Peyton

I spend a few hours comforting Ruby and reassuring her that everything is going to be OK. She falls asleep on the sofa, and I cover her with a blanket. I grab my phone from the coffee table, walking quietly across the flat and into the bathroom. I brush my teeth, wash off my makeup, and walk into my bedroom. I change into my pyjamas, lie down on my bed, and turn on my lamp. I still haven't heard from Sam, so I pick up my phone and send him a quick text.

Hey babe

You were amazing tonight

I'm in bed naked and waiting for you ;)

P x

As soon as I have sent the text, my phone starts ringing.

"Hey, babe, I'm so sorry I haven't been in touch sooner. We did a bunch of meet and greets with some fans, and then I got dragged to an after-show party with the boys."

I hear loud pumping music and voices in the background. He sounds more than a little drunk and my shoulders slump.

"It's OK."

He sighs on the end of the phone.

"Babe, I'm so fucking sorry. You know, I could still come over, my cock is still rock hard for you. I'm so horny right now, and you did say you were in bed naked and waiting for me." His voice drips seduction, and I laugh.

"It's OK, honestly. I'll see you tomorrow, and something came up anyway. Ruby had a crisis, and she needed me."

"OK, babe, I'll come by the shop tomorrow. I'll take you for lunch and make it up to you then I promise."

I smile to myself. "OK, I'll look forward to it."

I hear voices in the background and the phone crackles.

"Peyton! It's Jax, hey, I don't know what you've done to our boy Sammy, but he is love struck!"

Jax laughs hysterically, and I laugh at his drunken words.

"It's good to know, honey!"

"Listen, I'm fucking in love with Ruby. You need to get her to call me, and I need to see her," he slurs, and I pause, not knowing how to react to Jax's revelation.

"I'll tell her, Jax."

He laughs again, and I hear Sam shout, "I'm sorry about that, Jax is wasted."

"So are you by the sound of it!"

We both laugh.

"It's to numb the pain of not being with you, baby, you're amazing."

"You're such a smooth talker!"

"True story. Look, I have to go. I'll talk to you tomorrow, bye."

He hangs up abruptly before I get to say goodbye. After I get off the phone, I get ready for bed and soon fall into a deep sleep.

The next morning my phone ringing rudely awakes me. I open my eyes sleepily and look at the clock: it has just gone seven AM. I moan and pick up the phone without looking who it is that is calling.

"Hello, this better be good. Do you know what time it is?" I say groggily.

"Peyton Leigh Harper, since when have you been going out with a rock star?" my mum's shrill voice comes through the phone.

"What? Mum, what are you talking about? Who told—"

She cuts me off, "It's all over the newspapers and the internet, your picture is all over the front page," she snaps. I'm instantly alert and bolt upright.

"Mum, I have no idea what you're talking about. You woke me up."

She sighs. "I'm sorry, sweetie, I don't like finding out news about you second-hand. You know I'd rather hear it from you."

I rub the sleep from my eyes before I say, "I know, Mum, I'm sorry. Look, I need to see for myself, and I promise I'll call you right back."

"OK, sweetie, love you."

"Love you too, Mum, bye."

I hang up the phone and jump out of bed. I run through the flat barefoot and Ruby is sitting at the breakfast counter in the kitchen sipping coffee while playing on her iPad. I stand in front of her with my arms folded. She shakes her head and narrows her eyes at me over her glasses, making me feel like I'm back in school.

"Well, tut, tut Miss Peyton, haven't we been a naughty girl?" She laughs and pushes her glasses further up her nose.

"My mum just called. Apparently, Sam and I are all over the newspaper."

She sips her coffee. "See for yourself, babe," she says as she pushes her iPad towards me.

"More than meets the ink, that's fucking original," I say sarcastically and roll my eyes, silently seething. I read on aloud.

"Lead singer of Rancid Vengeance, Samson Newbolt, was spotted in a steamy clinch with tattoo artist, Peyton Harper, daughter of 1970's pin-up Sophia Bailey and high-profile fashion photographer Max Harper. The pair were spotted backstage at the band's London gig last night. Newbolt has been linked to a string of famous women in the past, but sources close to the pair say, 'She's the one'. Newbolt is said to be 'love struck and very much smitten' with the pint-sized, inked seductress. The pair met when Harper tattooed Newbolt and his bandmates at the London tattoo studio Saint Sinner Ink, where she works for celebrity tattoo artist Seb Henry. Is this the girl who can finally tame the wild boy of rock? We hear the sound of wedding bells, breaking the hearts of thousands of Rancid Vengeance female fans!"

I push the iPad back to Ruby.

"Where the fuck do they get this shit from? How the fuck do they know all that? My name, what I do, where I work? Oh, my God, Ruby."

I feel myself starting to panic. Ruby gets up from her stool and puts her hands on either side of my face.

"Babe, please calm down. You know what the press are like. They're all fucking scum bags who make up shit because they've got nothing better to do."

I let out a breath. "What am I going to do, Ruby? Everyone's going to know. Look at the picture, for fuck's sake. He must have known someone was there, he had to."

Ruby pulls me in for a hug. "Look, babe, call him. There's no use thinking the worst when he's not here to defend himself."

I look at her and put my hand to her forehead. "Are you feeling all right? That sounded very diplomatic for you."

She laughs. "I'm feeling fine apart from this fucking morning sickness. I'm making an appointment later."

My face drops, and I nod. Before I can say anything else, my phone starts ringing again.

"Peyton, I am so fucking sorry," Sam says before I even say hello. He sounds upset, and his voice is filled with panic.

"We're all over the front page, Sam. *Fuck*, how did they know some of that stuff? Did you know someone was photographing us?"

I hear him gasp, and he sounds genuinely shocked at my accusation.

"What the fuck? *No,* of course I didn't. I swear! You have to believe me, babe. I'd never do anything to purposely jeopardise us, *ever*, you mean too much to me."

I pause and put my hand to my head. "What are we going to do, Sam? They know everything, my name, where I work, what I do. Who the fuck told them all that?"

I feel myself start to panic and Ruby mouths 'deep breaths' from across the room. I take a deep breath and wander into my bedroom.

"I'll get Tate, our P.R guy, to sort it, issue a statement, do an interview. I don't know. Please believe me. I didn't know anything about this. I'm more shocked about this than you are, trust me," he says in a rush.

"The first I knew about it was my mum calling me this morning. I wasn't even out of bed."

He laughs. "I bet that was one hell of a wakeup call for you!"

I laugh too, and I hear a knock on the flat door. I stand in the doorway of my bedroom as Ruby opens the door. Danny walks into the flat waving the newspaper around with a pile of newspapers and magazines under his arm.

"Oh, my God, babes. You and the rock star, who knew!" he shrieks in a pitch that is way too high for this time of the morning and I roll my eyes.

"Look, Sam, I have to go; my friend Danny is here."

I hear the smile in his voice when he says, "OK, babe, I'll see you at lunch. I'll come by the shop around twelve, depending on my schedule."

"OK, bye."

I hang up the phone and Danny spreads the newspapers and magazines over the coffee table in the living room.

"You're everywhere, darling, you're a celebrity!" he says dramatically. "If you get invited to any celeb parties you *have* to take me with you, babe! It would be *totes-amaze balls* for my TV and modelling career."

I laugh. "Don't get ahead of yourself, Dan, bloody hell."

He jabs his finger on the newspaper. "You, my lovely, are dating one of *the* most famous rockers in the world and *I'm* getting ahead of myself? Fucking hell, darling, you're practically wanking him off in some of these pictures!"

I take a closer look. The picture on the front page shows Sam and me in a clinch, I am looking up at him; we are both smiling, unaware that we are being photographed and my hand is clearly visible on his crotch. I flush with embarrassment and put my head in my hands.

"*Fucking bastards,*" I shout at no one in particular and grit my teeth. I sit down on the sofa in the middle of Danny and Ruby. They both put their arms around me.

"What am I going to do?"

We spend the next half an hour dissecting the pictures and stories in the newspapers. Some say I am a publicity stunt, and some say I am a one-night wonder; it doesn't help my nerves and the feeling of anger bubbling up inside me. I am so fucking angry—not at Sam, but at the person who took these pictures of us sharing an intimate moment together. I know I should expect it because he is a worldwide superstar and one-quarter of a famous rock band. It comes with the territory, but part of me hates that our private lives are out there for public consumption and for everyone to judge.

I look at the clock and get up from the sofa. I leave Ruby and Danny gossiping on the sofa while I grab a shower and get dressed for work. Once I am showered and dressed, I go out into the living room, grabbing my jacket and my bag.

"I'm off to work now, or I'll be late."

Ruby smiles. "OK, sweetie, are we meeting for lunch today?"

I pull a face. "Sam's taking me for lunch; we kind of need to chat about the whole newspaper situation. I'm sorry."

Her smile fades, and she nods. "I understand, babe, it's totally fine. I'll see you when I get back from work. I'll pick up some wine, and we can have a proper girlie chat."

"Bye, babe. Bye, Danny."

Danny waves. "Don't forget your sunglasses! Hugs, sweetie."

I smile to myself and leave for work. I drive the ten minutes to work, glad that I don't have to endure the twenty-minute tube ride. I park the car next to Seb's red BMW Z4 in the car park and go into the shop.

"Mornin', honey bunny," Seb greets me.

"Morning, pumpkin."

He has my coffee waiting and sits in his chair with his bulging, tattooed, muscled arms folded.

"Someone's quite the celebrity this morning, babe."

I shake my head. "Don't you bloody start. I've had it from my mum, Ruby, *and* Danny this morning already. I came here to get away from it for a while."

He laughs. "I'm not judging; you know I'd never do that. If you need to chat I'm here for you, even if it's just to vent and get stuff off your chest."

"Thanks, honey, I really appreciate it."

I hug him and go to the back of the shop to stow my stuff away. I take off my coat, and I'm ready for the day ahead. I am about to go out into the shop when my phone starts ringing.

"O-M-F-G, Peyton!" my older sister, Eden, screams down the phone. *Great, that's all I need.* "Why didn't you tell me about you and Bolt? He's a hottie!"

I roll my eyes and imagine her dramatically fanning herself with her hand.

"Hey, sis, I'm fine, thanks for asking, how are you?"

She giggles. "Hey sis, how are you? Now spill, I want all the gory details about you and Bolt."

"There's nothing to tell, honestly. Sam and I met when I tattooed him at the shop. He asked me out, we had dinner, and now we're sort of dating. That's all there is to it, no major drama, Eden."

She gasps. "Oh, my God!" she screams again, and I'm not sure I can handle her shrieking this early in the morning.

"Can I be a bridesmaid?"

I roll my eyes.

"That's exactly what Ruby said, and I'll tell you exactly the same as I told her, don't get ahead of yourself. It's early days. I'm not sure I want to date someone whose private life is splashed all over the papers."

"Oh *please!* Stop playing the martyr, sis, it would be so great for your career; you could go and tattoo in America or somewhere exotic, get away from that God awful tattoo shop."

I wondered how long it would be before she started on me.

"How many more times, Eden? I'm happy working here with Seb."

I hear her sigh audibly down the phone, which is definitely my cue to go.

"Look, I'm at work, and my appointment has just arrived, I'll call you when I get chance," I lie.

"OK, sis, maybe we can meet up soon, we can double date. Jonah and I, you and Sam."

"Yeah, maybe. Talk to you soon, babe."

"Bye, sis, love ya."

"You too, Eden, bye."

I hang up the phone and stomp out into the shop.

"Is everything OK?" Seb looks at me with concern.

"Yeah, just my sister being a judgemental bitch as usual."

"That's sisters for you. Unfortunately, you can choose your friends but not your family, right?"

I nod. "Yeah, that's very true." I manage with a smile.

"You've got two appointments this morning, none scheduled for this afternoon, so you can take the afternoon off if you want to. You deserve it."

He smiles warmly, and I'm grateful for the opportunity to have a rare afternoon to myself. I take a sip of my coffee and welcome the familiar caffeine hit as it slides down my throat. An hour later, my appointment arrives, and it is a relatively small tribal butterfly tattoo on a young woman's shoulder blade.

When the stencil is all set, and I'm ready with my inks to begin, she looks at me curiously.

"Aren't you the girl in the newspaper with Bolt from Rancid Vengeance?"

I wondered how long before someone bought it up.

"Yeah, that's me."

She is lucky that she has her back to me.

"Oh, my God, that is *so* cool. It must be awesome dating a rock star."

I roll my eyes and let out an inaudible sigh.

"Yeah," I give her a one-word answer not wanting to elaborate and carry on tattooing her. An hour and plenty of idle chit-chat about Rancid Vengeance later, I am finished doing her tattoo. I put a layer of Vaseline on her tattoo and wrap it up, then take off my rubber gloves, put them in the bin, and go over to the reception desk where the till is. She pays me the money, and I give her an aftercare sheet. She takes it and smiles.

"Thanks so much for doing my tattoo, Peyton, see you around."

She winks and leaves the shop. I roll my eyes at Seb, and he laughs. Half an hour later, I have wiped down my station and have it set up for my next client. I go to the back of the shop and check my phone. I have several missed calls and a text from Sam.

Hey babe

Meet me at that pizza place down the street from your shop at 12:30pm

Looking forward to it

S x

I smile and instantly relax as I read his words. I go back out into the shop, and my next client has arrived. Two hours later, I am finished with my second and last client for the day. I wipe down my station for the final time today and get my stuff from the back of the shop. I pull on my jacket, grab my bag, and hug Seb.

"Thank you so much for giving me the afternoon off, Seb. I really appreciate it."

"Anytime, babe, you deserve the break. Now, go and do some girl shit!"

I laugh at Seb's dry sense of humour. I hug him, and he kisses me on the cheek.

"I'll see you tomorrow, honey."

He winks, and I leave the shop. I breathe in the fresh air and walk towards the pizza restaurant. As I am walking down the street, I see a familiar face that I would rather avoid. My ex, Callum. He spots me straight away, and his face lights up. He is tall, his eyes are the same light brown, he is still lean, tanned and muscled, and his hair is a lighter blonde and longer than before, resembling a surfer boy. He smiles, and it makes my skin crawl.

"Peyton."

I am tempted to walk right past him, but I don't.

"Hey, Callum, how are you?" I say tightly, and he nods.

"Yeah, I'm great, thanks. How are you?"

I nod and smile. "Yeah, I'm fantastic, thanks."

He looks me up and down.

"Looking good as always, baby cakes."

I visibly shudder at his pet name for me, and I can't believe he is standing in front of me acting as if he did nothing wrong.

"I wish I could say the same for you. You're a slimy bastard Cal, and you fucking cheated on me. You shagged that filthy slut behind my back, and you have the balls to stand in front of me as if nothing happened? Just when I thought you couldn't sink any lower, I bump into you here of all places. I'm seeing someone new, and he's *not* you, he's nothing like you. You damaged something in me, Callum. I'm terrified to let him get close to me because of *you*."

I jab him in the chest, and he actually has the balls to look shocked at my outburst. Every time I see him, he makes me so angry and what he did comes to the forefront of my mind—it makes my blood boil.

"I'm really fucking sorry, Peyton, I really am. I saw Ruby and your mum a while ago, I got the whole story. I hated myself when I heard, but if you think I was a filthy cheat and a liar spinning you a line, Sam fucking Newbolt, or Bolt whatever they call him, he is a new breed of scumbag. I know because the girl I cheated on you with is his *sister*. There's stories all over the internet and in the papers about you seeing him. Google images fucking loves you."

I scowl and feel like I have been punched in the chest. Inside, I feel like I want to cry, but I hold my own.

"You actually have time to sit and Google me? Wow, you really need to get a life, Cal. How do I know you're not lying about Sam's sister?"

He takes out his phone and shows me a picture. As soon as I see the picture, I feel bile rise up in my throat. The picture is of Callum and a beautiful, striking, dark-haired female who looks like she could be a model, which I'm assuming is Sam's sister. She bears an uncanny resemblance to him, and Sam is in the centre of the picture smiling back at me. They all look so happy and carefree. I feel my whole world crashing around me as I take in the image before me—I feel like I have been slapped in the face. I take a deep calming breath to stop my guts vacating in the middle of the pavement.

"It was taken when Savannah first took me to meet her parents; he'd just got home after a tour."

I feel the hot sting of tears behind my eyes, and I swallow back the lump in my throat, not wanting to give him the satisfaction of seeing me cry. He goes to brush my arm, and I flinch away from him.

"Don't you dare fucking touch me, Callum Kennedy," I manage to choke out.

"Look, Peyton. I'm so fucking sorry I cheated. I never meant to hurt you, and I definitely didn't mean for you to walk in that day."

I shake the image of him having sex with another girl from my mind. Wishing I could erase the image for good.

"But you should know Sam is a player. He tells women exactly what they want to hear. I know because I've been out partying with him and I've seen it first-hand with my own eyes. You deserve to know what a prize prick he is."

I laugh bitterly. "Takes one to know one, Cal."

"I deserved that one totally."

I look up to the sky and compose myself.

"I was fucking pregnant with your baby, Cal, and all the time you were cheating on me. Tell me one thing, where were you when I was having the miscarriage? Were you with her?"

He hangs his head.

"Are we really going to do this in the middle of the fucking street?"

I look defiantly up at him. "If we have to, yeah."

He lets out a breath.

"Yeah, yeah I was. Is that what you want to hear? I was *fucking* her; I was *balls deep* in her while you were losing our baby," he says coldly, and I slap him so hard across the face, my hand stings.

"I deserved that one, too. Look, yeah, I was a shitty boyfriend."

I can't stop the tears from rolling down my cheeks, but I quickly brush them away.

"I tried to fucking kill myself because of you, Cal."

My voice is shaky with tears, and he is stunned into silence.

"I-I-I had no idea, Peyton."

I take a deep breath. He puts his hand to his mouth and shakes his head.

"I didn't know, I ..."

Somehow, I know he is going to say sorry again.

"Don't you dare say you're fucking sorry, Cal. I'd lost our baby, I'd lost you, and my whole world came crashing down around me. I'd lost everything that I ever cared about."

He goes to walk towards me, and I take a step back.

"Don't, I have to go. I'm late for a lunch date."

I turn to leave, and he grabs my wrist, glancing down at the large, ugly white scars that mar my wrist.

"Meet me. Meet me for a coffee. We can't just leave things like this, baby cakes."

I snatch my wrist away and shake my head. "No, fuck you! I've got nothing else to say. Goodbye, Callum."

I turn around and walk quickly off down the street with my head held high wiping my tears on my sleeve as I walk. I walk into the pizza restaurant, and the hostess smiles tightly at me.

"Good afternoon, madam. How can I help you?"

I clear my throat knowing I must look a mess and paint on my best fake smile.

"I'm here to meet Sam Newbolt?"

She straightens her skirt and pushes her hair away from her face.

"Yes, madam, Mr. Newbolt is waiting for you. If you'd like to follow me, it's right this way."

She smiles, and I follow her to the table. Sam is sitting in a corner booth at the back of the restaurant; he is smiling and looking relaxed with his arms spread out over the back of the booth. Cole is guarding the booth, and he tips his hat as I approach.

"Good afternoon, Peyton." He smiles, and I smile back.

"Hey, Cole."

Sam stands up and smiles. He takes one look at me, and his smile fades. He holds me at arm's length, regarding me intently.

"Hey, you've been crying. What's wrong, babe?"

I shake my head, and it takes all my strength not to cry again. I get into the booth, and Sam sits next to me. I go to move away from him, and he gently grabs my wrist. His face is filled with worry and concern.

"Baby, please talk to me. What's wrong?"

I don't speak, because if I do, I know I'll break down.

"OK, fine. Cole," Sam says calmly, and Cole leans into the booth. "Could you bring the car 'round and drive us to my place? Have the restaurant box up some pizzas to-go, please?"

Cole nods, ever the professional, and smiles before he leaves. I look up at Sam, my eyes brimming with tears as he strokes my face.

"What's wrong, baby? I hate to see you this upset. You're killing me here, please talk to me, and tell me what's wrong."

I shake my head, and a stray tear rolls down my cheek. He wipes it away and clenches his teeth. I take a deep breath trying to compose myself, but it isn't helping.

"Someone's upset you, babe, and when I find out who it is, I'm going to fucking *end* them. I'll make sure they never hurt you again."

There is something in the way he says those words that chills me to the bone. Those words make me instantly believe that he would hurt anyone who laid a finger on me. I shake my head again and swallow a lump back from my throat. I look at him and manage to tell him what's wrong.

"The girl who Callum cheated with, he says she's ... *your sister*. Is that true?"

His eyes darken, and he avoids eye contact. I know straight away that it's the truth and I feel like I have been punched in the gut. Panic rises in my chest. *Please, God, don't have a panic attack here.* I close my eyes and take a few deep calming breaths.

"*Fuck!* I had no idea he was your ex, babe. I swear, not until I saw the picture of him in your flat. I was going to tell you eventually, but I just wanted to protect you."

I scoot around the other end of the booth and get up from my seat. In a flash, Sam is in front of me leaning down. He is so close I can feel his breath on my cheek.

"Please, Peyton, you have to believe me. We've had so many fucking setbacks with our relationship so far. Was it him who upset you?"

I am silent, and he tilts my chin up to face him.

"Look at me, I'll ask you again. Is it Callum who upset you?" he asks sharply, and I nod. His face turns angry, his nostrils flare, and he clenches his fists.

"I'm going to fucking *kill* him," he says too calmly for my liking, and I reach for his hand, stroking his knuckles softly.

"Please don't do anything stupid, Sam, he's not worth it. It was nothing, really, I'm just being silly. I just bumped into him on the way here."

He takes a breath. "So, he's the reason why you're in this state? I'd hardly call that nothing," he spits out angrily.

I get up, and we head towards the exit of the restaurant. As we step outside, there is a group of paparazzi waiting for us. Sam puts his arm possessively around my waist and pulls me towards him to protect me from the flashes. I hold my head down, and Cole pulls up at the kerb just in time in a silver Aston Martin V8 Vantage with tinted windows.

"Sam, are you and Peyton an item? Come on, mate, just one picture."

Sam pushes the lens impatiently away from us and swings the car door open. I climb in, and he crowds in behind me. He slams the door, and we speed off down the street.

"I'm so fucking sorry about all this, babe."

I shake my head. "It's not your fault, it's who you are, and it comes with the territory. I get that, I really do. I just can't stand you keeping stuff from me. I'm hurt that your sister was the one who took my ex-boyfriend from me. I'm so fucking angry right now."

I raise my voice and grip the door handle of the car so tightly my knuckles turn white. He strokes my face.

"If I could shield you from all this" He gestures around us "The press, your ex, the fact that the girl who turned your world upside down is my sister, my fame. I would in a heartbeat, babe, you have to believe that, and I want you and only you," he says huskily. "You're the best thing to happen in my life in a long fucking time. I get so lonely out on the road, but you're like the sunshine, Peyton, a light in the darkness, a rose among the thorns."

He nuzzles my neck. I burst into uncontrollable tears at his words and the depth of feeling I feel for him.

"Hey ..."

An adorable yet sexy look of concern washes over his features.

"Shhh, please don't cry, I hate to see you cry. It tears me apart."

He moves closer to me, and I am intoxicated by his scent. His closeness in the intimate space of the car makes me feel oddly horny. Tucking a strand of my hair behind my ear, he nuzzles my neck again. I sniff and dry my eyes on the sleeve of my jacket. Suddenly, I don't feel upset anymore, I feel bold, and I climb onto his lap. I wrap my arms around his neck and kiss him passionately on the lips, pressing my lips eagerly to his. His hands snake around my waist, and he runs one hand gently up my spine.

"Not here, baby, you're more to me than that. You deserve silk sheets, champagne, and strawberries for the first time I take you. I want to take my time devouring every inch of your body, slowly and sensually."

I look into his eyes. "Don't you want me, Sam?"

He bites his lip as if trying to restrain himself.

"God, of course, babe. Don't ever think that I don't want you. I fucking want you more than you'll ever know, more than my next breath," he whispers and pushes his hips into me, allowing me to feel the evidence of his arousal. "Does that feel like I don't want you?"

I shake my head.

"I need you to take it away Sam," I whisper to him, and he nods.

"I know, baby, and I will. I promise you. Just not here, you're not like any of the other women I've been with, you deserve to be treated ... right."

He strokes my face, and I climb off of his lap. Defeated, I resume my position next to him, and before I click my seatbelt in place, the car pulls to a stop. Cole parks the car, gets out, and comes around to open Sam's door. Sam climbs out, and I climb out of the other side. We are in an underground car park; Sam walks around to my side and reaches for my hand. He interlinks his fingers with mine, and we walk over to a lift. Cole pushes the call button, and the lift is there within seconds. We all get into the lift; Cole presses the button for Sam's place, and the lift starts to ascend. Sam has wrapped his arms around me and is holding me protectively as we silently rise up to Sam's floor. The lift comes to a halt, and we step out into a large foyer area minimally decorated in accented black and white. It looks very modern and very masculine with black and white floor tiles and a black glass table in the corner. I look around, and Sam smiles at my awed reaction.

"You like?"

I nod in approval. "Yeah, it's ... not what I imagined."

He laughs. "You haven't seen the rest of it yet!"

I smile, and he leads me across the foyer floor. He unlocks and opens a large, black, oak door. He gestures for me to step in before him. I step in, and the living room is a large open space with a huge black corner sofa against the wall dominating the space with a huge canvas of what I recognise as the boys' first album cover over the sofa. What astounds me is the wall of floor-to-ceiling glass doors at the furthest end of the apartment that leads out onto a balcony terrace. I can see the o2 arena, The Cutty Sark, and an array of tall buildings from his window—the view is breath-taking and looks out across the city. I walk slowly over to the window and look out.

"It's beautiful, isn't it?" He slides his hands around my waist from behind.

"It's ... breath-taking," I voice my thoughts aloud.

He rests his head on my shoulder. "Just like you."

He twirls me around and pulls me close to him. I bury my head in his chest—I feel safe in his arms.

"So, are you going to tell me what that dickhead Callum said to you to make you so upset?"

He looks down at me. *Way to ruin the moment.* I pull away and walk across the apartment, needing some distance from him.

"Peyton, talk to me, please don't walk away from me."

I spin around, suddenly angry with him for asking. The mood completely changed from a minute ago.

"You've got no idea what it was like for me when he cheated and to find out that girl is your sister. What do you expect me to say, Sam? I really don't get it."

I stop myself from calling her worse names, and he shakes his head.

"I had no idea, baby, I promise. Sav is ... She's strong-willed, determined and if she sees something, or someone and it belongs to someone else, she's like a dog with a bone: she doesn't give up until it's hers." He hangs his head. "You have to believe me, babe."

I shake my head. "Tell me one thing, Sam, is everything you've ever said me been a lie? You're telling me what I want to hear just to get me into bed?"

He looks shocked and hurt by my outburst, but I don't give him a chance to speak.

"He was with her when we lost our baby; he was in bed *fucking* her when I was in the hospital in agony and in bits because our baby died," I choke out, my voice thick with tears. He goes to step towards me, but I hold my hand up. "No, don't, Sam, please just *don't*."

He flops down on the sofa in defeat and scrubs his hands down his face.

"He showed me a picture of you. Him and your sister on his phone, she's ... pretty."

He maintains eye contact with me.

"Callum and me, we're not friends; I tolerate him for Sav's sake—"

"Take me home, Sam."

He gets up from the sofa and comes towards me.

"You don't mean that, babe. Please, I want you to stay and talk to me. Let me in, don't push me away."

I shake my head. "No, we've been through enough these past few days. This relationship is *over* before it's even begun. It's too much, Sam. I can't, my heart can't cope. I'm done."

He goes to the door, hanging his head in defeat and pushes an intercom.

"Cole, yeah, could you come and take Peyton home please, mate? Thanks."

He releases the button, and I go to open the door. He spins me around and pushes me against the door, his hands on either side of my head, pinning me to the door, so I can't get away. His face is inches away from mine, and I bite my lip.

"God, I want you so fucking badly it hurts; I can't think of anything else. I dream of being inside you, of seeing the expression on your face when I make you come," he whispers huskily, and I'm not sure if I'm in the presence of Sam or Bolt. I avoid eye contact, and he thrusts his hips into me. I feel his erection straining against his jeans push into my thigh.

"Look what you do to me, and you haven't even touched me. No woman has ever had the effect that you do."

Just speaking in that whispered husky voice is making me want him so badly. I know that if I look at him, I am going to give in to my body's urges and turn into a puddle at his feet. I shake my head.

"Bolt ... don't."

He looks at me as if I have just slapped him in the face and he recoils away from me.

"Do you really think I was being Bolt then?"

I look at him unwillingly.

"Everything I've said and done has come from Sam, not from Bolt. Bolt would have charmed you and had you in his bed and screaming with pleasure the day we met. He would have turned on the charm, had his way with you, and told you to get your knickers on and fuck off afterwards, no post-sex cuddling, no emotion, *nothing*," he snaps out, and I grip the door handle. "If you want to go, go. I won't stop you, but before you leave, know this, it's just you now, Peyton, *just you*."

I lean my head against the door and close my eyes. I breathed deeply trying to fight the strength of the emotions he evokes in me. I grip the door handle harder until my knuckles turn white, then I open the door and leave.

"Fucking fuck!"

I hear Sam shout and a loud crash as the door closes. I walk out into the foyer, avoiding eye contact with Cole, and walk straight past him into the waiting lift. I wait until the doors close until I break down in uncontrollable tears. By the time the lift stops, I have just about composed myself, and I step out into the underground car park. I see a door at the far end that leads out onto the street and go towards it. I push the door open and into the fresh air, and I walk away from Sam's house and out of his life for good.

12

Peyton

I get back to our flat and open the door. Ruby is lying on the sofa with a hot water bottle on her stomach softly sobbing. I throw my bag down and rush over to her. Crouching down next to the sofa, I stroke her hair and she looks pale. As she looks at me, I know that she went through with the abortion.

"I did it, Peyton."

I look sympathetically at her and hold her hand.

"Why didn't you call me? I would have been there for you."

She shakes her head. Seeing her like this breaks my heart.

"For you to talk me out of it?" she sobs, and I stroke her face. "I feel empty, Peyton."

I nod and place a kiss on the back of her hand. "I know, babe, I know."

I swallow back the lump in my throat. It breaks my heart to see my best friend like this.

"I'll make us some coffee."

I get to my feet and take off my jacket. I hang my coat up on the hanger and go into the kitchen. Ruby follows me as I switch on the coffee machine and get my favourite personalised purple 'Peyton keep calm and drink coffee' mug from the cupboard. She changes the subject and places her black 'Rock stars do it better' mug on the worktop.

"How come you're not at work? Skiving?"

I lean my head against the cupboard.

"No, I didn't have any appointments, so Seb gave me the afternoon off."

"How was your lunch date with Sam?"

I would rather not talk about it.

"Babe?"

I shake my head. "Please Ruby, just don't," I snap.

"Come on, what happened, babe? Talk to me."

"I bumped into Cal."

She turns to look at me, silently disapproving.

"Please tell me you're fucking joking."

The coffee machine finishes, and I pour the steaming hot black liquid into both mugs.

"Wish I was. Look, Rubes, you don't need to listen to my problems you've got your own to deal with."

"Don't be silly babe; it will take my mind off my own shit for a bit."

Smiling, I say, "Turns out, the girl Cal cheated with is Sam's fucking sister."

Her mouth drops open, and she puts the milk and sugar in her mug.

"Fuck me, Peyton, what are the odds? The slimy little wanker."

She goes into the living room and sits down on the sofa. I pour the milk into my coffee and spoon in two sugars. Stirring it, I walk carefully to the sofa. Ruby scoots her legs over, and I sit down next to her.

"He was with her when I was losing our baby."

Her face turns angry. "You fucking what? Just wait until I see him. I'll make sure he never fucking has kids, the cheating little fuck nugget."

I laugh at her reaction and take a sip of my coffee. I welcome the caffeine boost; it instantly calms me.

"I met Sam for lunch, but I was so upset after bumping into Callum, so we didn't stay for lunch. He took me back to his place."

Ruby raises her eyebrows knowingly. "Did you finally fuck him?"

I hit her arm playfully. "Ruby! No, I didn't, I told him it was over and that I didn't want to see him again."

She sits up slowly. "Are you shitting me? Peyton, you have a hot rock star falling over himself for you, and you're telling him you don't want to see him again? What the actual fuck!"

I shake my head. "I know, all of it, it was too much. All the press shit, him, he is too intense, the fact that his sister is the one who took Callum from me, and there's something about J.D that creeps me the fuck out."

She nods. "I agree, my lizard brain tells me that J.D is definitely bad news, just be careful, babe," Ruby warns, and I know that she is just looking out for me.

We spend the rest of the afternoon on the sofa, eating Ben and Jerry's ice cream and watching chick flicks, opting for *Love Actually*, *The Holiday* and *Mamma Mia*. I needed some girl time and a chance to talk with Ruby properly—these past few days have been such a whirlwind.

By early evening, Ruby has gone to her room for a lie-down and I'm in the flat on my own with a large glass of wine catching up with *Vampire Diaries* on TV. The door knocks softly, and I realise I am not expecting anyone. I open the door, and Sam leans into the doorway, his tall, powerfully-built frame filling the space.

"I couldn't leave it like that, babe, I had to come and make it right."

I look up at him, and he smiles. His smile melts me instantly, and he backs me into the flat. He swings the door closed and pushes me against it, gripping both of my wrists with one of his hands and pinning them above my head. His mouth finds my neck—he bites me gently, reminding me of the night of our date. Kisses are peppered from my neck to my collarbone until his other hand finds my breast. He gently squeezes it in his hand and fondles it through my clothes, stroking my nipple piercing. A wicked smile crawls onto his features, and I feel his erection digging into my pubic bone. He thrusts his hips forward, making me moan with pleasure.

"*Fuck,* Peyton, I want you so badly."

He kisses me on the lips frantically as his hand moves from my breast to my pussy. I writhe in his arms.

"Sam," I moan breathlessly into his mouth.

"Tell me to stop, tell me you don't want this, and I'll walk out of that door right now. You won't see me ever again, and that's a promise," he whispers, and I shake my head.

"I want you, Sam, so badly. *Fuck,* I wanted you the moment I first laid eyes on you."

He smiles and pops the button on my shorts with one smooth move of his hand.

"That's what I thought, babe."

He winks, pushing the zip down and reaching into my knickers. His long finger finds my slick folds, and he pushes it deep into my pussy. I gasp and moan so loud he frees my wrists and places his other hand over my mouth.

"See how wet you are for me, baby?"

He smiles seductively moving his finger slowly in and out of my pussy with ease.

"God, you're so tight. Imagine what my cock will feel like buried inside you."

I moan into his hand, and his lips find my neck. A fiery trail of kisses burns from my neck down to my breastbone, nipping as he goes. I stroke his erection through his trousers, and he moans into my heaving breasts.

"*Oh, Jesus,* that feels so good," he whispers huskily. He swiftly moves his finger from my pussy, and in one lithe move, he throws me effortlessly over his shoulder. He carries me into my bedroom, closes the door, and throws me down on the bed. With an effortless grace, he climbs onto my body like a panther stalking its prey. His lips caress me gently on the lips and move down my body. Suddenly, my shorts are pulled down, and my tights follow them into a heap onto the floor. I sit up and fumble with the zip on his jeans, pulling the denim down his muscular legs and kicking them off the end of the bed. He strips his t-shirt off to reveal the body of a perfectly sculpted Greek God—narrow hips, a heavily tattooed muscular chest, a six-pack to die for and a nipple piercing. I lick my lips at the sight of him—he smirks.

"Like what you see?"

I nod eagerly, and he throws his t-shirt on the growing pile of clothes on my floor. Within seconds, I am naked except for my knickers on my bed with him staring at me with appreciation.

"God, you're so ... fucking beautiful," he whispers.

"You're not so bad yourself, rock star."

I gasp as he carries on trailing kisses over the material of my knickers and down to my inner thigh. I'm aching for him; my whole body is burning with desire.

"Tell me what you want."

I pant as he nips a sensitive spot on my inner thigh, "I want you."

"How? Tell me, baby, tell me."

"I want your cock inside my pussy. Now."

"Good girl, your wish is my command."

He pulls my knickers down my legs, and they join the pile of clothes on the floor. The bed dips as he gets off the bed to remove his jeans and his boxers. My eyes widen at the size of the erection that springs free. He is huge, at least eight or nine inches in length if not bigger; he is hung like a donkey!

I must have a look of trepidation because he says, "I won't hurt you, I promise. I'll go slowly, and I'll be gentle."

He grasps his steel erection in his hand and strokes himself.

"Play with yourself. Show me how you make yourself come."

I shake my head. "I want you to make me come, Sam."

He winks. "All in good time, beautiful." He carries on stroking himself. "Show me," he growls.

I find something about the sound wild and erotic, making me want him even more. I never thought I would want a man as much as I want him. His eyes lock on mine, and he drops his hand from his growing cock before he gets back on the bed. He kneels between my legs and grasps his erection again.

"Now, show me how you make yourself come. I need to see you."

His voice is deep and commanding. I instantly do as he says, and he smiles playfully. I slide a finger down into my already soaking wet folds and begin to rub myself. I stroke my nub in deliberate slow circles and he moans.

"Oh, fuck, that's so fucking hot."

I moan as I watch him stroke himself. There is something so erotic and intimate about pleasuring ourselves in front of each other. Oddly, I don't feel embarrassed.

"God, look how swollen you are for me. Keep going, baby, I need you wet and ready for when I take you."

My slow circles become frantic as I moan and writhe on the bed.

"Sam, oh, God, Sam. Please," I moan out his name in desperation.

"I know, I know. Don't stop."

He gasps as he strokes himself, never breaking eye contact and I bite my lip.

"If you bite that lip once more I won't be gentle, I will fuck you *hard*."

I release my lip, and his voice is enough to make my pending orgasm rise to the surface. I feel it deep within my aching core, and I subconsciously bite my lip again. He drops his erection and lifts me up, stopping me abruptly.

"Do you have any condoms?" he rasps almost desperately, and I nod.

"In the top drawer," I say, breathless.

He reaches over into my top drawer and pulls out a foil packet, ripping it open with his teeth and sliding the condom onto his hard length. He pushes my legs open wider with his knee and pushes his cock deep into my pussy. I shriek at the sheer force, the size of him, and the feel of him filling me to the hilt. He puts his hand over my mouth as he moves in and out.

"God, you feel so good. You're so ... *Fuck*. You're tight," he gasps and takes his hand away from my mouth. I rake my nails down his back.

"That's it, touch me, I need to feel your hands on me."

My hands roam over his back and his shoulder blades. I squeeze his biceps and run my hands softly over his chest, loving how he feels underneath my touch. He is moving at a faster pace now, my body has adjusted to his size, and he cups my breast, kneading it in his hand. I moan, and pant as his pace quickens. He rams his cock deep into me, and when I pinch his nipple ring, he gasps.

"Oh, fuck me, you're amazing. Your pussy is like a velvet vice around my cock."

"Don't stop, Sam," I manage to pant out and he smiles lazily.

"Tell me."

I bite my lip, and he moves his hand from my breast to pull my lip out from the grip of my teeth.

"Tell me what you want, tell me what to do."

He lazily slides his cock in and out at a shockingly slow pace. I am left desperate and wanting.

"Sam, *please*." I try not to sound like a whiny child.

"Beg me," he growls, and I find it so hot.

"Look how wet you are for me; your pussy is soaking. Tell me what you want me to do."

I writhe under his touch. He trails his fingers down my stomach, causing goosebumps to appear over my entire body. I am burning for him—at this moment in time, I will do anything this man wants. I am aching for him to give me the release I need.

"Sam, please, *please* fuck me hard, make me come. I need you to make me come."

He smiles. "Good girl."

He rams his cock back into me, and I scream out. He quickens his pace, and I feel my orgasm rushing to the surface. He finds my swollen clit and rubs it in small circles. With one swift move of his cock, I feel my orgasm explode from me.

"*Fuck*, Sam. Oh, God, I'm going to come."

He pushes his cock into me to the hilt. "I've got you. Come with me, baby."

I scream out as my orgasm floods through my whole body, making me pant and quiver as he explodes into me at the same time. He leans down and bites my neck as he comes, trembling. Our orgasms subside, and he collapses, spent on top of me. We are both breathless and sweaty after our sex session.

After a few minutes, he pulls out of me, pulls the condom off, and knots it at the end. He throws it in the bin next to my bed and lies back down on the bed. As he scoots closer to me, he pulls me into him, and I lay my head on his torso; I feel the rise and fall of his chest. For the first time in a long time, I feel content and the happiest I have ever felt. Blissful and in the throes of a passionate, blossoming romance. He strokes my hair tenderly.

"Peyton, you're fucking amazing."

"Thanks, you're pretty amazing yourself."

I squeeze him, and the door to my bedroom knocks gently. I lift my head up from Sam's chest, and Ruby says quietly, "Babe, is everything OK?"

Sam and I both laugh silently.

"Erm ... yeah, everything's fine."

She giggles like a schoolgirl. "Glad you and the rock star made up, babe; you're made for each other."

I hear the smile in her voice as her footsteps cross the flat and a door closes. I resume my position with my head laid on Sam's chest and him stroking my arm gently. Enjoying his closeness and the heat from his body.

"Are you OK?" Sam looks down at me, and I nod.

"Yeah, I'm fine, thanks. Are you OK?"

He chuckles softly. "Yeah, I'm more than OK, babe, trust me."

We both laugh.

"Do you want to stay over?"

He strokes my hair and leans down to kiss the top of my head. "I'd love to, beautiful."

I smile, and I hear my phone ringing out in the flat where I left it. My ringtone of Avenged Sevenfold's *Seize the Day* growing louder as the phone continues to ring.

Groaning, I say, "Back to reality, baby."

I take my black, silk, kimono, dressing gown from the hook on the back of my bedroom door and put it on. The silk feels cool against my skin; I pull it tightly around my body and tie it at my waist, jam my feet into my UGG slippers, and Sam is watching me from the bed with his hands behind his head. Gloriously naked and with a smug grin plastered across his face. I open the door, and my phone stops ringing. *Bloody typical.* I pick up my phone and check who was calling—I have ten missed calls and a voicemail. *What could possibly be so important that would warrant that amount of communication?* Then I remember the small matter of mine and Sam's *'relationship'* plastered all over the newspapers and internet. I roll my eyes, frustrated at the whole sorry situation. Sam walks out of my bedroom wearing his jeans with the fly open—he is shirtless and walking barefoot towards me. He smiles, stops in front of me, and kisses me gently on the lips.

"Is everything all right?"

I shake my head, and concern mars his beautifully handsome features.

"I've got ten missed calls on my phone."

He rolls his eyes. "No rest for the wicked, babe."

We both smile at each other, and I listen to the voice mail.

"Hey, sweetie, it's only me, there's more photos of you and that handsome rocker of yours on the internet. You haven't called me back. I tried ringing Sebastian at the shop, but he said he had given you the afternoon off. Is everything OK, my darling? Give me a call back, you know how much I worry. Love you, bye."

It's my mum, I smile at her voice message, grateful that she cares so much. I dial her number and leave Sam clattering around in the kitchen, looking for something to cook for us.

"Hey, mum, it's me."

She sighs. "Hey, sweetie, *finally*. I've been trying to call you for an age. Where have you been?"

Having amazing sex with my gorgeous rock star boyfriend. But I don't say those words aloud. Instead, I clear my throat.

"Just catching up on some girl time with Ruby, she's ... had a lot to deal with."

My mum pauses a moment before saying, "Is everything OK, my darling? There's been more photos posted on the internet, of you and the rock star getting into a car."

I tighten my grip on the phone. "Yeah, everything's great. I haven't had a chance to look, Mum, I've been busy. Please don't worry about me. I'm fine, honestly. Eden called this morning."

She sucks in an audible breath.

"Yes, she mentioned she was going to call. Look, I think you should come home, have a family meal, all of us together. You can bring the rock star."

"Mum, his name is Sam, and a family meal sounds ... really great," I reluctantly agree. It's not that I don't like spending time with my family, it's just that me and my older sister don't get on. Our personalities are so different, and she is engaged to a barrister called Jonah Hunt who is middle-aged and *very* rich—his parents are billionaires and own a country estate in Surrey. She thinks that because he is ridiculously rich, everyone else is beneath her. We couldn't be more different.

"That's fabulous, sweetie; it's been so long since you came home. You can come home Friday evening for the weekend, get away from London for a while, it will do you good."

I smile and agree with my mum. I definitely think that a break from the hustle and bustle of city life would do me good, even if it is just for the weekend. Mum and Dad are semi-retired and live in Brighton, just an hour or so away from London. They live in a five-bedroom detached house with a swimming pool and an acre of land at the back of the house. It's amazing and was our family home until me, my older sister Eden, and my younger brother Dexter all moved out into the big wide world. I feel myself getting excited at the prospect of going home for the weekend.

"That would be really great, mum. I've missed you. It will be so nice to be home, and it feels like I haven't seen you and Dad in forever."

I hear the smile in her voice, and I can't remember the last time I saw my family. These past few months have been so busy.

"I know, sweetie, it will be fantastic to see you and to finally meet the boy who's stolen my little girl's heart."

Smiling to myself, I tell her, "Yeah, I really can't wait, Mum. Look, I have to go. Sam's trying to trash our kitchen by the looks of it."

Sam cocks his pierced eyebrow from across the flat, and I stick my tongue out at him. My mum laughs on the end of the phone.

"OK, my baby girl, we'll see you on Friday."

"See you Friday, Mum, love you."

"Love you, Peyton, bye."

I hang up the phone and Sam raises his eyebrows at me.

"Trying to trash the kitchen?"

He leaps athletically over the sofa and grabs me around the waist. He tickles me, and I scream, kicking my legs as he holds me with ease.

"I say we order Chinese and curl up on the sofa?"

He shakes his head. "Or we could go back to mine, snuggle up on my sofa, and order Chinese. Plus, now I owe you a tour of *my* bedroom." He winks and puts my feet firmly back on the ground.

"OK, that sounds like a plan."

I smile and walk to Ruby's bedroom, tapping the door gently.

"Ruby, it's me." I hear her sniff.

"Hey, babe, come in."

I open the door and walk into her bedroom. She looks up from her Kindle Fire and takes off her glasses as I sit on the edge of the bed.

"How are you feeling?"

She nods. "Better, thanks. I've got painkillers, a hot water bottle, and Jesse Ward. That's all I need, babe!"

I smile. The colour has returned to her cheeks, and she looks almost back to her normal self, at least from the outside.

"Are you sure?"

She looks at me with a pointed stare. "Yeah, I'm fine, honestly. Stop worrying. I'll be fine, I always am."

I smile, but something in the way she looks at me tells me that she's not being entirely honest with me.

"If you're sure? You know how I worry about you."

She rolls her eyes and puts her hand on top of mine. "You worry too much. I'm OK, honestly. Anyway, it's not me I'm worried about, you two sounded like you were enjoying yourselves!"

We both burst into a fit of giggles.

"Ruby, he's ... amazing." I sigh, collapsing back on Ruby's bed as we lie next to each other. She widens her eyes.

"Is he ... Fuck it. Is his cock big?"

I am embarrassed at Ruby's question, and then I nod. She giggles like a schoolgirl.

"Huge."

I put my hand to my open mouth, and we both laugh hysterically.

"I was just coming to tell you: I'm going back to Sam's place for a while."

She nods. "That's fine, babe. You don't have to check in with me, you know."

Despite her insistence, I know that she hates being on her own.

"I can stay if you want? You know how much I worry, and I know you don't like being here on your own."

"I'll be fine. Honestly, if I get lonely, I'll call Jax." She winks.

Sitting up, she gives me a hug, and I say, "I'll see you later or tomorrow if I decide to stay over. I'll call you or text you."

She kisses me on the cheek. "Love you, Peyton."

Getting up from the bed, I cross to the door before turning to blow her a kiss. "Love ya, Rubes."

I close her bedroom door behind me and find that Sam is fully dressed in the living room. He has his hands in his pockets, and he looks gorgeously awkward standing in my flat.

"I'm just going to pack an overnight bag."

He smiles and winks at me. "Good thinking."

I grab my Ed Hardy overnight bag and stuff in my pyjamas, knowing that I won't need them if Sam has anything to do with it! I grab a change of clothes for work tomorrow, spare underwear, my make-up bag, and my hairbrush, then zip up the bag and take it out into the flat. I rush to the bathroom to grab my electric toothbrush and then I am ready to leave. As I pull on my denim jacket, Sam picks up my bag.

"Bye, Ruby," I call.

Sam and I leave the flat and go down the stairs to the underground garage where he stops.

"I was going to call, Cole. I told him to go back home because I wasn't sure how long I'd be."

I raise my eyebrows. "We're going in my car; I am quite capable of driving. We don't all have personal chauffeurs."

"Touché!" His eyes widen when he catches sight of my car, whistling low. "Nice wheels, babe."

"I think so; she's my pride and joy."

He puts his arm around my waist, and tells me, "Don't say that too often. I might get jealous!"

We both laugh as I unlock the door. I climb into the driver seat; Sam opens the passenger door and throws my overnight bag in the backseat. He gets in, and we both fasten our seatbelts. Then I start up the car, and we pull out into the night.

13

Peyton

Half an hour later, we pull into Sam's parking garage at his apartment in Greenwich near to London's East Docklands. There are at least ten sports cars and at least ten superbikes parked in Sam's section. The cars range from Aston Martins and Bugatti Veyrons to Porsches and Mercedes. The superbikes range from Ducatis and Kawasakis to custom Harley Davidsons; it would definitely be a petrol head's wet dream! We both step into the waiting lift; he presses the button for his place, and when the doors slide shut, he backs me into the corner. He claims my mouth once again, and I melt into his arms. He holds me protectively to him as his tall frame towers over me.

"I owe you another orgasm!" he breathes seductively into my mouth, and I grin.

The lift comes to a halt, and we step out into the foyer. Cole is walking around without his hat and his tie on. He looks comfortable and at home. He greets me with a nod, and I start to wonder if he lives in the same building as Sam. I have so many questions I want to ask, but I keep them to myself for the time being. Sam unlocks and opens the large black oak door, and I am again struck dumb by the view looking across the city. I can see right across the city from Sam's window, and it looks even more beautiful at night. Sam puts my bag down and kicks off his shoes.

"Make yourself at home, babe, I want you to be just as comfortable here as you are at home. This is my sanctuary; somewhere I'm not disturbed, where I can be myself, just ordinary, regular Sam."

I smile and kick off my shoes too. He smiles back.

"Do you want some coffee or something stronger?"

I look at him. "Something stronger would be great, thanks."

He goes off into the kitchen, and I follow him, taking in my surroundings. His place is spectacular. I am taken aback as I follow him to his kitchen. It is huge and twice the size of my flat. The kitchen is all chrome, black and white, in clean accented tones. The worktop is black marble with a kitchen island in the centre with black lacquer stools around it. The cupboards are black, and the kitchen has the same view as his living room with floor to ceiling windows at the far end. There is a large glass dining table by the window with four high-backed, gothic chairs around it.

"You look stunned every time you step into another room here; it's adorable to see your face light up!" Sam says with a laugh.

I lean against the kitchen island and watch him as he opens his large silver fridge. There is a selection of pictures adorning the fridge, from pictures of his band, band magnets, and pictures of what looks like his family. I move closer to the fridge and take a closer look as he opens it. He takes out a bottle of white wine.

"Is white wine OK for you?"

I nod as I carry on examining the pictures.

"Is that The Lightning Bolts?"

I point towards the picture of the massive seventies rock band. I remember my mum and dad talking about them and listening to their music when I was a kid. They were a big deal back in the seventies, the Green Day of their era, rock mixed with a bit of Sex Pistols-inspired punk. Sam opens the wine and takes out two glasses.

"You're familiar with them, huh?"

I nod, and he smiles.

"Yeah my mum and dad used to play their music to get me to sleep; their music was always playing when I was growing up. They were huge fans back in the day." He pours the wine in the glasses as he continues, "The drummer, Marlowe, he's my dad."

I look at him with wide eyes and examine the picture more closely.

"Wow, your dad was a drummer, that's incredible. No wonder you became a rocker."

He smiles and hands me a glass. I take it from him with a quick, "Thanks."

I take a sip, feeling the cold liquid slide down my throat and warm my stomach.

"Me, my older brother, and older sister went on tour a couple of times with him when we were younger. It always fascinated me seeing him perform, the atmosphere, the way his fans adored him. I grew up around the music industry, it's in my blood. My dad and his bandmates are my heroes; they influenced our earlier stuff."

I smile at his enthusiasm. He hops up gracefully and sits on the worktop. I am standing opposite him leaning against the kitchen island, regarding him intently.

"My dad always took it in his stride. He never let the fame go to his head, and he always told me to follow my dreams, that he'd support me no matter what if I wanted to pick music as a career. I was rubbish in school at everything except music; it was as if it ... spoke to me in some way. I was in bands from an early age—my dad taught me drums and guitar, my mum made us take piano lessons—but I sang as well. I grew up with Jax; we lived next door to each other, and I went to school with Lucas and Brody. We were all best mates, more like brothers, really, and we decided we were going to form a band. We were called the Spunk Monkeys!"

I laugh at the name and listen attentively to his story, fascinated by hearing him tell me about his dad and how his band finally hit the big time.

"We rehearsed in my dad's studio and in Jax's garage; we did loads of free gigs for our mates, for the neighbours where we lived, for our school, for local clubs and pubs. It was so hard in the beginning, and I wanted to make it without the influence of my dad. But the truth is, I would never have made it without him. Jed Dalton was The Lightning Bolt's manager, but he passed away ten years ago. J.D inherited the record company at the age of twenty-seven, and he was looking to sign a new band to give his flailing record label a boost. My dad told him that I was in a band and it went from there. I was twenty, and I was going to be in a famous rock band."

He shakes his head at the thought as if he can't believe it happened and looks at me.

"So, that's how we made it. It was like a whirlwind: we went from just regular young guys to full-blown rock stars. It was completely mental."

He gets down from the worktop and walks over to me, kissing my forehead and grabbing my hand.

"Let's go and chill on the sofa. I want to just forget being me for a while and enjoy being with you."

I melt at his sweet words, as he grabs the bottle of wine from the worktop and leads me into the living room. He sits down on the sofa and pats the space beside him. His mobile starts ringing, but he silences it and rejects the call, which I find odd, but I keep my mouth firmly shut.

"Come and sit down, babe, make yourself comfortable."

I sit down next to him, and we both tuck our legs up underneath ourselves at the same time. We get comfortable, and I take a long sip of my wine.

"So, what's the deal with you and J.D?"

His pauses as he takes a sip of his wine and his smile fades. "You noticed the tension between us, huh?"

I look at him and nod slowly, gauging his reaction.

"It's kind of obvious, he keeps ... threatening me."

He clenches his teeth and balls his fist.

"I've warned him to stay the fuck away from you, babe. He won't hurt you—he is all talk, and he hasn't got the balls. If he even touches a hair on your head, I swear to God I will fucking kill him, you have my word."

His demeanour changes as he speaks about J.D, but I don't push him to tell me.

"When I was twenty, when he was signing us, we ... we had sex."

I almost choke on my wine. "*What?* You and J.D?"

I know my voice is a pitch higher than normal and he nods shamefully.

"That's pretty fucked up, isn't it? I fucked my manager to further my career; he told me that he had always liked me, being Marlowe Newbolt's son. He was always at family gatherings with his dad Jed, and he was always 'round at our house. We started to become friends; there's only seven years between us. He and his dad were a calming presence in our family. But when he was signing us, the power went to his head, and he said he could either make us or break us as band depending on what ... On what I could offer him."

I scowl and shudder at the thought of Sam and J.D.

"Sam, you don't have to tell me, baby." I brush his arm reassuringly, and he shakes his head.

"No, it's fine, I want to tell you the whole truth, I don't want any secrets or lies between us. I want total honesty all the way, not after earlier, when you found out about Savannah and Callum... When I thought I had lost you for good. I thought I'd fucked up so bad, then you walked out. All I wanted to do was go after you, but Cole stopped me."

"I just panicked, that's all. All Callum ever did was lie to me. I couldn't bear being in another relationship where my partner felt the need to lie to me."

He puts his wine glass down on the table and takes my hand in his.

"I would never ever lie to you. I didn't tell you about Sav and Callum because I knew how cut up you were about him. That first night when I took you for dinner, and you told me about what he did, I could see in your eyes how hurt you were just talking about it. I didn't ever want to see that look in your eyes while you were with me, and I wanted to protect you." He gently kisses the back of my hand. "Please understand that was the only reason I didn't tell you. When I saw that photo of you and him together, I recognised him straight away, and I wanted to fucking kill him for doing that to you. The next day, I went 'round to my sister's house where he lives with her, and I was going to seriously hurt him if Sav hadn't stopped me. I had my hands around his throat, I saw red, and I was so fucking angry."

He clenches his fist at the thought, and I can see in his eyes how much he wants to protect me.

"I feel ... protective of you, Peyton, you're so fragile and so fucking beautiful, you take my breath away. Even the paps from the other day, I wanted to fucking hurt every single one of them for pointing a camera in your face. You're in their radar now, and it's all because of me, so it's my duty to protect you."

I see the passion in his eyes as he says those words and I snuggle closer to him. He wraps his arm around me, and I am encased in his warmth. I rest my head on his chest.

"Now, where were we? Oh yeah, J.D."

I feel his whole body tense at the sound of his name.

"He said he could either make us or break us as band depending on what I could offer him. We were in his studio on the sofa; he put his arm around me and stroked my face, telling me he had always had a soft spot for me. Before I knew it, he was kissing me, and I was kissing him back because I didn't know what the fuck was going on. He got up, pulled the blinds and locked the door; I was young and so naïve back then. He kept telling me that he would make sure we made millions by the time we were twenty-five as long as I did what he asked. I was so desperate to make it in the music industry and to further our careers, I did what he told me."

He picks up his glass from the table and downs what is left.

"I sucked him off, and we had sex in his studio that night, but we both dismissed it afterwards, and he agreed to go along with it. Forgetting it ever happened. But since then, any girl who has got close to me, he gets so angry and jealous. He does everything in his power to push them away, so they end up either selling their story to the press or dumping me all because of him and his dirty fucking scheming. I promise you I won't let him do that to us."

I see him visibly become angry as he is retelling the story, but I stay silent since I don't know what to say. I am content with sitting here listening to him. The sane part of me is telling me not to judge, but the other part is telling me the complete opposite.

"He told me he was in love with me, and I told him straight that I only did it because I wanted to further my career and that I wasn't gay. He got so angry he threatened to tell the world that I was secretly gay, but I convinced him not to. I told him I would tell everyone that his record company was about to go bankrupt if he ever breathed a word. I stopped being the naïve gullible boy he knew, and ever since then he has gone back to being just J.D: managing our schedules, overseeing our tours, the usual stuff managers do. He means well, and I don't think he means to, but he just needs to let go of the past like I have."

I pull away from him and look at the pained look on his face.

"Sam ... I don't get why you're fucking defending him. He took advantage of you, and you can't let him manipulate you like that."

He pours us both another glass of wine.

"He doesn't manipulate me anymore, babe, believe me. That was a long time ago, it's like I was a completely different person back then."

I can't wrap my head around the revelation he has just told me, so I stand up and walk over to where I left my coat. He looks puzzled as I pull on my coat.

"I should go ..."

"What the fuck! Please don't go. I tell you something massive like that and all you want to do is run? I was twenty, Peyton, what fucking choice did I have?"

The other part of my otherwise sane brain takes over.

"That's bullshit; of course you had a fucking choice, Sam! You might not have had your millions back then, but at least you had your dignity and your self-respect."

He shakes his head. "I had nothing back then, I was at a difficult period in my life, and I was so desperate for fame and fortune. I had a hunger for the fans chanting my name, to see the banners in the crowd, to hear a crowd of people singing my songs back to me. I saw the way the fans idolised my dad, and I wanted that so fucking badly. J.D just gave me a shortcut."

When I look at him and see the way his eyes light up at the mention of his fans, I start to soften and understand more of why he did what he did.

"Look, if you want to go, I can't stop you."

I take a long sip of my wine and take off my coat. I sit down, not wanting to leave while he is in a sharing mood. I notice that the wine is making him open up.

"He inherited Diamond Records from his dad Jed after he passed away like I said. He's been our manager for ten years now, but lately, he's been letting things slide. He let the record company go bankrupt because he let the money, the power, and the fame go to his head. He thinks he's untouchable because he's the *great* Jed Dalton's son. The guy who owns our record company now, Alistair Simpson, he bought the record company from Johnnie and kept him on as our manager, but Alistair's been more of a manager these past few months, even though he normally takes a back seat. J.D's more interested in drinking himself into oblivion, drowning in his own self-pity and snorting thousands of pounds worth of cocaine. He's become a fucking liability; his dad would be turning in his grave."

I'm shocked at the revelations that Sam is sharing with me. I'm still silent, and I'm rendered speechless at the lengths that J.D would go to just to make Sam's life miserable. As Sam goes on, I begin to hate J.D more with every passing moment.

"He turns up here sometimes, drunk and off his face usually, banging on my door at all hours in the morning, begging me to open the door so we can talk. I used to let him in just to keep the peace, and at first, it was nice having some company other than Jax and the boys, but he made a pass at me. I went crazy and threw him out. Now, Jimmy the guard at the front desk refuses to let him anywhere near the building."

He takes a long sip of his wine.

"Do you want something stronger than wine, babe? I know I do. I think I have some vodka, tequila or whiskey? I have a limited selection; I haven't stocked up in a while."

I shake my head; my stomach is starting to feel fuzzy and warm. The wine is quickly having an effect on me, and I'm not normally such a lightweight.

"Fucking hell. I'm sorry, I think I've got a touch of the verbal's tonight, babe. You've hardly said a word."

"I like listening to you talk, your voice does something to me, and I could listen to you all day."

He raises his eyebrows. "Are you drunk?"

I laugh. "Maybe a little tipsy, it's just something that Ruby said when I first told her about tattooing you guys, she said you could make women orgasm with just your voice."

He raises his eyebrows and laughs hysterically. "OK, wow, that's ... *really flattering,* but deep down, I'm an ordinary guy who just got lucky."

I look at him as if to say *'are-you-shitting-me?'*

"You're Sam Newbolt, you're in one of the world's biggest rock bands, you've sold millions of albums and played all over the world. You're so far from ordinary."

It's times like these when we're alone that he shows me his vulnerable side. He wanders back into the kitchen, and while he is gone, I take advantage of his absence and walk around his impressive apartment. I take in the minimal decor, the black, white and chrome sleek look of the accessories. I sense that Sam didn't decorate this place himself, as all the rooms are similar in décor—clean and stark. He comes back with two bottles in his hands.

"You like the apartment then, babe?"

I smile and spin around to face him. "Yeah, I love it. I'm sorry, I don't mean to be nosy."

"You're far from nosy, babe. I'm sorry, I should have given you the grand tour, I'm a rubbish host, give me a sec."

He sprints over to the table and puts the bottles down. He is back at my side in seconds.

"Where do you want the tour to start?" he asks seductively, and I know he is hinting at round two in the bedroom.

"How about your studio, if you have one?"

He raises his eyebrow.

"Of course I have one, I'm Sam fucking Newbolt!" he says cockily, but I know he is teasing by the cheeky grin on his face bringing out his cute dimples. He leads me down a corridor with framed album covers hanging on the walls. He grabs my hand and unlocks a door at the end of the corridor. It's impressive; it has a full-size drum kit, two electric guitars, and a microphone stand behind a wall of glass. There is a full mixing desk with two iMac computers on the table. I look around, awe-struck by my surroundings. On the walls are gold and platinum discs in frames and I am again reminded of the contrast in our lifestyles.

"You like?"

I nod and look at him.

"Everything about this place amazes me, Sam."

He smiles and sits down on the leather chair that is at the desk.

"It's also soundproof." He winks cheekily, and I chuckle softly. He spins around to face me and pulls me down on his lap. "It doesn't have to, I'd be happy to live in a cardboard box as long as I'm with you."

He kisses me deeply on the lips.

"Peyton, you're *everything*. You're beautiful, funny, and you make me feel alive. I've never felt like this about anyone in my life before, it's kind of scaring the shit out of me, but it feels good."

He smiles, and the depth of feeling for this man overwhelms me. Even though our lives are poles apart and I have so many insecurities, I still want our relationship to stand the test of time. He runs his hand up my spine.

"What are you thinking about? You're sweet when you get that look on your face."

"Thanks. Just thinking about us. About how different our lives are, you with your entourage around you it's kind of *intimidating* at times, if I'm honest."

He folds his muscled arms and crosses his legs at the ankle.

"Intimidating? And I have an entourage?" He raises his eyebrows and laughs. "I'll sack them all if that's what you want. Just say the word."

My eyes widen, and I shake my head. "No! I didn't mean that"

He shrugs, stands up, and leads me out of the studio. He locks the door behind him, abruptly ending our conversation. We walk back down the small corridor where he opens another door.

"After you."

He gestures for me to step into his bedroom, and I am stunned into silence. A king-size four-poster bed with black and silver gothic drapes around it centres the room. Black silk sheets adorn the bed, and I see what he meant when he said I deserved silk sheets. There are two, gothic, black-embossed bedside tables with mirrored tops sit on either side of the bed. Throughout Sam's apartment, I notice a running theme of stark, black and white with matching accessories.

"Welcome to my boudoir!"

He laughs and bows dramatically as I take in the surroundings. I laugh at his humour.

"I don't bring women back here, you're highly honoured!"

I smile at being the only woman he has brought back here to his sanctuary.

"This is the en-suite bathroom."

He opens the door, and I walk in. The bathroom has black and white mosaic tiles on the walls, and the large bath takes up the entire back wall. Suddenly, I hear a phone ringing, and Sam rolls his eyes.

"No rest for the wicked, babe."

We leave the bathroom and go back out into the living area. Sam picks up his mobile.

"Hello, oh hey, yeah."

He holds up his finger indicating that he will be just a minute, and I resume my position on the sofa. He wanders off around the apartment talking on his phone, so I finish my wine and check my phone. I have a voicemail—I swipe my finger across the screen and listen.

"Peyton, it's Cal, I wasn't sure if you'd still have the same mobile number, so I'm not one hundred percent certain that you're going to get this. But I really wanted to apologise for the way I behaved today, it was bang out of order. I'm so sorry for everything that happened between us. I really want us to meet up and talk properly, not just argue like a pair of kids in the street. Look, I know you're with Sam and I'm with Sav, but we need closure on the whole you and me thing. Please call me back, baby cakes."

I sit open-mouthed at listening to Callum's message, and I feel the colour drain from my face. I can't believe that he has the nerve to call me after everything that has happened between us. Even though I'm not with him anymore, he still manages to fuck with my head. Sam comes back into the living room; he crouches down in front of me and cups my cheek in his hand.

"What's wrong, are you OK?"

I hang up the phone and put it down on the table.

"Everything's fine, honestly."

I put on my best fake smile, and he narrows his eyes at me.

"Don't lie to me, we agreed no more secrets. Plus, the fact that you look like you've seen a ghost kind of gives you away."

"Nothing gets past you, does it, Sam?"

"Nope! Just call me Sherlock Holmes! Tell me what's wrong, babe, you looked like you'd seen a ghost when you hung up the phone."

I clear my throat before saying, "Cal left a message on my voicemail."

Sam's demeanour becomes angry. I see his body visibly tense as he sits down next to me.

"What did that fucker say?" he asks through gritted teeth. I hand him my phone, and he listens to Callum's message. As soon as it finishes, he hands the phone back to me.

"Are you going to meet him?"

I shake my head. "No. God, I don't know, he fucks with my head every time, Sam. We said all we needed to earlier I have nothing more to say to him."

He puts his arm around me and squeezes me reassuringly.

"What was your relationship like with him?"

I look up at him, and a pained look crosses my face. It hurts to remember what it was like with Callum to begin with. He was so sweet, he was good-looking in a boy-next-door kind of way, and he treated me like a princess—we were so in love.

14

Peyton

Past

It was a Friday night. Ruby and I were at a club in Camden called Fifty-Five. We needed to let our hair down after a long week at work. My dark hair tumbled in loose waves down my shoulders. I was wearing a short, leather, panelled skirt, fishnet tights, heels, and a black, halter-neck top with diamante skulls all over it. My best pulling outfit. We were both single and more than a little tipsy. Ruby was pole dancing in the club, and there was a group of men gathered around watching her open-mouthed. I was confident and bubbly, but I wished I were more like her as far as men were concerned. I was a little shy around men; I had been single for so long I had forgotten what it was like to date and be in a relationship. That was when I saw him: a tall, toned, and tanned blonde man staring in my direction. He was with a group of his friends, and one of them was whispering to him. He didn't take his eyes off me. I turned my head, thinking he must have been looking at someone else, and then I looked back at him. He smiled and lowered his eyes. I smiled back, and he cocked his head to the side. I took a sip of my drink for some Dutch courage and slowly walked over to him.

"Hey," I said over the pumping music.

"Hey yourself."

His friend nudged him, winked, and left us to it.

"I saw you watching me from over there."

He leaned his head down, and I could smell his sweet Davidoff Cool Water aftershave.

"I'm Callum, but you can call me Cal."

He offered his hand, and I took it. He lifted my hand to his lips and kissed the back gently, causing me to smile at the sweet gesture.

"I'm Peyton."

"It's a pleasure to meet you, Peyton. So, what brings a beautiful girl like you to a place like this on a Friday night? I haven't seen you here before."

I took another sip of my drink, enjoying the attention Callum was showing me.

"No, me and my friend just decided we needed to let our hair down, we've both had kind of a mad week at work!"

He nodded. "You look stunning, by the way," he shouted over the music as his eyes travelled down my body.

"Thanks."

"Can I get you a drink?"

I nod. "Yeah, please, that would be lovely."

He gestured to the barman.

"Same again for the lady. Cheers, mate."

He got me a large Absolut vodka and cranberry, my drink of choice. He pushed it towards me and smiled.

"Here you go, love."

I smiled warmly, and he clinked my glass. "Thank you, Callum."

He smiled back, and I was disarmed by his wide, boyish smile.

"My pleasure, Peyton."

After an hour or so chatting to Callum, I felt like I had known him forever, we had so many things in common, and for the first time in a long time, I was comfortable being around him. He was charming, good-looking, and he made me laugh. I looked around the club, and Ruby was nowhere to be seen—she had more than likely copped off and gone back to some guy's house, without any regard for my safety. Great, cheers, Rubes. Callum looked at his watch.

"I should go home. I need to be up early for work in the morning. Look, I'd really like to take you out, Peyton. I like you a lot, and I don't usually click with women like I have with you, I feel like I've known you all my life."

I smiled, flattered at his kind words. I suddenly felt drunk and bold. I leaned in to kiss him gently on the lips. His lips were so soft, and I thought maybe I was drunker than I realised. I pulled away and giggled childishly.

"I don't want to take advantage of you, Peyton; I want to treat you like a princess, I want to wine and dine you. A woman as beautiful as you deserves to be treated with respect."

And that line was what hooked me on Callum Kennedy.

15

Peyton
Present

I am suddenly back in the room with Sam, and he strokes my hand.

"Babe, whoa! I lost you back then. Where were you?"

I look at him confused and shake myself back to the present.

"I was remembering what it was like when I first met Callum. We met in a club. He was so sweet and caring back then; he had the kindest eyes and a smile that would light up a room. He was so charming and such a gentleman. After a few dates, we slept together, and kind of got into a routine of me staying at his or him staying at ours. Callum was *safe*, he was ... everything to me."

Sam sits on the sofa listening attentively to me retell my story, and he pours us both large vodkas.

"After two years or so of being together, I got pregnant. We were so happy, or so I thought. But by the time I found out, I was already three months gone. I went for our first scan with Ruby, and when I told Callum, he was so distant. I thought he might feel *something* when I showed him the scan picture of our baby growing inside me. He asked me if I wanted to get rid of it because he wasn't ready to be a dad, and it wasn't the right time. We argued that night; he trashed the flat, stormed out, and left me in his flat on my own. I was all set to go ahead and be a single mum then I doubled over with crippling stomach pains, and I was bleeding heavily. I knew straight away that I was losing my baby and I was in his flat on my own. I didn't know what else to do; I managed to make it to a phone, called Ruby, and called an ambulance. I was hysterical and in total agony by the time they got there. Ruby was my rock that night. I don't know what I would have done without her. She was there for me when it should have been Callum."

My voice cracks and a tear rolls down my cheek. Sam wipes it away with his thumb and strokes my face. "I fucking promised myself I wouldn't *ever* cry over him again and he has done it twice in one day."

I laugh bitterly and down the vodka, relishing the burn as it slides down my throat.

"He showed up at the hospital the next day, no emotion, he just said how sorry he was, but his eyes told me a totally different story. I knew something was off with him, it was as if he wasn't even affected that our baby had just died."

Sam's eyes darken, and he downs his vodka. He pours us both two more.

"What an absolute fucking prick. I'd never have left you, Peyton; I'd have been there for you every single step of the way."

I sniff and smile at his kind words. He takes my hand reassuringly in his.

"I'm damaged, Sam, he damaged something inside me. I'd have done anything for him. I was so in love with him, I forgave him for so many things, but walking in on him fucking another woman was the final straw. He broke my fucking heart."

We both lean back on the sofa, and I snuggle into the crook of Sam's neck as I sob softly. At that moment, I have never felt more vulnerable, and I hope deep down that Sam doesn't hurt me the way Callum did.

"Hey, shhh, he is not worth your tears, angel. As long as we're together, I don't ever want to cause you tears and pain. I want to see you smile every single day. I want to wake up next to you and feel your presence in my heart. I can already see myself settling down with you, growing old with you."

He smiles and tucks a strand of my hair behind my ear. I am comforted by his words and the more time I spend with him, the more I can see us having a future together. He makes me feel alive, like I could take on the world by just looking into his eyes. I get lost in his touch and feel the warmth of his body. Sam makes me feel safe, and nothing can hurt me while he is around. It is a welcome feeling, but every time I think that we could have a future together, something comes along that jeopardises it.

At that moment, I promise myself that I am going to relax around him and just go with the flow. With that thought, he gets up and drags me up with him.

"Come with me, I've got a surprise for you. I want to show you something that I think will make you feel better."

We both run through his apartment like a pair of teenagers in love. I am giddy with excitement as he takes me to the foyer and drags me into the lift. He pushes the button labelled 'R', which I assume is for the roof.

"Where are you taking me?"

He looks down at me and interlinks our fingers together. "You'll see. It will be worth it, I promise."

He kisses me gently on the lips, and the lift comes to a halt. We step out, and he pushes open a door. I follow him and am shocked at what I see in front of me. He has brought me up to a roof garden; there are plants and bright, exotic flowers everywhere. But what shocks me the most is a large hot tub hidden behind a black partition surrounded by greenery. At the far end of the roof garden are a BBQ area, a hammock, and a modern, wooden, seating area looking out across the city.

"Surprise!"

I bite my lip and clap excitedly. All Sam's apartment has to offer renders me speechless.

"I wanted to save the best for last, baby. I wanted to show you how much you mean to me."

I melt at his kindness. "I'm ... speechless. It's beautiful."

"No woman has ever been up here. Just you, Peyton. I own the whole building, I occupy the whole second, third, and fourth floor. Cole lives on the first floor, there's a gym on the fifth floor, Jax lives on the sixth floor, Lucas lives on the seventh, there's another studio and a few offices."

I widen my eyes, shocked at the full extent of Sam's wealth. He doesn't brag and is very humble about his fame. Sam starts to take off his t-shirt and his jeans.

"Are you coming in, babe?"

I smile shyly and take in Sam's body, committing it to memory. His body is Adonis-like—he is toned, muscled, and his body is covered in the most amazing, intricate tattoo designs. The colours are vivid, bright, and very fitting for Sam's personality.

As he steps into the hot tub, I get a view of his arse—tight and to die for. I bite my lip and feel the heat between my legs. I want him so badly; when I am around him, I turn into an insatiable nymphomaniac, and I have never been like that around a man before. It is very refreshing and extremely liberating.

It is a welcome feeling from how I felt telling Sam about Callum just minutes ago. He crooks his finger at me.

"Coming in?"

I suddenly feel shy at being naked in front of him.

"Don't be shy, babe, no one can see. It's just us. Just you and me, I promise."

The steam rises as he sits in the hot tub and I start to take my clothes off. I strip off my t-shirt, my shorts, and my tights. I turn my back to unhook my bra and take off my pants giving him a glimpse of my back tattoo of black and grey angel wings covering my whole back. I spin around, walk towards him and step into the hot tub. The water is hot, steaming, and bubbling. Sam slides over and wraps me up in his arms. I grasp his erection under the bubbles as a thank you for bringing me up here to his private hideaway.

"God, *Peyton,*" he hisses and kisses me deeply on the lips. I move my fist up and down his shaft under the water. He nips my neck with his teeth and moves his hand under the water, sliding his finger into my pussy with ease and slowly moving it in and out.

I moan softly in his ear, "*Sam.*"

He kisses my collarbone and introduces another finger in my pussy. Moving two fingers in and out, working up a rhythm, and working me up into a sexual frenzy.

"*Jesus,* I love it when you say my name."

I kiss him deeply and run my other hand down his hard muscled chest. Feeling his tight abs under my touch.

"That's it, baby, *yes,*" he hisses as I carry on stroking his solid erection, the water splashing as my hand moves up and down.

"Stop, baby, *please.* I'm close to coming, and I need to fuck you. I need to be inside you so god damn badly."

"Are on the pill? I'm clean; I was tested a few weeks back, I promise. I never fuck without protection, but I want to fuck you without a condom so badly. I need to know what you feel like with nothing between us," he says breathlessly, his fingers still pumping in and out of my soaking wet folds.

"Yes, I'm on the pill," I say, panting, and I feel him smile a satisfied smile against my neck.

"Climb on top of me, baby," he whispers. I comply and settle onto his lap, straddling him. He takes my nipple in his mouth and laps it with his tongue, making my nipple into a hard erect bud as he nips it gently. I gasp with pleasure, and he guides his hard cock into my pussy. I adjust to his length and move up and down, building up a slow, sensual rhythm. He holds me around the waist and helps me move with him, all while kissing me and moaning into my mouth.

"*Jesus fuck*, you feel so fucking good. You're so wet and tight."

I love the way his body feels underneath mine. He drives his cock deep into me, and I scream in ecstasy, "Sam, *please.*"

He takes my nipple in his mouth again and nips my piercing.

"Tell me what you want, baby."

He bucks up, driving his cock in and out at a faster rhythm.

"I want to come all over your cock, Sam."

He growls, and with each deep drive, he hits my G-spot each time.

"I'm close, Sam, I'm so close," I pant. He smiles against my nipple and bites gently.

"I know, angel, I can feel you. I've got you," he whispers, slowing and quickening the rhythm, driving me insane with pleasure and burning hunger. As he lifts and releases me, I feel his balls slapping against my bottom as he plunges into me faster. We are both moaning softly, and I feel myself trembling with desire. I can feel my orgasm building and pooling somewhere deep within my core. He rams his cock into me, keeping the pace fast and frantic as we both near climax. I cry out, my breath coming out in ragged pants. He quickens his pace, and I feel my orgasm explode through my whole body.

"Sam, I'm coming," I cry out. He pushes his cock up deep inside me.

"Peyton, *Jesus* fuck, I'm going to come."

My eyes flutter and my whole body trembles as he pumps his seed inside me, growling in my ear as he comes. I bury my head in the crook of his neck, breathless and spent. He runs his hands up my spine and holds me to him.

"God, Peyton, that was ... *Fuck,* that was an epic shag!"

I chuckle softly into his neck and lift my head up, almost forgetting that we are in his hot tub on the roof of his apartment building. The cool wind blows, and I shiver against him. I climb off him, wincing as he pulls his cock out of my sensitive folds. I sit in the hot tub next to him, and he lazily drapes his arm around me.

"You're fucking ace."

"Thanks. You're not so bad yourself, stud!"

He kisses the top of my head. "I can add sex in a hot tub as the hottest sex I've ever had." He raises his eyebrows and smiles that breath-taking smile. He subconsciously twirls my hair around his finger. "I'm just glad I walked into the tattoo shop that day, because that was the day that totally changed my life."

I smile shyly at his sweet words and rest my head on his shoulder. I suddenly feel so tired.

"Tired, angel?" I nod. "I must be wearing you out!"

Sam gets out of the hot tub, pulling me up with him. He grabs two warm towels from underneath the hot tub and helps me out, wrapping me in a towel and carrying me back inside. He goes down a set of stairs with me in his arms and through his apartment, into his bedroom before setting me down on my feet.

"I'm going to grab a quick shower before bed, want to join me?"

How could I refuse a shower with the most gorgeous man I have ever laid eyes on? I nod, and he grabs my hand, leading us both into the walk-in shower. The water is pleasantly hot—Sam is being so tender and sweet, the perfect boyfriend and lover. I think he could be good for me. In fact, I know it has only been a few days, but I have felt the best I have ever felt. He makes me feel things I haven't felt in a long time—I finally feel alive. I catch sight of my reflection in the glass of the shower cubicle, and I'm glowing. The post-sex afterglow and the love of an amazing rock star. I think Sam Newbolt might be *the one*.

16

Peyton

The next morning, I wake up in Sam's bed and am completely naked. He was right about the silk sheets; they feel soft, cool, and so decadent against my skin. I roll over sleepily, and my muscles are deliciously sore after our marathon sex session. I reach out for him, but he isn't lying next to me. I sit up with a start, hear the toilet flush, and then he walks back into the room. He is already dressed wearing grey jogging bottoms, a white vest, and bare feet. His hair is wet and spiky; he has a white towel around his neck and a cup of coffee in his hand.

"Good morning, sleepy head."

"Good morning, rock star."

We laugh together as he takes a sip of his coffee

"I made you some coffee, babe."

"You weren't there when I woke up."

He looks at me. "I don't sleep too good, angel. I was in the studio writing, then I went for a long run and worked out in the gym for a while. I woke up early and didn't want to disturb you. You look so peaceful when you're asleep."

I pat the bed next to me; he comes over and sits down on the edge of the bed. He puts his cup down and wraps me in his arms. I breathe him in—he smells so good, of his special Sam scent, coffee, and faintly of sweat from his work out.

"Did you sleep well, babe?"

I nod and smile. "Yeah, like a log. I could so get used to these silk sheets."

He laughs. "Yeah, once you go silk, you never go back!"

His smile is infectious, and I don't think I will ever get tired of seeing it. I look at the clock, I leap out of Sam's arms and out of bed when I see that it says eight forty-five.

"*Shit*, why didn't you wake me sooner?"

He laughs. "You're funny when you're stressed! I thought you deserved a lie in after I wore you out last night."

"I need to be at work in an hour, I'm going to be so late. On the plus side, at least I won't have to wait for my morning shower. Ruby has a morning routine, and she takes forever in the bathroom!"

He smiles and kisses me gently on the end of my nose. "Bathroom's all yours, angel."

In the bathroom, I take a hot morning shower. When I emerge, I am feeling energised and ready to face the day. I towel dry my hair and get dressed for work. Today, I opt for black cropped jeans, a black and white polka dot dress and black Converse trainers. I apply my usual, light, natural make-up and tousle my hair in the mirror, as I don't have my straighteners with me or the time to mess around. Sam is leaning casually in the doorway watching me get ready.

"See something you like, rock star?" I ask seductively and wink cheekily at him.

"God, you're so beautiful. How did I get so lucky?" He comes and stands behind me, wrapping his arms around my waist.

"Maybe you were a saint in a previous life!" Laughing, I turn to face him. "I'm going out of the city at the weekend, to my mum and dad's in Brighton. Do you fancy taking off for a while? Just you and me? I know it's a bit soon, but I'd like it if you could come."

He kisses me gently on the lips and smiles. "I would love to. I have a rare weekend off, and that sounds so ... *normal.* I've been craving normal. You lose track of what's normal when you're on the road and living out of suitcases."

"That's great, I can't wait, and my mum and dad are dying to meet you."

He pulls a face. "Should I be worried?"

I shake my head. "My family are all amazing apart from my sister. I love her to bits, but she's a colossal pain in the arse."

He laughs. "OK, pain in the arse sisters I can deal with, but next week we've got our album launch at a club in town. It's our tenth anniversary, so it's kind of important. Would you be my date?"

He takes my hand and kisses the back gently. I smile.

"Why yes, kind sir, I would love to be your date."

He bows dramatically in front of me and twirls me around in his arms. It's times like these when I feel like we're a normal couple. When as soon as we get outside our relationship is in the public eye for everyone to pull apart and judge. I push that thought to the back of my mind and grab my Voodoo Vixen bag ready for work.

"I'm going to be late for work, Sam."

I kiss him tenderly on the lips and walk out of his bedroom. He follows close behind me.

"I can meet you for lunch if you want to. I'm going to be laying down the final vocals for our album today, but I should be done by this afternoon."

I take his coffee from him and take a sip, welcoming the caffeine boost.

"I think I'm going to meet Ruby. We need a girl chat, and she's going through some stuff."

He nods. "OK, I'll pick you up after work then, babe. We can come back here and have dinner."

"Sounds amazing. Look at us being normal!"

"If only it could be like this all the time."

He picks me up and spins me around, kissing me passionately. I leave for work in a good mood, go down to Sam's parking garage, and unlock my car. I get in, crank up the stereo listening to P!nk and make the fifteen-minute journey to work. I pull into the shop car park and practically skip into the shop.

"Mornin', honey bunny," Seb greets me in his usual manner as I breeze in.

"Good morning, pumpkin, it's such a beautiful day," I say in a sing-song voice. Seb looks genuinely shocked to see me in such a good mood. Good moods for me have been very rare recently.

"Someone's in a good mood this morning, babe."

"Yep, life's all good for once."

I can't stop myself from smiling; Seb gets up and hugs me tightly.

"Love looks good on you, darlin'. I'm so happy for you I really am. Now, stop bloody smiling; you're making my jaw ache!"

Laughing, I skip to the back of the shop to stow my stuff away. I take off my coat and go back out into the shop. Before I ask Seb about appointments, he jumps in.

"Three small tattoos this morning and two this afternoon; one is a large back piece. Busy day today, sweetie, no rest for the wicked!"

I nod. "Busy is good!"

I sit down in Seb's leather chair, cross my legs, and spin myself around. I pick up my cup of Starbucks finest and take a long sip.

"I take it you stayed over at Sam's last night?"

I nod. "Yeah, it was amazing; he has a roof garden and a hot tub."

Seb raises his eyebrows. "Flash bastard!"

The morning session flies by, and before I know it, it's lunchtime. My final morning client walks out of the shop happy with my work. I grab my jacket and bag from the back of the shop, check my phone, and find it highly unusual that I don't have my usual lunch text from Ruby. I walk out of the shop with no particular lunch destination. I look up, and there is a familiar face walking towards me. It's Callum again. Twice in two days. *Great*, that's all I need. I go to walk around him, but he grabs my arm.

"Twice in two days. It must be fate, baby cakes." When he sees the expression on my face, his smile fades. "Peyton, look, we need to talk."

I snatch my arm away from him. "Don't fucking touch me. I told you yesterday I've got nothing else to say to you."

He looks at me and tilts my chin up to face him, but I avert my eyes away from him.

"Look me in the eye, Peyton, and tell me you've got nothing to say. You were pretty vocal yesterday, I didn't get the chance to put my side out there."

I shake my head. "So you can lie to me some more, Cal? I don't fucking think so." I raise my voice and hold my index finger up to him. "No! No! I'm not letting you get inside my head again it's not happening; you've done enough damage."

He sighs. "Look, babe, all I want is a chance to tell you my side. I practically buried my head in the sand and didn't get to tell you how fucking sorry I am and why I did what I did to you."

I hang my head. "I'm sick of hearing sorry from you, Callum, sorry doesn't fucking cut it after what you did. You're with Savannah now, just go and be happy in your little love nest together, with your perfect little life and forget we ever happened. I'm moving on."

He smiles sarcastically. "Moving on with Newbolt, yeah OK, we'll see how long that one lasts."

I go to slap him around the face, but he grabs my wrist and stops me before my hand connects with his face.

"Go for one coffee with me, Peyton, you owe me that. Please."

Defeated, I step back from him and snatch my arm away from him.

"I don't owe you anything, Callum, but just one coffee then you fucking walk away," I say coldly, and he holds his hands up.

"OK, one coffee, and I'll walk away. You'll never have to speak to me again."

I am silent and walk a few inches away from him. We go into a greasy spoon cafe called The Breakfast Club, five minutes around the corner from the shop. I sit down at a table in the corner by the window and put my phone on the table in front of me.

"Usual, coffee two sugars, loads of milk?"

I want to say no, but I smirk and nod. "Yeah, please."

He smiles. "Some things never change, baby cakes."

I roll my eyes, and he goes over to the counter to order the coffees. He places the order and comes back over to the table, sitting opposite me.

"You're looking good, Peyton."

He smiles a flirty smile. A short, plump, middle-aged woman with greasy blonde hair and a moody look on her face comes over and puts the coffees down on the table.

"Can I get you anything else?" she asks in a bored tone, and Callum shakes his head whilst never taking his eyes off mine. She shrugs and walks away, leaving the awkward atmosphere unfolding between Callum and me.

"So, how long have you and the rock star been an item? Looks pretty serious from what I've seen in the papers and on the Internet."

"What was it you used to say? Never believe anything you read in the newspaper apart from the date?" I snap.

"Is it your time of the month, babe?"

He smirks. *Fucking smarmy bastard.* I clench my fist under the table, and it takes all I have not to launch myself across the table at him.

"Say what you need to say, Callum, I need to get back to the shop."

"OK, if that's what you want. Look, I wanted a chance to say sorry, and before you jump in, I am genuinely fucking sorry for hurting you, I really am. It was unforgivable; I have spent the past couple of days thinking of nothing else. I was such a shitty, insensitive, heartless bastard, and I deserve everything you throw at me. I was a crap boyfriend, and I don't blame you. When I found out our baby had died, I thought it was punishment for me cheating on you."

I almost choke on my coffee. "Are you actually fucking serious?" I spit out.

"Peyton, I need you to know why I did what I did. When you told me you were pregnant, I was fucking scared. Actually, I was terrified. Yeah, we'd talked about kids maybe in the future, but we were being careful, and I wasn't ready to be a dad. I thought you had gotten yourself pregnant to trap me. When you showed me the scan picture, I thought I would feel different, but I felt *nothing*. I'd been seeing Savannah at the gym for a few months before we actually hooked up, she would come for a workout at first a couple of times a week and then more regularly. She was being flirty, she would always stop to chat, and we got to know each other. Well, friendly banter at first, then it led to more. When I found out you were pregnant I went straight to the gym to get away, I was snapping at everyone at work, being a complete prick to be around. She came into the gym and sensed something was wrong."

I roll my eyes. *Here we go, typical Callum spinning me lie after lie.*

"I broke down on her in the changing rooms, told her everything, I was so fucking messed up, I don't know what happened. We ended up at a hotel around the corner, and we had sex. It instantly took my problems away, and it made me forget for a while. I was terrified of being caught, and we started meeting up at hotels stealing moments together where we could, but know it was never ever in our bed. I couldn't do that to you."

I raise my eyebrows. "And I'm supposed to be grateful for that?" I spit sarcastically.

"Hear me out. I wanted to tell you, but when I got the call that you were in the hospital having a miscarriage, I ended it with her. Literally told her I didn't want to be with her and that I wouldn't leave you for her."

I slam my cup on the table. "And this conversation is helping how, Callum? Ease your fucking conscience, telling me all the sordid little details? How fucking dare you?"

"No, I want you to understand, Peyton," he says calmly, and I shake my head.

"No, if you left her as soon as you got the call that I was in the hospital, why didn't you show up until the next morning? I needed you, Callum, I fucking needed you with me, and I was grieving for our unborn baby all alone."

My eyes glaze over, and I swallow back the lump in my throat, not wanting to give him the satisfaction of seeing me cry in front of him. He reaches across the table for my hand, and I quickly snatch it away.

"I'm so sorry, I need you to believe that. I went to a bar and got completely wasted because I felt weak that I couldn't be the strong one, and I couldn't be the rock you deserved."

I sigh audibly and take a sip of my coffee.

"I got completely wasted and passed out in a bar; I don't know how I got home that night. I turned up at the hospital the next day, and I didn't know what to say to you. I was hung-over, you were crying and completely inconsolable. Ruby was shouting the odds at me, your dad and your brother wanted to punch me, your mum was staring daggers at me, and I was a total fucking mess. I know that's no excuse for my behaviour, but the day you walked in on us, I didn't intend for it to happen that way. After you got out of the hospital, I didn't know what to say or how to act around you. You'd sit in the flat with the curtains closed crying all day."

"Don't you dare fucking lay that one on me, Callum. I was grieving for our baby. I felt like my whole world was falling apart. You had an affair with another woman behind my back, and I walked in on you shagging her. It's as simple as that. You don't need to spin me some bullshit excuse. I needed time to get over that and then I walked in on you. My whole world crashed down around me. I felt so alone. Not only had I lost a baby, but I'd also lost the man I loved as well." A tear escapes and rolls down my cheek.

"I'm not blaming you, baby cakes, you have to believe me. I was grieving in my own way too, and it wasn't just your baby."

As those words pass his lips, I want to smash his stupid smug face in.

"You're un-fucking-believable, Callum, do you know that?" I say through clenched teeth. I am so angry with him, so I finish my coffee quickly and pull on my jacket.

"Where are you going?"

I narrow my eyes and drop my phone in my coat pocket. "You don't get to ask me that, you've got no fucking right. I listened to your pathetic story like you wanted, now I'm going back to work."

He puts his hand on top of mine and looks me in the eyes.

"Please don't go, you tried to kill yourself because of me."

He lowers his voice. *Low blow, Kennedy.*

"It was all my fault, I know that now, and I couldn't leave things like we left it yesterday. Talk to me, just five more minutes, please."

I pull my hand away.

"I tried to kill myself because I couldn't see another way out. I had constant nightmares, and I was on anti-depressants. I medicated because I felt dead inside, and I pushed everyone away, people who wanted to help me. I was a total and absolute mess. I slashed my wrists, took an overdose, and fell unconscious in the bath. Ruby found me just in time; I would be dead if it wasn't for her. A minute longer and I wouldn't have made it. I was *lucky*, apparently," I say bitterly as I wipe my tears away, hating my emotions for betraying me in front of my cheating ex-boyfriend. "I saw a counsellor for a few months, and the rest, as they say, is history. So now you know how weak and pathetic I became all because of you. I'll never *ever* forgive you for what you did, Callum. I have to go now."

I stand up defiantly and push my chair back. I go to walk past him, but he grabs my arm.

"You're not pathetic or weak. There's not a day goes by that I don't regret everything I've done, and the way behaved. I've never stopped loving you, baby cakes."

He looks up at me, and I don't know whether he's lying or telling the truth, but I don't stick around to find out.

"Goodbye, Callum."

I walk away from him and run out of the café, and around the corner with my head down, sobbing. I want to get away from him. I *need* to get away from him. I run into the shop, thankful there aren't any customers, and run to the back quickly. I shield my face from Seb, put my head in my hands, and sob. Seconds later, I feel a presence behind me, and a large hand brushes my arm.

"Hey, honey, what's wrong? Come on, talk to me."

Seb's voice soothes me. I turn around and sob into his chest. He envelopes me in his arms and rubs my back, resting his chin on top of my head.

"It's OK, I've got you, sweetie. It's going to be all right. I'm here." He strokes my hair, and I look up at him. "Who's upset you, darlin'?"

I shake my head, unable to get the words out.

"Come on, sit down with me."

He leads me over to the sofa where we both sit down.

"What's happened? You're scaring me here, and I haven't seen you like this in such a long time, honey." He tucks my hair behind my ear and wipes my tears away.

"Callum," I choke out, and Seb stands up.

"I told you to tell me if that fucking prick ever bothered you again, babe," he says through clenched teeth. I grab his hand.

"Seb, he's not worth it. Please, it isn't your fight."

"Yes, it is my fight. You're like my little sister. If someone upsets you, they upset me. It's just the way I roll," he jokes, and I manage to laugh through my tears. He wipes my tears away with the pad of his thumb. "See, that's better. Look, if you need to take the afternoon off, I can call in some favours to cover your appointments?"

I smile and shake my head. "I need to work, Seb. It's fine, thank you so much for the offer, though. I need to keep my mind occupied."

Seb smiles and kisses the top of my head. "Take as long as you need, babe, your station's all set up for you."

I kiss him on the cheek, and he goes back out into the shop. I splash cold water on my face and dry off with a towel. Checking my reflection, I'm angered to see my eyes are red and puffy. I put a little concealer to hide it and slick on some lip-gloss, then force a smile at my reflection and take a deep breath. I check my phone, and I have a text from Sam.

Can't wait to see you later angel

Counting down the hours

S xx

I smile at the thought of seeing him again, and it is as if the events of lunchtime have just melted away. I stow my phone away and go out into the shop, quickly focusing my mind back onto my work, and start my afternoon tattooing session. I dedicate my afternoon to tattooing a semi-professional footballer—a lion and a union jack with a football in the centre. It is a large tattoo and takes me over five painstaking hours to complete the line work. I am glad of the distraction, almost forgetting about the dramas of the day. At the end of the day, I am wiping down my station and setting up ready for tomorrow. Seb comes over to my workstation.

"I told you I'd do that for you, babe."

I smile. "It's OK, Seb, I've got it."

He brushes my arm. "If you need to chat, honey, you know I'm here."

I carry on wiping down my station before saying, "Yeah, I know, and that means the world to me, it really does."

He takes a pile of paperwork into the back of the shop. The door of the shop opens, but I don't look up.

"We're closed."

The door closes, and I look up. Callum is standing in the shop.

"Callum, I said all I had to this afternoon."

He holds up my bag, which I didn't even realise I had forgotten.

"You left this in the café." He smiles, and I take it from him, keeping my face impassive.

"Thanks."

He nods. "You're welcome."

He stands with his hands in his pockets, and I hear Seb's heavy footsteps coming towards me. He stands a few inches behind me, his stance loose and predatory as if he is waiting for Callum to make one false move towards me.

"Is everything all right? Do you want me to get rid of him?"

I put my hand on his hard, heaving chest. "Everything's fine, babe, honestly."

I look up at him and smile. The way he looks at me says he's reluctant to leave me alone in the shop with Callum.

"I'll just be in the back, honey." He winks at me and jabs his finger at Callum. "If you lay one finger on her, or say anything to upset her ever again, I swear to God I will fuck you up."

There is something in the tone of Seb's voice that makes me believe that he would carry out his threats.

"Someone's protective. Is he your bodyguard now? Does Newbolt know?"

I roll my eyes. "The number of times you fucking accused me of cheating on you with Seb and the whole time you were the one who was cheating, unbelievable."

I finish setting up my station for tomorrow and Callum takes my hand in his.

"I meant what I said, Peyton, I've never stopped loving you. There's not a day that's gone by when I don't think of what could have been, we'd have a baby son or daughter now."

I pull my hand away. "Don't."

He leans his face down towards mine and strokes my hair.

"Tell me you still don't get that feeling when I'm near you," he whispers, and I step back.

"I feel *nothing* for you, Callum."

Leaving him seething, I go to the back to gather my things. When I get back into the shop, he is still standing there with his hands in his pockets.

"Can't you take a hint? I don't fucking want you here, I don't want you in my life, and I definitely don't want you turning up here screwing with my head. I went for a coffee with you earlier because I thought you might have had something to say that I hadn't heard before. But it's always the same with you, Cal, same old lies, same old bullshit, and same old you. I don't want to see you again, so stay the fuck away from me."

He looks at me and takes my hand in his. "Now look me in the eye and say it."

I look him straight in the eye and snatch my hand away, repeating my earlier statement.

"I feel *nothing* for you, Callum. I don't want to ever see you again. Is that clear enough for you?"

He looks genuinely hurt by my admission, but after everything he has put me through, I want to draw a line under the whole Callum and me thing. I want to focus on my future with Sam.

"OK, you'll never have to see me again, Peyton, that's a promise."

He turns to walk away.

"Callum," I call out.

He turns back around and a whole year of pent-up anger towards him comes bubbling to the surface. I punch him hard in the face, catching him off-guard, and he stumbles backwards just as Seb rushes out from the back of the shop. I raise my fist to punch him again, but Seb holds me firmly back with his iron grip. My hand is stinging and sore, but I feel so much better. Callum's nose is pouring with blood. Seb shields me from him.

"I suggest you get the fuck out of my shop, and if I catch you within even a hundred feet of her again, I will fucking kill you," Seb says, his voice dripping with menace. Callum holds his hand up in silent defeat, walks out of the shop, and continues off down the street.

"Are you OK, babe? That was some punch! I'm going to start nicknaming you Rocky Balboa!" He laughs, and I join him. "Come on, I'll wrap that hand for you, babe."

He takes me into the kitchen area at the back of the shop, runs my hand under the cold tap for me, then takes out a bandage and wraps my hand with it. There is a silent understanding between Seb and me, that says he has my back and he'll always take care of me.

"There you go, just put some ice on it when you get home and if it gets worse, go to the hospital."

I nod. He smiles, and I kiss him on the cheek.

"Thanks, Seb, I will do. You're a diamond."

"See you tomorrow, honey."

He kisses me on the forehead, and I leave the shop to drive back to my flat. Parking the car, I go up the stairs, open the door and am greeted by the sound of low guttural groans as I step into the flat. I walk further in and kick off my shoes. I see Jax on the sofa with his arms spread out across the back, his head thrown back and his eyes closed.

"*Oh, fuck yeah*, that's it, baby, take me all the way."

I am shocked at what is unfolding in front of me. Ruby is on her knees in front of the sofa giving Jax a blowjob. Standing there with my mouth open, I don't know what to do or where to put my face.

"Ahem," I clear my throat. Jax's eyes fly open, and Ruby looks up with a mischievous grin on her face.

"*Jesus! Shit*! Peyton! I didn't—"

"It's OK, honestly," I say with a laugh as I shake my head.

Ruby stands up with her hands on her hips; she is wearing a black and red corset with matching black, French knickers, stockings, and suspenders with her long dark hair tumbling down her back.

"Hey, babe, I didn't realise you'd be home yet," she says in her singsong voice that I have become accustomed to. I hang up my coat and throw my bag on the floor.

"Clearly," I say sarcastically. Jax zips up his trousers and stands up, trying desperately to hide his hard-on.

"I'm so sorry, Peyton."

"It's fine, really." I smile, a little too brightly. I go into the kitchen and turn on the coffee machine. Ruby follows me and starts speaking as if the incident from a few minutes ago never occurred.

"Good day at work?"

I put my hand to my head. "Long story, Rubes."

She frowns and puts her hand on my shoulder. "What happened to your hand?"

I take my cup from the cupboard and put it down, then lower my voice so Jax doesn't overhear us.

"I hurt my hand punching Callum's face."

Ruby laughs hysterically. "About fucking time someone wiped that stupid smug grin off his smarmy face." She jumps up, sits on the worktop, and regards me intently. "Should you really be meeting Callum behind Sam's back, though, babe? Sam's good for you. It's obvious that he is really into you and he treats you right. I haven't seen you this happy in a long time; don't let that prick ruin it. I'm saying this as your best friend, Peyton."

I know she means well, and she is my best friend, but the pressures and dramas of the day surface. I suddenly feel intense anger and a deep bitter resentment towards her.

"Look, Ruby. I really don't need you to fucking judge me right now, especially after you aborted your baby," I spit out angrily. She looks genuinely shocked and taken aback by my outburst.

"Oh, OK, so that's what this is all about, me getting rid of my baby because I'm not in a stable relationship because I'm not ready to settle down and be a mum? I'm sorry that's fucking inconvenient for you, Peyton. I thought you were my best friend and best friends don't judge each other"

I look at her with fire in my eyes. "No, this is about you being a selfish fucking bitch and refusing to face up to your mistakes, refusing to take responsibility for your actions. I *lost* my baby, Ruby, and there's you just getting rid of yours because it's an inconvenience for you. I'd do anything to have my baby here with me right now."

A lone tear escapes my eye, and I wipe it away before she speaks again.

"I can't believe you just said that to me, Peyton, after everything we've been through together. You're judging me just because I made the right decision for me, well fuck you."

She wipes tears from her eyes, gets down from the worktop, and storms off into her bedroom. Jax looks at me, and I shake my head as he follows her. I punch the cupboard door with my sore hand and relish in the pain that follows, wishing I had had time to go to the boxing gym after work. Suddenly, my phone starts ringing.

"Hello," I say wearily and instantly perk up when I hear Sam's voice on the other side.

"Hey, are you back home? I dropped by the shop hoping I would catch you on the way home but Seb said you'd just left."

"Yeah, I'm back at the flat, babe."

He pauses and clears his throat. "Cole's outside your place."

I smile to myself and say, "OK, babe, I'll get my stuff together, and I'll see you in a while."

I hear the smile in Sam's voice when he says, "I can't wait, angel, see you soon."

"See you soon, honey."

I hang up the phone, go into my room, and throw a few things in my overnight bag. I slam the door of the flat more to let Ruby know I'm pissed off and run down the stairs. I am in such a bad mood and have the events of today going through my mind at a hundred miles an hour. Everything from the meeting with Callum and the argument with Ruby. The only redeeming quality of the day is seeing Sam.

When I get out into the street, I see the weather has changed and is pouring with rain. I see Cole parked at the kerb, and before he can get out and soak himself to let me in, I open the door and climb in.

"Hey, Cole."

He tips his hat and smiles in the interior mirror. I lean back heavily in the seat—I can't wait to see Sam. Ten minutes pass, and we are pulling up outside the front of Sam's building, which seems unusual for Cole as he normally pulls into the parking garage underneath the building. I open the door, step out, and go inside. The security guard at the black marble desk looks up as I step into the building; he smiles and nods as if in recognition. I smile back, push the button for the lift, and step in.

The lift comes to a halt, and I step out into the foyer of Sam's apartment. I walk over and knock on the wooden door; Sam comes to the door and opens it. His hair is perfectly mussed and spiky, he is barefoot, wearing loose ripped jeans and a white shirt with three buttons undone. He looks dazzling. I throw my arms around him, and his face lights up as he sees me and kisses me as if it's the last kiss we'll ever share.

"I've been looking forward to seeing you all day, baby."

My face lights up, and he narrows his eyes at me. He holds me an arm's length away from him and regards me intently.

"Something's wrong, honey."

I take off my shoes and jacket and put my bag down on the edge of the sofa. Before I even look up, Sam is standing in front of me, his six-foot-four frame towering over me. He lifts my bandaged hand to his face and rubs his thumb over my knuckle. I wince in pain, and he clenches his jaw.

"What happened to your hand, babe?"

I put my other hand to my head and look up at him. "I ... punched Callum."

His nostrils flare as his eyes widen in anger. "Has he hurt you? If he's harmed even a hair on your head, I swear to God I will fucking kill him."

I stroke his face to calm him. "He didn't touch me, babe, honestly. Those boxing lessons were so worth it. He ended up worse, trust me—I think I broke his nose," I say with a smirk.

Sam smirks as well then goes into the kitchen to get us both a drink and an ice pack for my hand. He hands me a large, cold glass of wine, and the clean, crisp taste of the wine helps the dramas of the day melt away instantly. I flop down on the sofa, and we cuddle up. He strokes my hand.

"I'm so sorry I didn't call, today's been hectic at the studio. I tried to make lunch, but I haven't had a spare five minutes all day, and I called as soon as I could."

I shake my head. "It's OK. I know you're busy; I don't expect you to drop everything just for me. Today has been the day from hell, I couldn't wait to see you."

He takes a long sip of his wine, and a look of concern mars his handsome features. He looks so relaxed and ... *hot*.

"Is everything OK? Do you want to tell me about it?"

I take a deep breath. "I had a row with Ruby, and I bumped into Callum again. I was going to lunch, and we bumped into each other on the street near the shop. He practically rail-roaded me into having coffee with him, he said he needed to explain why he did what he did to me. He started spouting off some bullshit how he was terrified that I was pregnant and how he wasn't ready to be a dad. He was trying to make out like he was the victim."

Sam's mouth drops open. "That guy is un-fucking-believable."

"So you're not mad that I went for coffee with my ex?"

He laughs. "'Course not, why would I. Like I said in that note, everyone is entitled to a past."

I brush his arm and kiss him gently on the lips at his thoughtfulness and understanding.

"We had coffee, he talked, and I had a go at him, I practically ran back to the shop in tears because of him. He showed up when the shop had closed saying he still loved me and then I punched him in the face."

Sam narrows his eyes. "I said if he ever made you cry or feel like that ever again I'd kill him. He can't keep getting inside your head like that, babe, and he's got no fucking right," he spits out angrily. His hand reaches out to stroke my chin. "He doesn't see how fragile you are. You put on the confident, bubbly, tough girl act like you did when we met, but I can see right through it. You're vulnerable, funny, intelligent, and incredibly beautiful. I'm one lucky motherfucker!"

I giggle shyly and place my hand over his. "All I kept thinking when I was with Cal today was why couldn't I have met you first?"

He smiles. "I would have romanced you properly: hearts, flowers, bedroom window serenades, the whole nine yards!" Laughing, he becomes serious once more. "What exactly did he say to you? It must have been bad for you to punch him, babe."

My smile fades. "He kept apologising for what he did, spinning me the same old Kennedy bullshit. He must get it from his dad."

Sam strokes my face with the back of his hand soothingly. "I'm nothing like him; I need you to believe that, angel. I need you to trust me. I'd never hurt you like that ever."

I look into his eyes and know by the look in his eyes that he is being sincere. I know I can trust Sam one hundred percent—he's the total opposite of Callum.

"I was an absolute mess when I lost our baby, and I needed him. He abandoned me when I needed him the most, and I don't think I'll ever be able to forgive him for that. No matter how hard I try, and no matter how many times he says sorry, I wasted three fucking years on him." I avert my gaze to the floor.

"Do you want to talk about it? I'd totally understand if you didn't want to tell me all the sordid details, but I'm here for you, angel."

I smile, and something inside me says that maybe I need to talk about it with Sam in order to move on with my life.

17

Peyton

Past

Today. I'm going to tell Callum today. I'll go home, cook him dinner, sit him down, and then I'll tell him. He'll be happy, I know he will. That's what I told myself anyway. I was standing outside the hospital with my—our—twelve-week scan of our baby. I was there with Ruby, and it shouldn't have been her I was there with, it should have been him. Hearing his or her heartbeat and seeing our baby growing inside me for the first time, I was so overwhelmed. As I was looking at the screen with tears in my eyes, Ruby squeezed my hand and screamed with excitement. I suddenly realised that I was actually terrified of what Callum was going to say. It shouldn't have been that way, I should have been over the moon ... Well, I was, but we should have been in it together, like a normal couple. Happy and excited to have created a brand new life together.

But he had been so distant lately—he had been so busy with work, he didn't talk to me anymore; he was not the man I fell in love with. Gone was the sweet, charming man who paid me compliments, the man who sent me flowers at work every single day, the man who left me post-it notes around my flat, the man who made my heart skip a beat every time he walked into a room. He had been replaced with a completely different man altogether. He was cold, distant, moody, and he didn't talk to me. He had even taken to sleeping on the sofa for the past few weeks putting it down to me being so restless in the night. He was withdrawn and unhappy, refusing to acknowledge me or any problem in our relationship. He constantly accused me of having an affair with Seb, asking me to quit my job at the shop because he didn't trust Seb. I received constant accusations; the slightest thing he was shouting and causing unnecessary arguments.

Three months pregnant, I had a little life growing inside of me, and it had to be the best feeling in the entire world. If Callum didn't want to know, then I'd made a decision to bring the baby up on my own. I could be the best mum in the world. Not every child had to have a mum and dad, right? That's what I told myself, anyway.

Ruby had been there from day one, through the chronic morning sickness and she was with me, holding my hand in our bathroom when I took the test, and those two little blue lines changed everything. I'm not going to lie, it was a complete shock at first. As soon as I adjusted to the idea of motherhood, I was wandering around the shop in a euphorically happy baby bubble. My happiness was short-lived because as soon as I got home, Callum and I had a massive row. I thought it was best not to tell him about the baby; it was too soon. Things between us were strained enough, but now, three months in, I was struggling to explain the baggy clothes and getting dressed where he couldn't look at me too closely. He deserved to know, I just needed to find the right moment.

After the hospital appointment, Ruby drove me back to Callum's flat, and I laid down for a while. I couldn't sleep, though, I kept going over and over it in my mind of what I was going to say to him. I took a hot relaxing bubbly bath, and by the time he finished work, I was feeling a little more relaxed, sitting on the sofa with my legs tucked underneath me with a mug of hot chocolate and marshmallows in front of the TV.

"Hey, Cal," I greeted him brightly. He grunted.

"Is there any beer in the fridge, I've had a bitch of a day at work." His voice was cold.

"Cal, please, babe, come and sit down. I need to talk to you."

He came back into the living room and cracked open his can of lager, taking a sip before he said, "So talk."

He didn't look me in the eyes, so I took his hand in mine, and he pulled away. Great start.

"Please, don't be mad, Callum."

He finally looked at me; his eyes were dark and brooding with bags underneath them marring his usually boyish features.

"I'm-I'm ... pregnant."

He actually looked like a deer caught in headlights, dumbstruck into silence.

"Say something then, babe." I smiled but as he got to his feet, my smile faded.

"Fuck me, what the fucking fuck were you thinking? We've always been careful, how the— Have you done this to trap me? Is that it? Our relationship is on the brink of ending so what, you stopped taking the pill? Please enlighten me, Peyton, because I don't fucking understand."

"Callum, I'm carrying your baby, and you're accusing me of trying to trap you? Believe me, I'm as shocked as you are."

I pulled the scan picture out of my bag and showed it to him.

"Look, this is our baby. Look, Callum."

I grabbed his face between my hands and forced him to look at the picture in front of him. He glanced at the scan briefly and shoved me away.

"Get the fuck away from me, Peyton. I really can't be around you right now."

I stood in his living room with my mouth hanging open. I actually couldn't believe his reaction. Following him into the kitchen, I cried, "Don't fucking walk away from me, Callum. I've got your baby growing inside me."

I grabbed his hand and placed it on my growing bump. He snatched it away as if I was on fire.

"You've got no idea at all, Peyton; I'm not fucking ready to be a dad. I can barely look after myself. Work is busier than ever, you're busy with the shop. Maybe it's not the right time for us to bring a baby into the world."

I narrowed my eyes at him as he leaned over the worktop.

"Maybe you should consider ... you know ..."

I shook my head and something about the tone his voice instantly made me know what he was about to say. But I feigned ignorance, wanting to hear him say the words.

"No, I don't know, Cal."

He glanced at me. "A ... termination."

My eyes widened in shock at his admission.

"I can't believe you just fucking said that, Callum, this isn't just your baby. I'm three months pregnant, he or she is a part of me now, and I can't just get rid of it because it's an inconvenience for you." My voice grew shaky and my eyes glazed over.

"Don't lay a guilt trip on me, Peyton. I'm really not in the mood right now," he spit out, and I grabbed his arm.

"Well, tough shit, I don't give a fuck that you're not in the mood, we're going to talk about this whether you like it or not."

He snatched his arm from my grip. "I said I can't fucking deal with this now, Peyton. Anyway, how do I know you haven't been shagging someone else? Seb, for instance. How can I be sure it's even mine?" he raised his voice a few decibels louder and a look of pure disgust formed on his face. I looked at him open-mouthed.

"Here we fucking go again. For the millionth time, I'm not sleeping with Seb. He is my boss for God's sake. This baby is definitely yours, and I'll take a DNA test to prove it if I have to. You're being pathetic and childish as usual. You need to fucking grow up and take responsibility for once in your God damn life, Callum," I screamed at him. I could feel the anger burning inside me. He slammed his hand down on the worktop, and I jumped at the sound.

"Take responsibility. That's rich coming from you. You're what ... three months pregnant? Why the fuck am I only just hearing about it now?"

I hung my head, knowing he had a point.

"I don't know I-I was fucking scared of how you'd react, and I was right, wasn't I? I expected you to at least be happy."

A tear rolled down my cheek.

"Happy? How the fuck can I be happy? I'm ... Christ, I don't know what I'm feeling right now. When you showed me the scan picture back then I should have felt something, but I felt—" he stopped, and I brushed his arm, silently begging my Callum to come back to me. He looked me in the eye. "I felt nothing."

His voice was hard and cold. It was at that moment I knew I had lost him. He moved across the room, dragging his hands down his face.

"Don't fucking walk away from me, Callum. I'm your girlfriend, and we've been together for three years. Doesn't that mean anything to you? You've been distant for weeks, is there someone else? Have I done something wrong?"

I moved closer to him until I was standing right in front of him.

"Don't you find me attractive anymore, baby? You've hardly touched me recently, sometimes I can hear you tossing and turning on that sofa. All I wanted was for you to come back to bed and hold me, make love to me like you used to. Don't you miss that?"

Even as I said the words, I heard the desperation in my voice, and I hated myself for being so needy. I took his hand and placed it on my breast, hoping to evoke some feeling in the shell of a man in front of me.

"See, Cal, it's me, Peyton, your girl, the woman you love," I whispered trying to sound seductive, and the voice in my head was going crazy. *Stop acting so needy and desperate.*

He looked at me, and his face turned angry. He looked as if he was about to explode, and I had never seen that look on his face before. Deciding to step away from him, he went crazy. He completely trashed the flat, and I was cowering in the corner, screaming and sobbing hysterically for him to stop. The extent of his temper had me shaking with fear, and I didn't know what to do. The look in his eyes was terrifying, and I had never seen him that way before. Something told me that there was more to that side of him than me telling him I was pregnant.

After what seemed like an eternity, he stopped and looked around. The flat was completely trashed, the sofa upturned, photos of us were strewn around the room, there was glass everywhere, and the flat looked like a bombsite. He stopped, and his eyes widened as if he had just suddenly come to his senses. His eyes locked on mine cowering and shaking in the corner. He put his hand to his mouth.

"Oh, my God, baby cakes, I'm so sorry."

He offered me his hand to help me to my feet, but I slapped his hand away.

"Get the fuck away from me, Callum," I managed to choke out. My voice was shaky, and I was in complete and utter shock. I couldn't believe he would do something like that. Callum was usually so calm, gentle, and laid back, but watching him then was as if I was in the room with a virtual stranger. He held his hands up in defeat and ran out of the flat, slamming the door behind him. I got to my feet, and sharp stomach pains crippled me. I clutched my stomach and looked down—blood was seeping through my pyjamas bottoms.

18

Peyton
Present

I am instantly jolted back to the present, and my face is wet with tears.

"I can't go through that pain again, Sam. I don't think I'll come back from it if you hurt me the way Callum did."

Sam shakes his head and pulls me into his hard chest. "Shhh, it's OK, angel, I'm here."

I suddenly feel like a huge weight has been lifted from my shoulders just by sharing with Sam the agony I went through. At that moment, I know that my future is with Sam and that everything is going to be all right as long as I have him at my side.

The rest of the week passes without any more dramas or run-ins with Callum, but the silent treatment from Ruby remains. I have been hiding out at Sam's place all week since the argument with Ruby; it has been heaven spending time with the man in my life and hot, nasty sex on tap!

I finish work at lunchtime on Friday afternoon, and I'm so excited to be leaving London for the weekend. The hustle and bustle of the city is a little hard to take at times. It's been so long since I saw my family, so I am looking forward to seeing them and catching up with my mum, dad, my brother, Dexter, and my sister, Eden. I am also looking forward to finally introducing them to Sam; it has been a while since I introduced a new boyfriend to my family. I am optimistic that they will love Sam just as much as I do.

I packed my weekend bag last night, so I didn't have to rush after work. It is a welcome change for me to be organised for once! But I still have to go home for a few things, and I come home to Ruby crying.

"Rubes, hey."

She sobs, and she collapses in tears in my arms. "I'm so sorry, Peyton."

I stroke her hair, and say, "Hey, it's OK, babe, I'm sorry too. I didn't mean to be such a bitch."

She shakes her head. "No, everything you said was true. I was a complete fucking bitch to you, I know that. I hate it when we fight."

I tuck a strand of her hair behind her ear. "It's OK, honestly, babe, I hate fighting with you too. Now, do you want to tell me what's wrong?"

She sniffs and wipes her eyes on her sleeve. "Fucking Isaac fired me."

I look wide-eyed at her. "What? Why the fuck did he fire you?"

She pulls away from our hug and walks over to the sofa. "His fucking wife found out about us, she found a hotel booking on his bank statement and saucy underwear stuffed down the backseat of his car, which was totally nothing to do with me." She smirks which tells me it was most definitely something to do with her! "She went mental, threw him out of their house, froze their bank accounts, and she's filing for divorce. She's taking him for half of everything: the company, the house, his other businesses, the lot. He practically dragged me into his office this morning. He was fuming saying it was my fault that his wife found out about us. I'm sorry, but how the fuck was it my fault that he can't keep his dick in his pants? It wasn't as if I made it obvious that we were shagging. I was discreet, I was happy to just be his bit on the side."

I roll my eyes that she actually thinks so little of herself. *Poor Ruby.*

"Don't judge me, babe. I was happy being his bit on the side, I didn't ask him for anything. I didn't hang on his every word like some dumb bimbo, I didn't expect him to leave his wife for me and declare his undying love for me, either. It was just sex, quick fumble in his office, blowjob under his desk, it wasn't as if it was serious, and we both knew that. Now I'm getting the blame for his frigid wife finding out he was getting it elsewhere. If she had looked hard enough, she would have found out he was also seeing prostitutes, high-class call girls and visiting brothels. I told him about the baby and the abortion totally in the heat of the moment, and then he just fucking lost it. He started calling me a filthy whore and a gold digging slag, and then he fired me."

She flops down on the sofa, and I sit down next to her.

"He can't just fire you for sleeping with him, he is just pissed that his wife found out. You could take him to an industrial tribunal for unfair dismissal.

He can't do that to you, babe. There's laws against that. Just because he is a powerful businessman doesn't mean there are loopholes."

She shakes her head. "Isaac isn't just a powerful businessman—he's practically a billionaire, he's extremely clever and sly, he's precise, and he makes sure his arse is covered. I can't do fuck-all about him firing me, babe; he'll make sure I never work in advertising again. I'm screwed either way. I'll be joining the dole queue and sitting on my fat arse watching Jeremy Kyle every morning," she says with a sigh.

"Then go back to college, retrain in something you actually enjoy rather than just something you're good at."

She smiles. "How do you manage to always be right, Peyton?"

I smile back. "What can I say? It's a gift!"

"Aren't you supposed to be going to Brighton to see your parents?"

I nod and look at the clock.

"Yeah, I need to go and pick Sam up then we're heading off. Are you sure you don't need me to stay, babe? I can cancel and reschedule for next weekend if you need me. I don't like leaving you on your own."

She kisses me on the cheek.

"Thanks for the offer, but I'll be fine. You're the best friend any girl could wish to have, you know, offering to give up your weekend for me, but it's not necessary, sweetie. I'm going to get my shit together, go out, and get wasted! Maybe booty call Jax!"

I laugh. "Sounds like a plan, honey."

I get up off the sofa and grab a quick shower before I leave, reapply my makeup, and grab the bag that I've packed.

"I'm going then, babe. Call me if you need anything. If it's an emergency, my mum and dad's number is on a post-it note on the fridge."

She smiles. "OK, babe, I know the drill! Have fun. Don't do anything I wouldn't do," she says with a wink.

I roll my eyes playfully and leave the flat, looking forward to our weekend away.

The traffic is heavy for a Friday afternoon, and it takes us longer than usual to get into Brighton from London. As soon as I see the sign 'Welcome to Brighton', I instantly relax and smile. I feel like a kid again, excited to get to my mum and dad's seaside retreat. The journey there is filled with light-hearted conversation, an epic selection of road trip music, Sam's eyes on me, and the occasional tender touch on my leg. I turn into my mum and dad's driveway, and Sam looks up at the impressive house in front of him.

"Jesus fucking Christ!"

I laugh at his reaction, then pull onto the gravel driveway, cut the engine, and we both get out of the car. I open the boot to get our bags out, and Sam grabs them from me. He puts his arm around my waist and pulls me to him.

"Don't be nervous, they don't bite!" I wink, and he smiles.

This is a totally different side of Sam—the sensitive, shy, vulnerable and unsure side of him that craves approval from meeting new people. I find it endearing and a welcome change from the Sam from back in London—the in-demand rock star. I have a key, so I let myself in, and as we step inside the hallway, I know I am finally home. The hallway is welcoming; it has dark wooden flooring and pictures of all of us as kids adorning the walls.

"Nice pigtails!"

Sam laughs, and I hit him playfully on the arm.

"Mum, dad, I'm home," I call out.

My mum comes out of the kitchen and throws her arms around me.

"Darling, it's so good to see you, it's been forever. Why didn't you call us to tell us what time you'd be arriving?"

She pulls away and smiles brightly. I look at my beautiful mother; she looks so different. Her hair is cut into a short, dark-brown, highlighted, spiky style, she is bronzed and wears black rimmed glasses to frame her violet eyes. She looks great for her fifty-two years, and the resemblance between us is apparent. I smile, glad to be back in my family home.

"We wanted to surprise you, Mum."

My mum smiles warmly, and Sam stands awkwardly next to me.

"This must be the *very* handsome rock star I've heard all about."

I feel myself blush while Sam smiles his bright, dazzling smile.

"Mrs. Harper, I'm Sam, it's a pleasure to finally meet you."

She shakes his hand, and I can tell that she is smitten by the way she looks at him.

"Sophia, please. Mrs. Harper makes me sound so old!" she says, and Sam chuckles.

"Sophia, thank you so much for inviting me. You have such a beautiful home."

She smiles. "You're very welcome. Peyton, I believe you've found something rare, darling. A famous rock star with manners. They weren't like that in my day."

I roll my eyes and Sam looks at me for support.

"I'm sorry, I should have explained before. My mum used to be a model in the seventies."

Sam looks impressed and nods. "You look ravishing, Sophia. If I didn't know, I'd think you and Peyton were sisters."

Flattery will get you everywhere with my mum, Newbolt!

She blushes, fawning over him.

"Put him down, Mum!"

We all laugh, and my dad comes down the stairs.

"Peyton, sweetheart."

My face lights up as I see my dad. I was always a daddy's girl.

"Dad!"

I run up to him and throw my arms around him. He picks me up and spins me around.

"How's my little girl doing? Look at you. Love looks fabulous on you, sweetheart!"

I laugh and feel like I'm a kid all over again.

"You must be Sam. Max Harper." My dad grasps Sam's hand in a firm handshake, and Sam nods.

"Pleased to meet you, Mr. Harper."

My dad smiles and claps Sam on the back. "We're on first name terms in this house, so call me Max. Come. Let me show you some of my photographs in my studio, Sam, leave these two girls to catch up."

Sam nods nervously, kisses me on the cheek, and my dad whisks him away. I go into the kitchen with my mum. The kitchen has been renovated since I was last here. Grey tiled floor, rustic stone worktops, a breakfast bar with white lacquer stools, an AGA cooker, and a bright open plan dining room leading out onto the garden decking.

"Coffee, sweetie?"

I nod. "Yeah please, Mum, that would be lovely. I've missed your cups of coffee."

I sit at the breakfast bar and fold my arms as my mum puts the kettle on.

"It's so good to see you, sweetie, it's been so long. You're looking gorgeous as ever, my beautiful little girl, and Sam seems like a very nice young man. His photos don't do him justice! I want all the gossip." My mum laughs, and I smile a genuine smile.

"There's nothing to tell, Mum. He and his band came to the shop, I tattooed him, he asked me out, we went for dinner, and it went from there. He makes me so happy, Mum, I think he might be the one," I gush.

"I'm happy that you're happy, darling, just make sure you don't rush into things, that's all I'm saying. I don't want to see you hurt again like you were with Callum."

I hang my head at the mention of his name, and I hate to see the look in my mum's eyes at the memory of how I was when we split up. It is a part of my life I would rather avoid.

"I came here to get away from him to be honest, Mum. I keep bumping into him. It's like everywhere I go, he's there. We met for coffee a few days ago, and he was lying as usual about how sorry he was for cheating on me."

My mum shakes her head. I conveniently leave out the part about the woman he cheated with being Sam's sister. My mum puts my coffee down on the worktop.

"The bloody bare-faced cheek of him, after everything he put you through."

I take a sip of my coffee and swiftly change the subject.

"Where's Dex and Eden?"

My mum sits opposite me and takes my hands in hers.

"Dexter is working, he should be here later, and Eden is at some charity function with that posh fella of hers. She is not coming over until tomorrow then we can have our family BBQ together. Your dad got some of those steaks that you like."

I smile and my mouth waters at the thought of rare steak cooked on the BBQ with stilton and mushroom sauce and chips. One of my favourite foods! My stomach growls loudly, reminding me I haven't eaten today.

"Let me make you a sandwich, darling. You look like you haven't had a good meal in a while."

I laugh and roll my eyes at my mum's concern.

"I see your dad's taken a shine to Sam."

I sip my coffee, and I don't think I've been this happy to be home in a long time. My mum opens the fridge and sets about making me a sandwich.

"How have things been with you, Mum?"

She nods. "Things have been great, sweetie, we've not long got back from a trip to New York, and your dad has an opportunity coming up for a large fashion campaign. Fifty years old and still at the top of his game, not many people can say that. I've been doing a few shifts at the spa with Eden; it gets me out of the house for a while. I've been doing some consultations with a TV channel for a modelling show, this and that keeping me busy, honey! How are things at the tattoo shop with you and Sebastian?"

I smile at her sly change of subject. *I know where I get that trait!* I nod.

"Yeah, things are going really great right now, there's still just Seb and me at the shop, and Riley's due to give birth in a few months, so Parker's spending as much time with her as possible."

My mum smiles. "That's nice, darling. Should I be buying a hat sometime soon?"

I almost choke on my coffee and roll my eyes. "You're the third person to say that, Mum. It's early days. I've fallen hard for him, but it doesn't mean I want him to walk me down the aisle just yet!"

We both laugh, and she pushes a plate towards me with my ham and cheese sandwich on it. I devour the food on my plate, and by the time I take my last bite, Sam and my dad come into the kitchen. My mum is humming a tune while scrubbing potatoes ready for tonight's dinner.

"How are my girls doing?"

My dad smiles and takes his place behind my mum. He put his arms around her waist. After all the years they spent together, they're still madly in love with each other, and I instantly think I would love that to be Sam and me someday. Sam comes over to the breakfast bar and kisses me gently on the lips.

"Did you enjoy the tour of my dad's studio?"

Sam's face lights up, and he nods.

"Yeah, it was amazing. Your dad is so talented, and we could totally use him for our new album cover. J.D is being a pain in the arse about hiring a photographer after Brody slept with the last one. Needless to say, it ended badly when she caught him with a groupie in the dressing room, pants around his ankles!"

We both laugh, and my dad raises his eyebrows.

"Have men these days got no respect at all for women? Sam, you, my friend, are the exception to the rule. There aren't many men these days who are true gentlemen like yourself."

Sam smiles at my dad's compliment, and my mum laughs, rolling her eyes.

"Oh, Max! The men back in my modelling days were just the same. You're only young once."

I get up from the stool and jump down. Sam wraps his arms around me.

"Did you get the tour of the rest of the house?" I wink. Sam smirks and shakes his head. "Mum, I'm going to show Sam the rest of the house."

"OK, my love."

I grab Sam's hand, close the kitchen door, and take him out into the hallway. I push him against the wall and claim his mouth. I stroke his tongue with mine and rub his erection through his trousers. He pulls away.

"Easy, baby, your mum and dad are just through there."

I look up seductively at him.

"There's something erotic and dangerous about being almost caught," I whisper in his ear.

"You're so naughty!"

He cups my breast in his hand and strokes my nipple with his thumb. I gasp and instantly feel liquid heat between my legs.

"I can't keep my hands off you, the whole time I was with your dad I wanted to come down here, rip your clothes off, and fuck you so god damn hard."

His husky voice is like a hotline to my pussy, and I nip his ear excitedly.

"I need to be alone with you, Sam."

He grabs my hand. "Lead the way then, angel!"

Sam grabs our bags, and I take him upstairs. I swing open the door to my old bedroom. It still looks the same as it did all those years ago, apart from the clean bed sheets. My room is a light purple, with light wood laminate flooring, a double sleigh bed near the window, a desk with my old computer on, and a corkboard with a selection of passport-sized pictures on it of my brother, sister, and me and Ruby. Reminding me of the old times we all spent together. There is a small bedside cabinet next to my bed. Sam puts our bags down on the floor and takes in his surroundings. He looks gorgeous as always, and I don't think I'll get bored of seeing his beautiful face every time I wake up. I sit down on the edge of the bed and Sam pushes me down. He kisses me deeply and rubs my pussy through my clothes.

"*Sam,*" I moan into his mouth.

"God, I want you so fucking bad."

I smile and put my arms around his neck. I feel his mobile vibrate in his pocket. *Way to kill the mood.*

"*Fuck,* I'm so sorry, babe, I have to get this."

He gets up and sits down next to me. I sit up, and he answers his phone, exasperated.

"Hello, J.D. Yeah, I'm away with Peyton. Well, I fucking told you. No, I'm not coming back to London until Sunday evening. Tough shit, you'll have to do without me. We're all meant to be off for the weekend. Have you called any of the other boys? No, I didn't fucking think so. We all deserve a break, J.D; work can wait until Monday. That's none of your fucking business. It was my decision; I don't have to justify myself to you. No, end of. I'm hanging up now."

He cuts the phone off.

"*Fucking J.D.,*" Sam curses. "You know what?"

I look at him, and he turns his phone off. He opens my bedside cabinet drawer and slides his phone into it.

"There, a work free, and J.D. free weekend. Peace, quiet, and quality time with my girl."

He smiles and kisses me on the lips. I feel warm and fuzzy inside when he refers to me as '*his girl.*'

"We'll resume our sex-capades later, baby!" He winks and gets up from the bed. He pulls me to my feet and kisses my forehead. "Thought you were meant to be giving me the guided tour of Harper Manor?"

We go out onto the large landing area, which has cream carpet, and off-white walls. Adorning the walls is a set of my mum's modelling pictures from her heyday. Sam examines the photos.

"Wow, your mum was a stunner, babe; I can see where you got your good looks from."

He squeezes me around the waist. I take him along the landing and push the bathroom door open.

"This is the bathroom."

He nods at the basic bathroom with a large shower cubicle in the corner; a small half-circle shaped bath, a sink, and a toilet all in white and chrome. I show him the rest of the four bedrooms and point up to the loft.

"My dad's studio up there which you've seen, then there's my mum's office, a swimming pool in the conservatory, and a small gym next to my room."

He looks impressed with my mum and dad's seaside getaway. I hear the front door slam shut. My eyes light up, and I run down the stairs.

"Dex!"

My little brother Dexter looks up at me, and his face softens. "Sis!"

I jump into his arms, and we hug tightly. I am really close to my brother, and it is always good to see him. Sam comes down the stairs and hangs back, watching the reunion between brother and sister unfold.

"It's so good to see you, sis. You look different. Did you cut your hair?"

He smiles a bright smile. He is two years younger than I am, over six and a half feet tall, lean, and muscular. Dexter and I were always close when we were growing up. I was a tomboy when I was younger and always favoured male company over female. I couldn't, and still can't, handle the drama of having female friends, except for Ruby. She was different from other girls; we clicked straight away and became firm friends. Dexter pulls away from our embrace.

"Are you back here for the whole weekend then? Mum's been going on about you coming down all week!"

I laugh. "Yeah, we're here for the weekend. When did you come home?"

He smiles. "Beginning of the week, Grace is away at some clothes show until Sunday evening, so I came back home for a while, I've been commuting to work from here."

I nod. Looking past me, Dex looks Sam up and down. Sam comes over and wraps his arm around me.

"I'm Sam, Peyton's boyfriend."

Dexter nods, and they shake hands, sizing each other up. "Dexter. PC Dexter Harper, Peyton's brother."

I roll my eyes. "Stop with the pissing contest, Dex."

Dexter looks at me as if he is about to say something then he doesn't.

"So, you're the famous rock star everyone's been gushing about?" Dexter sounds bored, and Sam nods.

"Sure am, Constable!"

Sam smirks, and Dexter narrows his eyes. I can tell that Dexter has taken an instant dislike to Sam. I nudge him in the ribs, and Sam shrugs his shoulders.

"How's work?"

Dexter nods. "Yeah, all good, thanks, sis. Keeping me on my toes as always." He smiles. "I'm going to get changed, sis. I'll see you in a bit, and we'll catch up properly, I promise."

Dexter makes a cross over his heart, kisses the top of my head and runs up the stairs two at a time, bumping purposely into Sam as he goes. I grab Sam's arm.

"Babe, please try and get on with my baby brother, it would mean a lot to me. He's just doing the overprotective brother routine, that's all."

Sam holds his hands up in defeat, and my dad comes out from the kitchen.

"Did I just hear Dex come in?" I nod and smile. He gathers me into a hug. "He's been pining for his big sister, you know." He pulls away and pinches my cheek playfully. "Good to have you home, darling."

It makes me so happy to finally be back in my family home surrounded by my family and the man I have fallen in love with.

19

Peyton

We have a dinner of chicken wrapped in bacon with melted cheese on the top, jacket potatoes, and a mixed salad. The conversation flows easily, and by the time we have finished, I think Dexter and Sam are definitely getting along better. The boys go into the conservatory and sit at a table by the pool with a few bottles of beer. I hang back and help Mum with the washing up. We chat about anything and everything. It is so good being around my family again—I didn't realise how much I missed them living in London. Sam comes in, ending our conversation.

"Is everything OK in here, babe. Do you need a hand, Mrs. Harper?"

My mum looks up at Sam and brushes his arm. "I told you, call me Sophia, please!"

Sam laughs and looks to me for reassurance.

"Everything's fine, honestly, we're just finishing the washing up. Grab me a beer, and I'll be out in a sec."

I kiss him gently on the lips, and he rests his hand at the small of my back. An intimate yet tender gesture, which I love about him.

"How are things going with you and Dex?"

He nods. "Yeah, better, I think. Surprisingly enough, we've actually got stuff in common."

I laugh, and he strokes my hair. He grabs a bottle of Budweiser from the worktop and goes back out to the conservatory.

"I think he is a keeper, darling," Mum says as she strokes my face. "He's such a sweet boy; he's definitely smitten with you."

I feel my face heat at her words.

"Go and be with your man, I'll finish up here. I'll be out to join you in ten minutes."

As I walk out into the conservatory, I shout, "I hope these two aren't telling you any embarrassing stories about me!"

My dad and Dexter laugh.

"Of course not, sis. Would we do that to you?" Dexter sniggers.

I sit down next to Sam and move my chair closer. He wraps his arm around my shoulder and hands me my bottle of beer. I take a long pull on the bottle. We all sit in the conservatory beside the swimming pool chatting and catching up until well into the night.

At around eleven PM, my mum goes up to bed, and my dad takes Sam up to his studio to show him some more pictures, and I know Sam is keen to work with him. Dexter and I go out onto the decking outside in the garden and sit down around the table with our beers. The night is clear and pleasant, but I still turn on the patio heater before I lean back in my chair.

"So how are things with you and Grace?"

Dexter takes a sip of his beer and nods. "Yeah, we're all good, thanks. I'm going to take her to Paris for the weekend and ask her to marry me."

I clap with excitement. "Dex! That's great news, congratulations. I'm so happy for you. You and Grace are made for each other."

He beams. "I'm sure Grace will call you when we get back. She loves you. I'm sure she would want you to be a bridesmaid."

I'm so happy for my little brother. Grace and he have been together for around six years. They met in college—they were in the same Media Studies class. I'm sure Dex only took the class because of her! They would pair up on projects and Grace would come to our house for tea on regular occasions.

Grace grounds Dexter, and he is a calming influence on her feisty nature. Their personalities perfectly complement each other—he is the quiet one, and Grace is definitely the outspoken one. She is a tall, slim, and feisty redhead with curves in all the right places and a fiery personality to match the shade of her hair. Grace is a junior fashion designer; this is another reason why my mum loves her! She is always sending Ruby and me samples of her stuff, which also keeps us well up to date with the latest trends! She always well turned out and always dresses immaculately putting me to complete shame. Fashion has never been my strong point; I dress for comfort and whatever I feel looks good on me.

Dexter and Grace are like a Hollywood couple in the looks stakes with Dexter's chiselled cheekbones, tall, lithe, and muscular physique, blue eyes, and his dark hair. When they are out in public, they definitely turn heads. They are literally made for each other.

Dexter leans back in his chair and swigs his beer from the bottle.

"So, what's the low down on you and the rock star then, sis? Is it serious?" I smile coyly, and Dexter nudges me. "Someone's in *lurrrvvveee!*" Dexter teases. We both laugh, and I nod.

"I think he might be the one, Dex. He's amazing. He's ... *everything*, and he's *not* Callum."

"I'm so happy for you, sis. I'd never seen you so miserable while you were with Callum. It's good to see you smiling again, I mean actually smiling. I hated seeing you so upset and down all the time while you were with him. I wanted to punch the twat for making you feel that way. I was so worried about you, so was Mum; she would cry for hours on end after the phone conversations. I literally had to stop her from driving down to London on a few occasions because she wanted to bring you back here."

I look at Dexter. "I hate it when you guys worry about me. I'm a big girl, I can look after myself."

He nods. "Yeah, of course!"

I hit his arm playfully. "I hated the way he made me feel towards the end. I'm so scared to let Sam get too close in case he hurts me the way Callum did."

Dexter shakes his head. "That guy might be a rock star, but anyone can see he is besotted with you. Peyton this, Peyton that, I was sceptical around him at first, but that was before I got talking to him. He seems so *normal.*"

I say with a laugh, "He is. We might have had some hiccups, but everything is great right now, more than great."

He raises his eyebrows. "Don't tell Mum. She'll have you planning the wedding!" That makes the both of us chuckle. "That laugh sounds good on you, sis. Just go with your heart on this one."

"I've had so many doubts since we started going out. I can't seem to shake them off. He's a famous rock star for fuck's sake, Dex! I'm just ordinary. I don't think I'm worthy of him."

Dexter forcefully puts his bottle down on the table and looks sternly at me.

"You *are* worthy of him. Fucking hell, it's about time you had some happiness in your life. Please don't overanalyse things, sis, listen to me on this one, the way the guy looks at you, it's *sickening*."

After we laugh hysterically, I manage to calm down long enough to say, "He's gorgeous, he makes me laugh. He's amazing. The way he looks at me ... he makes me feel so safe and loved, Dex. I never felt any of that with Callum. I've cried so much over Sam, but that's because now he is in my life, I'm scared he is going to run in the opposite direction."

He tilts my chin up. "I spoke with the guy for twenty minutes. I was getting bored of hearing your name, and you're my sister! Trust me, he's not going anywhere. The doubts are all in your mind and stem from Callum treating you like shit for three fucking years. That would have an effect on anyone."

I cross my legs underneath me and take a long pull on my beer.

"It's been such a whirlwind, I haven't really had a chance to stop and think about it too much. I think he's the one, but I'm terrified I'm going to scare him away, Dex."

He turns his chair to face me and crosses his legs. "If you think he's the one, hold onto him, Peyton."

I smile. "How did you get so wise, Dex?"

He winks. "Years of practise!" Dexter gets up from his chair and asks, "Do you want another beer, sis?"

"Yeah, please."

He goes inside, and I lean back in my chair and think about the heart-to-heart with Dexter. He is my little brother, and sometimes I ask myself how he got old beyond his years. As a big sister, I should be the one giving him advice, but it seems to be the other way around. Everything he said about Sam is true; I deserve to be happy, and I vow from this moment on I am going to follow Dexter's advice. I am going to hold on to Sam, focus on a future for our relationship, and put Callum firmly in the past where he belongs.

20

Peyton

Dexter and I stayed up until the early hours of the morning catching up and having an overdue heart-to-heart. By the time I got to bed, Sam was already asleep, I crawled into bed next to him, and it felt so good to be in his arms. He looks so peaceful and content when he is asleep—a far cry from his hectic reality.

After probably the best night's sleep I have had in a while, we finally wake to the smell of bacon and eggs cooking downstairs.

"Good morning, angel."

Sam stretches his lean, muscular body and turns over to kiss me gently on the lips.

"Morning, gorgeous."

Sam smiles. "I'll never get tired of waking up to that smile, baby."

He lazily trails his fingers over my arm, my skin instantly goose bumping at his touch.

"Someone's feeling frisky this morning."

He laughs. "You have that effect on me, what can I say!"

I grasp his growing erection under the covers. He hisses and bites his lip. "*Jesus,* Peyton," he whispers huskily, and a soft tap on the door interrupts us.

"Sis, are you awake?"

Dexter is outside, and we both giggle at my brother's piss poor timing. I clear my throat.

"Yeah, I'm awake, Dex."

There's a pause.

"I was just wondering if you were coming down for breakfast."

"Yeah, I'll be down in ten minutes. I'm going to grab a shower."

I hear Dexter's footsteps across the landing and get out of bed before turning around to face Sam.

"To be continued!"

I wink, and Sam laughs. I grab my morning shower and relish the relaxing hot water on my skin. While I am washing the lather from my hair, I hear the bathroom door shut with a click and feel Sam's warm hard body press against my back. He reaches around and cups my breast, squeezing and massaging gently. He chuckles softly.

"I couldn't wait, baby," he whispers huskily. He slips a finger into my soaking wet cleft, and I feel limp against his hard muscled body. He pushes his finger in and out slowly and teasing. When I grasp his erection from behind me, he growls with pleasure. He doesn't speak, but he pushes me against the wall until the coldness of the bathroom tiles hits the front of my body. He pins my hand above my head, as water cascades between our bodies. He grasps his growing hard-on and finds my wet folds from behind, teasing my swollen pussy as I wiggle my arse against him.

"Patience, my lovely," he whispers in my ear and trails kisses from my neck to my shoulder, nipping my shoulder gently with his teeth. A soft moan escapes.

"Shhh, I've got you, angel."

I close my eyes and think to myself that I will never ever get tired of making love to this gorgeous man. He presses his hard, wet, slick body against my back and the hot water from the shower is trickling between us. Suddenly, he pushes his rock-hard cock into me. I gasp. His rhythm is slow, sensual and steady, as if he is savouring the feeling of being inside me. I contract my pelvic muscles around his cock and squeeze. He gasps and moans.

"God that feels so fucking good, baby," he whispers. "I love being inside you, you feel so good."

He thrusts into me, and I shriek at the feeling. He puts his hand over my mouth and quickens his speed.

"It's like my cock was meant for you. Look how we fit together."

He rams into me and cups my breast from behind. Moaning against his hand, I am so hot with desire for him as he alternates from quick thrusts to a gentler pace.

"Oh, Sam."

He moves his hand from my breast and finds my soaking wet pussy. He moves his finger to my nub and rubs it in deliberate, gentle circles, driving me crazy with lust.

"Beg me, baby, I love hearing you beg for it."

He slams into me.

"Sam, please, *please* make me come. I need you."

He slows his pace and continues rubbing my pussy in a quicker, more frantic motion. I can feel my orgasm rising to the surface.

"Peyton, come for me, *now*," he growls and as if on cue, I feel my orgasm rip through my whole body. I tremble against him, and his grip tightens around my waist to stop my legs from buckling underneath me. He quickens his pace, and I feel his hot seed spurting deep inside me.

We are both spent and leaning heavily on the wall. Our breathing perfectly in sync, and my heart is racing a frantic tattoo. Sam kisses me on my shoulder gently and spins me around to face him. He smiles and kisses me deeply on the lips. I am so lost in the moment, I close my eyes, nuzzle in the crook of his neck and let out a sigh.

Before I know what I am saying, I whisper in Sam's ear, "I love you so much, Sam."

My eyes fly open when I realise that is the first time I have said the *L* word. *Oh, shit.* I look up at him trying to gauge his reaction. He lets out a breath, and he pulls me closer to him.

"Peyton, I fucking *love* you. It was love at first sight. God, I love you so much, I think I might burst."

I swallow back another lump in my throat.

"You had me at, hey beautiful!" A nervous laugh bubbles up from inside of me. "My head is telling me not to, but my heart is telling me something completely bloody different, and this feeling terrifies the shit out of me."

"Me too. We'll figure it out together, baby, I promise."

I feel him smile into my shoulder. The depth of feeling I feel for him all over again suddenly overwhelms me, and I nestle closer to him. Both of us are content and satiated after our morning shower sex session.

We finish our shower, go back into the bedroom, dry off, and get dressed before heading down into the kitchen.

"Morning, Mum. Morning, Dad."

My mum smiles as she is cooking the breakfast. "Morning, sweetheart."

My dad looks up from his newspaper and smiles. "Morning, darling, sleep well?"

I nod. "Yeah, like a baby, thanks, Dad. Best night's sleep I've had in a while."

"Do you and Sam want some coffee? The kettle's just boiled, we haven't got one of those fancy pants coffee machines, so you'll have to make do with instant."

That makes me giggle. "Coffee would be great, thanks, Dad."

Sam perches himself on a stool across from my dad and rests his chin on his tattooed hands.

"Morning, Sam."

"Morning, Max."

I am happy to have the men in my life getting on so well. I make both Sam and myself a cup of coffee and smile to at the way Sam retreats into himself around my family. It is sweet to watch to see him transform from Sam the confident rock star to Sam the sweet, sensitive and shy guy. I put Sam's coffee on the worktop and take a long welcome sip of mine, enjoying the caffeine hit. "So, what have you two got planned for today then, sweetheart?" my dad enquires, and I look at Sam.

"I don't know. It's been so long since I've had a Saturday off I forget that you're supposed to relax!" I say with a laugh.

Dad joins in. "We're just enjoying having you back here, Peyton. Your mum and me we've both been so worried about you."

My gaze drops to the floor, and I think back to the conversation Dexter and I had last night. *Mum would cry for hours on end after the phone conversations.* I am about to speak, but the discussion comes to an abrupt halt at the shriek of my sister's voice.

"Peyton!"

She rushes in pulling a Louis Vuitton suitcase behind her. A wall of Chanel perfume suddenly hits me. She throws her arms around me, and I think to myself that the peaceful weekend I was hoping for has come to a premature end.

She pulls away, and we take each other in. My sister Eden never changes. She is taller than me by a few inches at five foot six, slender, with long dark brown wavy hair that flows down to her waist. She is flawlessly turned out wearing a shocking red trench coat, black skinny jeans, black sky-high patent heels, a white polka dot blouse, a pair of expensive Gucci sunglasses sitting on top of her head, and her signature burst of red lipstick. She smiles brightly.

"It's so good to see you, sis, you look amazing as always." She turns her attention to Sam. "This must be the famous Sam; I'm Eden, Peyton's older, better-looking sister."

She giggles, with a hint of contempt and jealousy in her voice. I roll my eyes and mouth 'sorry' to Sam as she shakes his hand. He winks reassuringly in my direction and clears his throat.

"Nice to meet you, Eden." Sam smiles at her, and she gets giggly.

"You're *so* much better looking in real life; the pictures don't do you justice."

She fawns over him, flicking her hair over her shoulder, and before Sam can reply, my mum walks over to us.

"Oh, Eden, leave the poor boy alone."

Eden laughs and hugs my mum. I roll my eyes at Sam, which is an involuntary reaction around my sister. I finish my coffee and grab Sam's hand.

"I'm taking you to some of my old haunts, and I'm going to show you around Brighton, babe."

Sam smiles and looks relieved. We grab our coats, and I pick up my car keys. Eden looks at me.

"You're not still driving that rust bucket around, are you? I thought dating a rock star he could have at *least* bought you a decent set of wheels, sis."

Dexter comes down the stairs just then saying, "Leave off, Eden. If it makes her happy, then who are you to judge? Just because you have Jonah wrapped around your little finger. We can't all afford manicures and flash cars."

Dexter brushes my arm as he walks past, and I am grateful for his brotherly intervention. Eden stomps childishly up the stairs, ignoring Dexter's rant, and we walk to my car. We both get in, and I start the engine.

"I'm so sorry about my sister, babe. She can be a little hard to take at times."

Sam smiles and takes my free hand in his.

"Unfortunately, I'm accustomed to girls like her. Some of our fans can be a little amorous and bratty at times. Don't worry about her, you are the most beautiful girl in my life, babe, and I'm looking forward to having you all to myself today."

I smile and get a fuzzy warm feeling inside. I haven't felt this good in a long time, and I'm going to savour it.

We spend the day hanging around some of the places I grew up in. First, we visit the beach. The tide is out, and the beach is looking particularly beautiful today. With the sunlight catching the water and shimmering like blue-green diamonds. The beach is pebbles instead of sand, and the familiar feeling of the stones underneath my feet reminds me that I'm home. Sam and I walk along the beach hand in hand. For the first time since we have been together, I actually feel like we are a proper normal couple. We sit down, and I sit between his legs, my back to his warm chest. He wraps his arms around my waist, resting his head on my shoulder, and pulls me close to him.

"We used to come here all the time when we were kids; we used to walk our dog Ziggy."

Sam looks at me. "You have a dog?"

"Yeah, he's a chocolate brown Labrador. He's gorgeous. He lives with Dexter and Grace. He's old now, though, bless him. I used to think he was my only friend when I was a kid, then I met Ruby."

I watch the waves ripple and lap at the shore.

"How exactly did you and Ruby meet?"

I smile at the memory.

"She was crying because she was too scared to climb to the top of the climbing frame, I hate seeing people sad, even back then. I was a fearless tomboy who always wanted to climb the highest. I went down to the bottom and showed her there was nothing to be scared of. We were best friends after that."

I am in a nostalgic, melancholy mood and snuggle closer to Sam.

"When I was a teenager or needed time to think, I'd come here to clear my head. There were so many times I just wished I could come back here after Callum."

He squeezes my hand. "Then why didn't you?"

I shrug my shoulders. "I don't know. I was scared of the 'I told you so', I wanted to so many times, just get in my car and keep driving. Mum and Dad's is so peaceful and ... not London." That makes us both chuckle. "But you've seen what Eden's like. I couldn't. She is jealous, shallow, driven by money, status, and greed. She's everything I despise, and she's my sister. How fucked up does that make me?"

Sam shakes his head. "It's not fucked up at all, babe, it's human. First impressions? Truthfully, I don't like her! That's nothing to do with what you've said, she just doesn't come across like a very nice person. 'I'm the older better-looking sister', what the fuck was that all about?"

I laugh and lean into Sam. He squeezes me tightly and kisses my forehead. I pull away from his embrace, clamber to my feet, grab his hand, and pull him to his feet.

"Come on, there's more of Peyton's magical mystery tour!"

We both giggle, and he chases me down the beach.

We spend the rest of the day visiting old haunts: my old school, the park where Ruby and I used to hang out in the summer holidays. We stroll around the Lanes, visit the famous Brighton Pier, and the church where my mum and dad got married. Even though Sam is recognised by his fans, it doesn't seem to faze him—it comes so easily to him. He speaks to his fans as if he has known them for years; he signs autographs and poses for pictures. He is humble and apologetic, but it doesn't stop Sam and me enjoying our time together as a couple and getting to know each other better. I find out that he was born in Southend-On-Sea and spent his early years there but grew up in Kent as well as touring around the country with his dad and his band. His mum, Lori, is American, he has a Husky called Ace, a passion for action movies, American motorbikes, and he keeps a journal. His favourite film is Dark Angel, his favourite actor is Morgan Freeman, and the person he considers as his hero is Milo Lightman from The Lightning Bolts. His favourite song is "Good Riddance (Time of Your Life)" by Green Day, his favourite album of all time is *Velvet Perfection* by The Lightning Bolts, and his favourite colour is black. By the end of the day, I feel like I have known him all my life and we are both in good spirits on the way back to my parents' house.

"Mum, Dad, we're back," my voice echoes through the house, and Eden bounces out into the hallway.

"Sis! You're back!" I smile tightly. "We're out in the garden; Dad's got the barbeque out and that ridiculous apron with the boobs on the front."

I laugh at the thought and take off my coat. Eden is in the hallway flicking her hair, flirting and fawning over Sam, giggling like a schoolgirl. I roll my eyes.

"I'm going to grab a shower and get changed."

Eden ignores me completely, twirling her hair around her finger. Sam moves away from her.

"Look we'll chat later, Eden. I should grab a shower too, and it's been a long day."

Her face drops, but she tries to hide it behind a fake smile. "Oh, OK. Later, then."

Sam salutes, and we both go up the stairs.

"Is she always like that?"

I laugh. "Yeah, unfortunately. We've never really been close if I'm honest. Dex and I have always been closer. I miss him so much being up in London, and he is like my ally as far as Eden is concerned!"

"I really like your family. They seem *normal* and so down to earth. My family are all mental and eccentric but in a really good way. You're going to love my mum and dad."

I suddenly feel bold and strip off my clothes. Sam crosses the room and is in front of me in two strides.

"You're not playing fair, angel!"

I run my tongue over my bottom lip in an attempt to look seductive.

"I'm a woman; you need to learn that we definitely don't play fair, rock star."

I wink and nip his earlobe. He swats my bottom as I walk over to the bathroom door, strips off his clothes, and follows me in. Twenty minutes later—after a mind-blowing quickie in the bathroom—we are both dressed and satisfied. We go out into the garden, and Dexter hands us both bottles of beer. My dad beckons Sam over; he kisses me on the cheek and walks over to my dad.

"Eden is being her usual dramatic self, banging on about her and that pompous twat of a fiancé." Dexter lowers his voice and pulls a face, "Sometimes I think she must be fucking adopted!"

I almost choke on my beer and slap Dexter playfully.

"That's our sister, Dexter James Harper, how *very* dare you!" I say mockingly. We both laugh, and Eden bounces over to us.

"Sis!"

She throws her arms around me and air kisses me, enveloping me in her Chanel scent.

"You look fab, that dress really suits you. I can't believe I had to find out about you and Sam from the internet. Why didn't you call me?"

Straight for the jugular. Typical Eden. I take a sip of my beer before I give her my answer, "I've been so busy at the shop. Lately, it's been non-stop."

She narrows her eyes as I mention the shop. "I can't believe you're still working for Seb in that grotty shop. Yeah, he's fit and all, but now you're with Sam. You could totally use your celeb connection, and you could *so* work somewhere more upmarket."

"How many times, Eden? I'm happy working with Seb; he's like a brother to me. I could never let him down like that, we make a good team."

Eden rolls her eyes. "Yeah because he wants to get in your knickers, Peyton."

I clench my fist at my side, and Dexter touches my arm in warning.

"Why do you insist on being such a bitch, Eden? She said she's happy where she is. I told you before not everyone can afford holidays on yachts in St Tropez and diamond encrusted engagement rings."

Eden narrows her eyes at Dexter and stomps off in a strop.

"Thanks, Dex," I say.

He smiles. "No need to thank me, I just hate the way she talks to you, that's all."

I look over to where my dad and Sam are, chatting easily and bonding over the barbeque. Sam smiles shyly in my direction, and I get butterflies in my stomach just looking at him. Eden goes over to him and stands uncomfortably close to him. I can tell Sam is trying to be polite, but the way she is brushing his arm and flicking her hair over her shoulder is beginning to bug me.

"Don't let her see that she is getting to you, sis."

I take a deep breath. "She's done this with every boyfriend I've had. She can't just be happy for me, she has to try and take what's mine every single fucking time, Dex. You would think she would have grown out of it by now. She's exactly the reason why I don't come home more often," I say through clenched teeth as my mum comes over to us.

"Is everything all right, sweetheart?"

I put on my best fake smile and nod, not wanting to cause a scene. "Yeah, everything's fine, Mum."

She smiles. "Have you and Sam had a good day?"

I nod. "Yeah, it was perfect, thanks, Mum. It's so good being back here. I miss you guys."

She hugs me tightly and says in a shaky voice, "We miss you too, darling." She pulls away from our embrace. "Can I get you another bottle? Maybe a glass of wine?"

"Yeah, wine would be great, please, Mum."

She puts on a smile and walks away from us.

"She really misses you, Peyton. God, I miss you being here. Yeah, it's peaceful, but now that we've all moved out, it lacks heart. We should definitely make more of an effort to come home more often."

Dexter smiles a genuine smile, and I am reminded of how much I miss my baby brother and being back in my family home.

Coming over to us, Dad says, "Hey, sweetheart, the food is almost done. I bought some of those steaks you love so much. Dex, could you come and give me a hand, please, son?"

Dexter nods, and my dad kisses me on the cheek. They both walk over to the barbeque area. I go inside and use the toilet, and as I flush the toilet, I hear voices outside.

"Eden, what the fuck? I'm with Peyton, I love her."

"Come on, Sam, rock stars always cheat on their girlfriends with groupies. What makes my sister so special?"

I open the door as Eden leans in and tries to kiss Sam. Sam grabs her wrists and pushes her away. I am shocked at the sight in front of me.

"Eden, what the fuck do you think you're doing?"

She pretends to look shocked.

"Peyton, he-he-came onto me. He tried to kiss me."

I shake my head. "No, he didn't. I saw exactly what happened. How fucking dare you? Keep your filthy hands off my boyfriend. You've always been jealous of me, Eden; you've always wanted what's mine ever since we were kids. You hate seeing me happy, you're jealous, and you're shallow. You're only with Jonah because he has money. You don't love him, because you're always on the lookout for something better, something that's mine. You've done it with every boyfriend I've had, you can't stand that someone like Sam actually wants to be with me and not you. You're trying to ruin what we have just because your life is such a train wreck, and you do it every single fucking time, Eden," I shout. Mum and Dexter come rushing in from outside.

"What's going on here, girls? What's all the shouting about?"

Eden is about to speak, and I hold my finger up.

"I just walked in to find her trying to kiss Sam."

My mum looks open-mouthed at Eden. "How could you do that to your sister, Eden? After everything she has been through."

Eden laughs bitterly. "After everything she has been through? She was with a complete psycho for three years, she got knocked up, and tried to commit suicide for attention. Big bloody deal."

I slap Eden hard around the face. I go to hit her again, but Sam and Dexter both hold me back.

"Eden, sometimes I think you must be adopted. You've really fucking excelled yourself today, trying to kiss Sam, being a complete bitch, *and* you've just managed to alienate the rest of your family. Well done." Dexter claps sarcastically, and mum slaps his arm.

"Watch your mouth, Dexter. Go and help your dad plate up the food outside, please, I'll deal with this."

Dexter looks at me, concern marring his boyish features. "Will you be OK, sis?"

I nod, and Eden rolls her eyes.

"Oh, please, she loves playing the role of the victim in all this. As if a guy like Sam is really in this because he loves her. He just wants the publicity of a relationship."

Sam steps in front of me, shielding me from Eden.

"I'm in this because I'm in love with Peyton. It might be hard for you to believe, but your sister is *everything* to me. She's everything you're not: she's beautiful, funny, talented and intelligent, she's genuinely nice, and the kindest person I've ever met. What you see is what you get, and I hope to spend the rest of my life with her. If you think I'm with her for publicity, then so be it. Believe what you want to believe. I know the truth, and Peyton knows the truth, that's all that matters."

My eyes glaze over at Sam's words, and I squeeze his hand.

"Fine! Take her side. I'm going!" Eden shouts childishly. She grabs her things and leaves in a huff.

"I'm so sorry for all that, Mum."

My mum shakes her head "Don't be silly, sweetheart." Mum hugs me quickly and leaves to go out into the garden.

"Thank you so much for standing up for me back there, honey."

Sam smiles warmly. "I meant every word, baby. I would never cheat on you or ever do anything to betray you. You mean too much to me."

He strokes my face and kisses me gently on the lips before we go back out into the garden. We spend the rest of the night eating, chatting, laughing, reminiscing, and catching up like a proper family. I am really enjoying being back here, and I will be sad to go back to London. Halfway through the evening, my mobile starts ringing. I excuse myself and get up to take it, expecting it to be Ruby.

"Hey, babe, I wondered how long it would take you to call me!"

There is a pause on the other end, and I am shocked at the voice who replies.

"I'm flattered, baby cakes."

My eyes widen. *Fucking Callum.*

"I thought you were Ruby."

He laughs. "It's OK, please don't hang up. I wanted to apologise about the other day. I was bang out of order. I haven't been able to stop thinking about everything that was said."

It's my turn to pause. "I can't believe you've got the cheek to actually call me after everything you said."

"You broke my fucking nose, Peyton; I had to lie to Sav about how it happened."

I stifle my laughter before saying, "The lies come easy to you, Callum; it runs in your family. Once a liar, always a liar."

"How can you say that? Look, we need to meet up again. I know you're at your parents' house, but when you get back to London. It's about time I started being honest with you about the way I acted when I found out you were pregnant."

I sigh. "I'm bored of this now. It's in the past, and I've got nothing more to say to you."

"No, you're going to fucking listen to me for once instead of shooting me down constantly. Yeah, I cheated, but I need to make amends for it Peyton, just give me one final chance. Please, that's all I'm asking."

I look up to the sky, let out a loud sigh, and say, "OK, I'll meet you for lunch on Monday."

He clears his throat. "OK, that was easy enough, our usual spot? In Finsbury Square?"

I smile involuntarily at the memory. "Yeah, around twelve thirty on Monday? This is your last and final chance, Callum. I mean it."

"Thanks, Peyton. I'll look forward to seeing you, bye."

Exasperated, I hang up the phone. I go back over to Sam and sit on his lap.

"Is everything all right, babe?"

I nod and plaster on a fake smile. "Just ... I'll explain later."

I wrap my arms tightly around his neck and breathe in his scent. He smells of mint, Joop aftershave, and his familiar Sam smell, which I love the most. It is comforting and calms me like nothing else before. Dexter makes a vomiting sound.

"Someone pass me the sick bucket!"

Laughter breaks out all around. We resume our family chat, and before I know it, the sun has gone down. Mum and Dad go inside, and Dexter takes a call from Grace, leaving Sam and me in the garden. I lead him over to the decking area, and we relax into a hammock at the bottom of the garden. I am comfortable lying in Sam's arms with him subconsciously stroking my arm and a blanket pulled up over us.

"Today has been ... *eventful*!" I say with a sigh, and we both chuckle softly.

"Dexter and I had a heart to heart last night. I miss him so much being in London."

Sam looks down at me. "Then I'm going to make it my mission to make sure you come back home at least once a month,"

I smile at his thoughtfulness.

"Have you been in touch with the boys since you came here?"

He shakes his head. "No, I switched my phone off because of J.D, babe; it's just you and me. I've enjoyed the peace and quiet, if I'm honest."

I look at him, and my curiosity gets the better of me.

"Tell me more about the boys; I feel like I hardly know anything about them."

"OK, where do I start? Brody is definitely the dark side of the band. If it's female, got tits, and a pulse—although we joke around that, a pulse is optional sometimes with him—he'll try to put his dick in it, photographers, interviewers, TV presenters. I'm actually surprised he didn't try it on with you at the shop the day you tattooed us, you fit his criteria! You name it, Brody's done it. He is also the biggest junkie of the band too. He has snorted lines of coke off stripper's arses, and he's popped so many pills I'm surprised he doesn't rattle when he walks, it's a shock that he's still functioning."

I am shocked at Sam's honesty about the dark side of fame, and it sends an unwelcome shiver down my spine.

"You see, Brody was born an addict, literally. His mum was a total fuck up, and she took drugs the whole time she was pregnant with him."

My eyes widen. "What do you mean was?"

He pauses before continuing, "She was a prostitute and died with a needle in her arm. She overdosed on heroin; Brody found her when he was ten. It fucked him up for years. It ate away at him. He would lose himself in the music, but he was so hurt and broken, he was just a frightened little kid. He started taking drugs at fifteen and spent his life in and out of children's homes, always having to look out for himself, but he's ... *Brody*. He's clever, so talented, has a photographic memory, and an IQ of one hundred and fifty-four. Watching him play guitar is fascinating, it's so effortless and something that comes so easily to him. He hardly has to practice, which is why he doesn't do rehearsals with us the majority of the time. One of the roadies sound checks for him, all he has to do is turn up on time. He's been in and out of rehab for the past ten years or so, and he has a sober sponsor called Lenny who's like a dad to him. He's an amazing person, he tries to keep Brody clean and on the straight and narrow, but J.D just makes it so God damn easy for him to get hold of the drugs. Brody asks for coke, his drug of choice, anytime of the day and like an idiot, J.D sources it and gets it for him. There's been nights where he has gone missing, literally just disappeared. He once was so fucked up on coke, we locked him in the dressing room and played a show without him. We made up some bullshit excuse that he was ill. He hides behind the bravado, the jokes, and his flamboyant dress sense. But deep down he is still that frightened, terrified, little kid who found his mum dead."

I lie in Sam's arms listening to him tell Brody's story, and my heart clenches in my chest. I can't imagine what it must have been like for a child to find his parent dead.

"Now Jax, he is my best friend—my wingman, my brother. We lived next door to each other when we were growing up. We were always causing trouble, but we always had each other's back. I spent my early years up until the age of four or five on a tour bus with my mum and dad, moving from place to place, but when the touring dried up, we moved into a house. Jax and me clicked straight away, we hung around together, we sat next to each other in school, and we shared everything. But we drew the line at girls. I briefly dated his sister Shay for a few years, which to this day he still doesn't know about. His family was an extension of my own. I trust him with my life, and I can tell him anything. We share hotel rooms when we're on the road. I'd do anything for that boy, and he has saved me so many times, I owe Jax my life."

My heart lurches.

"He saved you?" I will him to elaborate, and he clears his throat.

"That's a story for another time, babe."

He doesn't say any more about it, and I vow not to push him, so I don't say any more on the subject.

"Lucas came over from America when he was seven. He was an odd kid with an odd accent. He found it hard to fit in being the new kid; we saw him struggling, so we took him under our wing and welcomed him into our friendship fold. When we were fourteen or fifteen, we formed a band, like I told you before, and I'd never seen anyone play the drums like Lucas before—the way his face lights up when he has his sticks in his hands, the stick spinning trick he does before he goes on stage. He doesn't talk about his past at all, not even to us; he's extremely private and guarded. He's the quietest member of the band but also a total ladies' man and a massive party animal. The fans seem to like that he's the dark horse of the band. He brings an air of mystery to what he's about."

Sam smiles as he tells of his bandmates and I can tell there is a strong bond between the four of them.

"I could tell you so many stories of drunken debauchery and tour bus shenanigans, but I really don't want to scare you off!"

We both laugh, and Sam nuzzles his face in my hair. I feel the most relaxed I have felt all weekend and snuggle closer to him. He wraps his arms tighter around me.

"You could never scare me off, baby." I feel him relax underneath me. "What about Cole, what's the story with him? How did you meet?"

I let my curiosity get the better of me and take full advantage of the alcohol making him chatty.

"Cole's a good bloke, the best. He's ex-military and an ex-cop. In the early days, we didn't need security, but when we started to get more and more well-known, it was harder for us to even leave the venues without protection. He was the doorman at a nightclub where we went to celebrate our first album going straight to number one in the rock charts. Brody was drunk and off his face on pills, and he spilled a drink on this guy's girlfriend by accident. He copped a feel of her tits, and the guy started going crazy. He smashed a glass and was about to push it in Brody's face until Cole stepped in. He totally disarmed the situation, cooled everyone down—I had never seen anyone handle a situation as calmly as he did that night. I told J.D that we could use a guy like him and hired him on the spot. He owns his own security firm: C.B Security Corps—we're his biggest clients. He has around six or seven men working for him at the moment. They are all the best at what they do. We've become really close, and I consider him one of my best friends. He has a fiancée called Amy, who works for a magazine; she is Milo Lightman's stepdaughter from my dad's band. They have a four-year-old daughter called Addison—she's my goddaughter, and I love her to bits. He's tough and would give his life to protect us, but he's total mush around both of them."

I am enjoying listening to Sam tell me about the people close to him and relish the sharing mood he is in. Although, listening to his voice is making me oddly horny. I wriggle my arse against him and feel his hardness press against me.

"Feeling horny, baby? Is it me and my voice again?"

I hear the smile in his voice and giggle.

"What can I say? You have that effect on me, and your voice does something to me," I whisper, and he chuckles against my neck.

"Well, we can't have your needs going unsatisfied, now can we, Miss Harper?" he rasps and cocks his pierced eyebrow. I get up from the hammock and brazenly strip off my clothes leaving them in a trail leading to the swimming pool. I shake my hair loose from my scarf and dive into the pool completely naked. Sam stands in the doorway with his hands lazily in his pockets.

"Are you coming in?"

He licks his lips. "God, you're beautiful and completely insatiable!"

I laugh and ogle his tattooed body as he kicks his shoes off and strips off his clothes. His bum is pert and perfectly formed; it reminds me of a peach. Even with the lightning bolt tattooed on his left bum cheek, it has to be the best bum I have ever laid eyes on. I'll never get tired of exploring and ogling every inch of this gorgeous man's body.

He is standing gloriously naked in the conservatory. I go to the side of the pool and click a button that frosts the windows. Sam clicks the door so it is locked and dives into the pool. I look around for him, and he surprises me by popping up from underneath the water. He grabs me, and I wrap my legs around him. I can't get close enough to this beautiful, kind, and handsome man.

"What is it with us and water sex?"

We both laugh, and he runs his hands up my spine, causing my whole body to tingle and goose bump under his touch. He presses his lips urgently to mine, and his tongue strokes mine gently. I can't get enough of the way he makes me feel, he makes me feel wanted and beautiful like I could literally take on the world by looking into those sparkling green eyes.

"Make love to me, Sam," I whisper in his ear. He smiles that familiar panty-dropping smile, and he lifts me in his arms. Unexpectedly, he impales me on his waiting hardness, and I moan softly with pleasure in his ear.

"Shhh, I've got you, babe," he says against my skin, continuing to drive me up and down on his steel erection. He runs his fingers lazily down my spine, and I shiver against him. He chuckles against my neck, and I scrape my nails down his back, so hard that I think I have drawn blood and marred his beautiful body. He cups my face in his hands and looks me in the eyes. He is moving at a leisurely pace now, and his finger flicks over my nipple ring. I am gasping and panting as he pushes his cock further into me and I contract my pelvic muscles around him, squeezing him.

"Oh, fuck!" he moans. "You feel like heaven, Peyton."

He quickens his pace, and I can feel my orgasm building.

"Oh, Sam," I whisper in his ear and feel him smile against me. I nip his earlobe.

"Are you close, baby?"

I nod.

"Not yet," he pants and nuzzles his face into my neck. Placing kisses from my neck to my collarbone, kneading my breast in his large hand.

"Together, angel."

He moves his hand under the water and finds my sensitive clit. He strokes my nub in lazy circles, and I explode around him. I cry out in pure unadulterated pleasure, and he finds his release at the same time, spurting his seed into me. I squeeze my pelvic muscles around him, milking every last drop, and he growls into my ear. He stills, and I rest my head on his shoulder.

"That was fucking amazing."

My heart is pounding in my chest while Sam strokes my back.

"You're so beautiful, Peyton. You're everything to me. I can't imagine my life without you in it. I love you with every beat of my heart, and you complete me." His voice is husky and sincere. I feel a lump forming in my throat.

"I love you so much, Sam, I felt so lost and lonely before you came into my life, now I feel so alive."

He smiles. "See, we're not that different, baby, just two people seeking their other half."

I get the familiar butterflies in my stomach as he says those words, reminding me of how deep and hard I have fallen for this beautiful, handsome man. We dry ourselves off, go upstairs, and crawl into bed. I snuggle into the crook of Sam's neck, the place where I truly belong.

Over the course of the weekend, I have seen Sam in a completely different light—a relaxed, laid-back, regular guy who I feel like I have known my whole life. We have learned new things about each other, and I feel so much closer to him. After a tearful goodbye to my mum, dad and Dexter with promises to come home more often, Sam and I finally head back to our normal lives in London.

21

Peyton

Monday morning rolls around all too soon, and I wake to an empty bed after Sam reluctantly decided to go back to his place when we got back from Brighton. I grab my morning shower and go out into the living room. Ruby is sitting at the breakfast bar in her dressing gown. It is the first time since I got back that I have seen her.

"Good morning, babe." She smiles.

"Morning, Rubes."

"Good time at your parent's house?" she asks, flicking through the newspaper.

I nod. "Yeah, it was over too soon, though, babe."

"Judging by the rosy-cheeked glow, someone's in lurrvve!" she says in her singsong voice and giggles girlishly. "We need a catch-up, babe! I was at Jax's place last night; you would not believe how swanky it is!"

After agreeing that we need to catch up soon, I get dressed ready for the day ahead, nervous at meeting Callum for lunch.

"What are you doing for lunch today, babe?" Ruby asks when I come back out to the kitchen.

I avoid her eyes. "Meeting Cal."

I clear my throat, and she gets up off her seat. She comes over to me and narrows her eyes at me.

"Please tell me you're joking? You're meeting that fucking dickhead again?"

I zip up my bag and grab my car keys.

"I'm giving him one final chance to explain then that's it."

She rolls her eyes. "You must be a glutton for punishment. How many more fucking chances does that guy deserve?"

I kiss her on the cheek, knowing she can't be mad at me for too long, and leave for work. I drive to work and breeze into the shop, feeling refreshed after my time away.

"Mornin', honey."

Seb scoops me enthusiastically up into a big bear hug, and I inhale his familiar musky male Seb smell. I have missed it so much.

"Morning, babe, missed me?"

He laughs and releases me. "'Course I have, sweetness, the shop is never the same without you."

He smiles, and I kiss him on the cheek.

"Good to be back, babe."

The morning session goes by quickly with just a large phoenix back tattoo for a pumped-up, muscular, gym freak. It takes me almost six hours to complete the line work, and I am glad of the break when lunchtime finally comes around.

I grab my bag and leave the shop, promising Seb that I will bring him lunch back with me. As if on cue, my phone starts ringing, and I shudder when I see Callum's name flash up on the screen. I answer a little too brightly.

"Hey."

He laughs. "Hey, Peyton, it's Cal. Are we still on for lunch today?"

I sigh and check the time. "Yeah, I'm just on my break now."

I hear a voice in the background. It sounds oddly like my sister, but I push that thought to the back of my mind.

"I'll see you in twenty minutes then, bye."

He hangs up, and I stop off at Eli's to grab myself lunch to go, a bottle of orange Lucozade, and a bag of my favourite prawn cocktail crisps. Stocked up on lunch, I make my journey to Finsbury Square. I round the corner and see Callum sitting on a bench with his hands stuffed into the pockets of his familiar grey hoodie and wearing a white beanie hat. I watch him for a few seconds, his shoulders look broader than I remember, and I realise I am procrastinating. I take a deep breath and gather up the courage to go over to him.

"Hey."

His face lights up as he sees me and stands as I approach.

"Hey yourself."

He gives me an awkward one-arm hug, and we both sit down. We both take out our lunch and tuck in at the same time. Callum chuckles as he watches me.

"Lucozade and prawn cocktail, some things never change, baby cakes."

I pause. "Please stop calling me that, Cal."

He nods and says, "Sorry, old habits die hard."

I put my lunch down.

"Cut the fucking crap, Callum, just say what you need to say," I say a little more harshly than I mean to. He winces and turns to face me.

"Wow, I thought we could at *least* be a little more civil."

I take a long sip of my coffee and feel a little calmer.

"I've wanted to tell you this for ages; I just couldn't find the right words. I know how much you hate me, and I don't blame you at all for any of it. There was a reason why I flipped when I found out you were pregnant."

I lean back and roll my eyes.

"I'm tired of your bullshit, Callum. In fact, I'm bored of all the lies and the manipulation. Our relationship was toxic for three fucking years. I don't hate you anymore I pity you. You're with Savannah, and I'm with Sam, we've both moved on. Go and live your life and forget I ever existed."

I go to get up, and he grabs my hand.

"My mum died when she was giving birth to me. I found out that the woman who I thought was my mum was really my step-mum. I thought my whole life was a lie until my dad told me the whole story about my real mum. I didn't take it well, and I've had a pregnancy phobia ever since. I freaked out, and I was fucking terrified that you were going to die on me and leave me to bring that poor defenceless baby up by myself," his voice cracks and I am taken aback by Callum's revelation. I suddenly feel bad for not listening to him sooner. "I know I should have told you sooner."

I am speechless, and I'm sure look a little dumbstruck.

"Say something, Peyton," he says and takes a deep breath.

"I'm ... so sorry. I don't know what to say."

He laughs. "First time you've ever been speechless baby ca—" He stops himself finishing his sentence and looks to the floor. "I can barely look after myself let alone another life that was completely dependent on me to protect it and love it unconditionally. It was a totally alien concept to me, and then throw my mum into the mix; I was messed up for a long time. I know that's no excuse. I should have talked to you about it, but you have to understand, it was so hard. I just couldn't."

His eyes are glazed, and I know that he is being totally genuine. I stroke his arm reassuringly.

"It's OK, I understand now, Callum." That is all my brain can think to say to reassure him.

"Thank you so much for listening, all I've wanted for the past few months is for you to know the whole truth."

"I'm sorry I didn't hear you out sooner."

"It's OK. I hope after this we can be friends?"

I nod. "Yeah, we can be friends."

We shake hands and laugh awkwardly. *Friends with my ex? That can work, right?* I look at the time on my phone.

"Look, I need to get back to the shop, Cal."

We both stand at the same time.

"OK, thanks for today, Peyton; I appreciate the opportunity to finally explain things."

I nod, and he kisses me tenderly on the cheek.

"I guess I'll see you around?"

I smile. "Yeah, you can bet on it!" I wink, and he smiles. Just like that, we turn and go in opposite directions.

The next few days go by without any major dramas, and before I know it, it is Wednesday. Sam and I haven't seen each other since we returned from Brighton, but his daily texts have brightened my day and reassured me that I have not been far from his thoughts. I smile at his text as I get to the shop.

Good morning beautiful ☺

I miss you so much

Love you

S xx

"Mornin', honey."

Seb greets me with a cup of Starbucks finest when I walk into the shop.

"Morning, sweetie."

I hug Seb and go into the back of the shop to stow my stuff away. There is a large black box with a purple ribbon around it sitting on the table. Seb leans in the doorway with his arms folded.

"Who's the package for, Seb?"

He smiles. "Showed up about half hour ago, for you."

I look puzzled and begin to unwrap the ribbon. Opening the box, I take out the card.

Peyton

A little something for you for the album launch on Friday. Hope you like it; I saw it and instantly thought of you. I have no doubt that you'll look stunning. I'll be the luckiest man alive and proud to say that you're my girl.

Love you

S xx

I get the familiar butterflies and unwrap the purple tissue that is in the box. Inside the box is a black evening dress with a diamante halter neck, a purple sash around the middle, and a dramatic thigh-high slit down the left side. It is astonishingly beautiful, and I thank God for Sam's excellent taste. I take it out and run my fingers over the delicate material. Sam is right: it is stunning.

Seb laughs. "Wow, he definitely has excellent taste, babe."

With a shy smile, I reach for my phone and dial Sam's number.

"Hey, beautiful, I take it you got my gift?"

"Yes, it's stunning. Thank you so much, babe, I love it."

I can hear the smile in his voice.

"Glad to hear it, angel, I wanted to spoil you and make sure that you know you're always on my mind. I have been so busy promoting the album this week, we haven't had any time to ourselves. It's been non-stop. We've been working until at least midnight every night to make sure everything is all set for Friday."

"It's OK, you don't have to explain yourself to me, I understand. It's your job. You're a famous rock star, you do rock star things!"

We both laugh.

"I'm aching to see you; it feels like forever since I've held you. All I can think about is being with you and how you feel in my arms. If I can get away before Friday, I'll definitely try. If not, I'll make sure yours, Ruby's, and Danny's names are on the guest list, and I'll send Cole to get you at seven."

I smile at his thoughtfulness. Danny is going to squeal with excitement when I call him. Which reminds me, I haven't heard from him for a while.

"I miss you."

He sighs and says, "I miss you too, so much. Look, I have to go, angel. I'm sorry. I'll see you soon, I love you."

"Love you too, Sam, bye."

He hangs up the phone, and I dial Danny's number, suddenly feeling bad that I haven't been in touch sooner.

"Hey, stranger."

"Hey, sweet pea! Long-time no speak. I thought you had forgotten my number or something! Or has the rock star been keeping you tied to his bed and all to himself?"

"Something like that. Work's been mental, and we went away to my parents for the weekend. How are you, anyway?"

"Fabulous, darling. How's that gorgeous brother of yours?"

I roll my eyes and giggle. Danny has a little man crush on Dexter, much to my amusement.

"Yeah, he is all good thanks, babe."

"Still gorgeous and straight as always?"

I laugh. "Yep, as always, honey." He sighs dramatically. "How are you fixed for Friday? Do you want to come to Rancid Vengeance's album launch? Sam's put mine, yours, and Ruby's names on the guest list."

Danny shrieks, "*Oh, my god!* Do bears shit in the woods, babe? Of course I'll come; I'll be there with my knickers in the air as always! We need to shop! How are you fixed for lunch?"

I pause to think about it. "Yeah, I'm free."

"Fabulous! I'll swing by the shop at twelve. Have to run, baby girl, things to see, people to do, and all that! Hugs"

"Kisses. Bye, Danny."

The morning passes by in a haze of ink, and by the time lunchtime rolls around, I have six small tattoos under my belt. Not bad for a morning's work, and I am grateful to be kept busy. I am wiping down my station when Danny breezes into the shop. He is looking as stylish and preened as always in his bright-red skinny jeans, a black V-neck t-shirt, his signature black chunky knit cardigan, and black men's UGG boots.

"Hey, sweetie!"

I look up and smile brightly, pleased to see my friend.

"Hey, honey, I'll be five minutes."

Danny sits himself down in the leather chair at the reception desk and makes himself comfortable. He puts his feet up on the desk and starts filing his nails.

"No rush, baby girl!"

Seb catches my gaze and rolls his eyes causing me to smirk to myself. I finish wiping my station down, lay out some fresh paper towel across the leather bed, and go to the back to wash my hands. I grab my bag, my coat, and go back out into the shop.

"Finally," Danny says dramatically, and Seb smiles.

"I'm going to lunch, Seb."

He looks up. "Could you bring me back something, please, babe? The usual?"

"Yeah 'course, see you later."

Danny and I leave the shop, our arms linked and stroll off down the street.

"That man is the epitome of all things rugged; he is sex on legs, like a tattooed Mr. Darcy."

I laugh. "God, you need to get laid!"

He laughs and waves his arm. "How do you know I haven't already?"

I look at him, and he has that knowing look on his face.

"Come on then, spill!"

I enjoy spending time catching up and gossiping with Danny on my lunch break. We go shopping for Friday night, and I pick up a gorgeous pair of black, patent, peep-toe, Christian Laboutin heels in the sale, a black clutch bag with a skull knuckle-duster handle, and a pair of simple diamante studs. If it was left to me, I'd be wearing my Doctor Martens under my dress, but Danny insisted I buy a pair of heels, even though I almost never do heels and I feel I am going to regret the decision.

Danny goes all out buying a designer outfit, including skinny jeans, a leather studded Armani jacket, and black shirt. We even manage to fit in lunch at Swingin' Eli's all in the space of my lunch break. It is a welcome change, and I leave him vowing that we need to make time to catch up more often.

Back at the shop, the afternoon session breezes by just as quickly as the morning session did, fitting in four more small tattoos. By the time Seb flips the closed sign on the shop door, we are both pleased with the day's takings and how the day has panned out so far. We wipe down our stations in relative silence until Seb speaks.

"What have you got planned for the rest of the evening, babe?"

"I was just going to go home I have a date with a hot bath, glass of vino, and a blonde Viking vampire!"

"Are you not seeing Sam?"

I shake my head. "He's busy promoting his album."

He nods. "How do you fancy coming to the gym with me?"

I direct my gaze to him. "Is that your subtle way of saying I look like I've eaten too many pies?"

Seb is stuck for words, and I laugh hysterically.

"I'm joking, babe! The look on your face!"

Seb narrows his eyes, and we chase each other round the shop playfully. An hour later, I have been home to change into my gym gear. I am looking forward to a good work out and a proper chat with Seb outside of work. We get to the gym, and we secure two treadmills next to each other. I start with a brisk walk and ease into a gentle jog.

"So, things seem pretty good with you and Sam?"

"Yeah, things are really great, thanks. I really like him, Seb, and I've fallen so hard for him."

"Just be careful and don't rush into things, babe. I saw how upset you were when you were with Callum. I hated seeing you so miserable every day, and I wanted to smash his face in for making you feel that way. I care about you. I don't want to see you upset, or I'll have to bust out my secret ninja moves!"

Laughing, I say, "Thanks, Seb."

He smiles warmly, and I know Seb likes me a little more than he lets on, but I don't say that aloud.

"Look, I had an ulterior motive to asking you here tonight, babe."

I look at him trying to read his expression, but he doesn't give anything away. He definitely has a poker face.

"OK, sounds ominous."

He clears his throat. "I'm expanding the shop; I've just bought new premises."

I nod. "That's excellent news, babe."

He pauses. "That's not all; the shop is in California, which means I'll be splitting my time between here and the States."

I take in Seb's news with a shocked look on my face.

"Please don't look so worried, honey; your job is as safe as houses. I want you to manage the shop in London for me. You've worked so hard and earned your stripes, and I think you've got it in you to handle it."

My mouth forms a perfect O shape—I am genuinely shocked at Seb's proposition.

"I believe in you, Peyton; I trust you to run my shop. I wouldn't have asked you if I didn't think you could do it. You've proved you're a great friend and a treasured employee, the shop isn't the same without you in it. You and me, babe, we make an amazing team. I consider you part of my family."

For the second time this week, I am speechless. Seb wants *me* to manage his shop. *Little old me. Wow.* That is such a massive responsibility, but he is right, I have worked so hard to get to where I am. My reputation as one of the best female tattoo artists in the industry is unprecedented, and I have earned respect in an industry dominated mainly by men.

Seb cocks his head thoughtfully, and before I talk myself out of it, I blurt out. "Yes! Yes! Yes! I'd love to manage the shop, Seb!"

Seb's face breaks out into a dazzling grin.

"I'm so glad you agreed, babe! I was so worried that you'd turn me down."

Seb's statement has a double meaning, but I brush that aside.

"I'll run over the paperwork, and we can have a proper chat at the shop tomorrow, maybe go out and celebrate after work? Thank you so much, Peyton."

He smiles a wide genuine smile. I am so happy and honoured to be the manager of Saint Sinner Ink. We finish our work-out in two hours, and when we leave, I am exhausted. I can hear my bed calling. Seb drops me off home, and I am so tired I can barely function. I walk back into an empty flat; Ruby must be staying over at Jax's.

I take advantage of the peace and quiet and take a well-earned, hot, bubbly bath and enjoy a cold glass of white wine. An hour later, feeling relaxed, refreshed, and ready for bed I get out. I dry my hair and pull on my dressing gown. Just as I am about to call it a night, the door taps softly. I automatically think Ruby has forgotten her key and open the door. I look up at the figure filling the doorframe.

"Hey, baby."

Sam smiles his familiar dazzling smile, and my stomach flips. I am so happy to see him I jump into his arms, fling my arms around his neck, and wrap my legs around his waist. He carries me into the flat and swings the door shut.

"Happy to see me?"

I nod against his neck and breathe in his scent. He sets me down and kisses me gently on the lips.

"I've missed you so much, Peyton. You're all I've thought about since we got back. I tried so hard to get away, but the schedule has been so busy. J.D's been cracking the whip. I'm so sorry."

He envelopes me in his strong, muscular arms, I feel so safe and overwhelmed by his presence in our flat.

"I've missed you too, baby, so much," I whisper in his ear, and we kiss passionately. His tongue gently strokes mine, and I love the feel of his light stubble grazing my cheek. His hair is spiky and a little longer than the last time I saw him. I take in every inch of his muscular, statuesque body. I have missed everything about him—his touch, his kiss, and the way his arms feel around me. He decides to stay over, and we crawl into bed, snuggling against each other, enjoying our reunion.

The next morning, I wake to an empty bed. I reach over, and there is a black and white photograph of Sam sleeping laid on the pillow next to me. I smile and pick it up; there is a message on the back in Sam's familiar handwriting.

I'm so sorry I had to leave early

Had to get to a TV interview

Imagine I'm still lying next to you baby

See you tomorrow

Love you

S xx

I put the picture back on the pillow and get out of bed. I take my early morning shower, and Ruby is in the living room on the sofa watching early morning TV. As I am towel drying my hair, I glance at the TV.

"These guys have been in the music industry for ten years and are about to release their highly anticipated greatest hits album titled Tattoos and Tears on Monday. Famous for their guitar-driven, all-out rock anthems and husky-voiced vocalist, we are very pleased to welcome into the studio, Rancid Vengeance."

I see Sam, and the boys saunter casually into the studio and sit down on the bright yellow sofa. Sam looks gorgeous as ever wearing baggy jeans, a white vest, a black leather jacket, and a black beanie hat. He looks mouth-wateringly handsome, and the woman on the sofa is fawning over him. The other boys look handsome too. Jax's blonde hair isn't in its usual messed up bed-head style—it is gelled and perfectly styled. Brody is playing up to the camera and pulling faces with his black and blue Mohawk. Lucas is grinning and casually relaxing on the sofa. I am mesmerized by their chemistry and closeness as a band. I carry on getting dressed for work, opting for dark-blue skinny jeans, a Rancid Vengeance vest top that was given to me by Sam, and Doc Martens. I tousle my hair into loose waves choosing not to straighten my hair today. I apply natural make-up, and I am ready for the day ahead. I am about to go out of the door when the TV catches my attention again.

"So, Sam, it's been reported that you're dating the daughter of nineteen seventies model Sophia Bailey. Are those rumours true?"

His face breaks out into an ear-splitting grin, and I'm sure I hear the woman on the TV sigh.

"Peyton Harper, yes, it's one hundred percent true, we are dating."

The feeling warms me inside that he wants to give me my own identity to the world and his fans. I am someone other than just the daughter of Sophia Harper. He looks to the camera.

"If you're watching, babe." He winks and blows a kiss.

Ruby shrieks. "Oh, my God, babe! Did you see that?"

I grin and nod.

"Does this mean you're officially off the market? Do you think that will bother your legions of female admirers?"

Sam crosses his leg and leans back.

"Yes, I'm officially off the market. I hope it won't bother the fans, but if they're true fans, they'll be happy that I've finally found someone who loves me for me and wants to surround themselves with the madness of Rancid Vengeance!"

He laughs, and before I get distracted further, I head to work. The day goes by in a haze of paperwork and the handing over of the shop to me. I still haven't told anyone my news yet; I want it to be a surprise. By the end of the day, I'm still reeling by Sam's public declaration of his love for me, and I still can't quite believe my luck at landing a rock star. He is the sweetest, gentlest, most genuine man I have ever met; I must be the luckiest girl on Earth right now.

22

Peyton

Friday goes by in a flash, and before I know it, Seb has given me the afternoon off to get myself ready and prepared to tonight's album launch. I am actually feeling quite nervous at being publicly paraded around as Sam's new girlfriend. I get my hair and nails done with Ruby and Danny. By the time we are all freshly pampered and preened ready for our night out, we go back to our flat. We eat my favourite Chinese takeaway of chicken and king prawn curry with egg-fried rice and set about getting ready for the night ahead.

I grab a shower, reluctantly let Danny apply my makeup, and pull on my dress. Danny makes an excellent job of making me look sexy and sultry, with natural make-up, smoky eyes, lashings of mascara, and a splash of red lipstick. I look in the mirror and can't quite believe the reflection staring back at me. I have had my haircut and dyed back to my original dark-chocolate colour. My dark, glossy hair is loose and tumbling down in waves around my face and shoulders. The dress is figure-hugging and fits like a glove. It accentuates my curves and makes my boobs look phenomenal! Danny wolf-whistles.

"What have you done with our Peyton? She has been replaced with a total sex kitten! You and the rock star are *definitely* getting laid tonight!"

We all laugh and take some pictures of all three of us together. We definitely scrub up well. Ruby is wearing a black, lace, knee-length dress, sky-high black heels, her dark hair is poker straight and glossy, and she looks like she would be at home on a catwalk. Danny is looking extremely dapper in his outfit he bought on our shopping trip. His hair is perfectly styled into a side quiff, which seems to be his new way to style his hair. He is wearing black eyeliner, which makes his dark blue eyes stand out, and his golden tan completes his look for tonight.

He pulls on his newly-purchased, Armani, leather, studded jacket and asks, "How do I look?"

Ruby and I start giggling.

"You look beautiful, sweetie!"

We both kiss him on the cheek. I look up at the clock, and it is almost seven. I feel butterflies start in my stomach and I take a deep breath.

"Are you all right, babe?" Ruby brushes my arm.

"Yeah, babe, just really nervous."

She smiles and hands me a glass of rose wine.

"Here, drink this. You'll be fine, honestly, you're with one of the most famous rock stars in the world right now. If the public doesn't like you, then fuck them, babe!"

I take a long glug of the wine and smile at Ruby's optimism, but I can't seem to shake the feeling that something bad might happen. I take another deep breath and plaster a bright smile on my face.

"I have some news."

Danny and Ruby stop admiring their reflections and turn to look at me.

"You're not knocked up already, are you, babe?"

I narrow my eyes at Danny and slap his arm playfully.

"No! Of course I'm not pregnant!"

Ruby looks at me—she looks relieved.

"Come on then, spill, babe."

I smile. "Seb's expanding the shop to the States, and he has asked me to manage the shop in London."

They both start shrieking and whooping. They throw their arms around me, and we start jumping up and down.

"Congratulations, babe, that's fantastic! I'm so happy for you."

Ruby seems genuinely pleased for me, even in her current unemployment situation.

"Double celebration tonight then, babe, let's get wasted!" Danny says brightly and we all laugh. I have to admit I am in good spirits. I am grateful for having such amazing people in my life, my family, Ruby, Danny, Seb, and Sam.

The buzzer goes, signalling that Cole is here. We all head downstairs to the waiting dark limo at the kerb. Cole smiles warmly and tips his hat.

"Peyton."

I smile. "Cole, nice to see you again. These are my friends, Danny and Ruby."

He nods to both of them and smiles. He opens the car door and waits for us to get in before closing it behind us. It doesn't take us long to get to the exclusive venue Neon Nights, in the heart of the West End near to Leicester Square. Cole opens the car door and flashbulbs from the waiting paparazzi instantly blind us. I smile robotically at this surreal situation we have been thrust into. Danny is posing and putting on his best pout with Ruby. He is a total natural and plays up to the camera, loving the attention. We all walk arm in arm down the red carpet. I feel like a celebrity.

We get to the club's entrance, and I instantly recognise the doorman from the gig at the o2. He is tall and very muscular, broad across the shoulders, and looks uncomfortable wearing his dark grey suit. His hands are covered in large sovereign rings and look like they could do some real damage if connected with someone's face. He has a shaved head, and he smiles menacingly, showing a gold tooth at the front.

"You must be Peyton. I'm Skip, a friend of Sam's and security extraordinaire. He's expecting you, and I must say you're looking rather ravishing tonight, Miss Harper."

"Thank you. It's nice to meet you, Skip."

He lets us through the red velvet rope. We all step into the club, and it gives off the feeling of luxury and decadence. We walk further into the club, and my ears are instantly filled with Rancid Vengeance's familiar hits. Danny whistles.

"Le swank."

He looks mesmerized, and I giggle at his childlike enthusiasm. Ruby looks around.

"Wow, Peyton this place is amazing."

I'm speechless. The walls are decorated with opulent black and aubergine wall-coverings, the main area of the club is open with purple plush sofas all around the edges, and the tables are black granite and chrome. The fully stocked black granite bar takes up the whole back of the venue. Danny goes to the bar to get us some drinks, and I see Jax place his hands over Ruby's eyes. She spins around, he pulls her to him, and she throws her arms around him. They make such a cute couple, I smile at the two of them together, and Danny rolls his eyes. I see Sam standing at the end of the bar with the boys and a few people I haven't met before. He is standing with his one hand casually tucked into his trouser pocket, sipping a glass of amber liquid. I see Lucas nudge him and his face lights up as he sees me. He puts his drink down and his eyes cast down my body. He strides over purposefully, scooping me up into his arms.

"Hey, angel, you look … *Fuck*, you look absolutely stunning. Amazing. *Wow*."

I laugh. "Hey yourself, rock star!"

He sets me down on my feet and drinks me in.

"I've missed you."

I look up at him, and he is looking especially delicious tonight. He is in all his tattooed and pierced glory, looks as if he has two days' worth of stubble, and he looks ruggedly handsome. I resist the urge to run my fingers through his spiky hair. He is dressed somewhere in between Sam and Bolt tonight, and I start to wonder which one I am going to be graced with. Even though he has brought me as his date and publicly declared me as his girlfriend, my nerves are on edge. He pulls me into his hard chest and wraps his arms around me, breathing me in.

"God, I've missed you so fucking much, babe. I've been counting down the days."

He kisses me passionately on the lips.

"I've missed you too, Sam. After Brighton, I feel like we found out so much about each other, I felt so close to you."

His green eyes lock onto mine, and he tips my chin up.

"I've thought about nothing else other than being here with you tonight, finally going public about our relationship. That TV interview yesterday I got a little carried away. I was so excited about seeing you tonight I kind of lost myself for a second. That's what you do to me, Peyton, you make me lose myself. Being in your arms in your bed the other night was the most content I have felt in such a long time. Leaving you the next morning just about killed me, baby."

I look up at him, and my eyes glaze over at his sweet words.

"Everything about you overwhelms me, Sam. The way you look at me, the way you make me feel. Just seeing you from across the room I felt like I was about to melt into a puddle right in front of you!"

"Glad I'm not the only one, babe. I'm happy that you like the dress. I wasn't sure you'd like it, but as soon as I saw it, I thought of you."

"I love it, thank you so much, honey."

He leans down, and I am hit by his pure Sam smell. The smell I always miss so much.

"You look fucking gorgeous. You take my breath away, angel." He nuzzles my neck, and his lips skate across my shoulder. "When I saw it I thought of you and how amazing it's going to look in a pool on my bedroom floor."

His voice is husky and laced with a seductive promise. I feel heat between my legs, and I don't know how he manages to reduce me to a sex-starved nymphomaniac with just the power of his voice. I bite my lip, and he looks down at me, stroking my face as he releases my lip from my teeth. He shakes his head.

"Please don't bite your lip or I'm going to find a quiet corner and fuck you until you can't remember your own name," he whispers, and our reunion is interrupted by the presence of a couple. The man is tall—at least six feet tall, if not taller—slim but heavily muscled, with tribal tattoos on both arms, and dark-brown collar-length hair. His eyes are pale-blue, he has his ear pierced with a simple diamond stud, and if I were to guess his age, I would say he was around thirty. He looks extremely handsome, and I start to wonder if all the men Sam surrounds himself with are as good looking. I suppress my smirk.

"I'm so sorry to interrupt, mate."

Sam shakes his head. "Not at all. Alistair, this is my beautiful girlfriend, Peyton. Peyton this is our record company boss, Alistair."

I smile, and we shake hands.

"Pleased to meet you, sweetheart. This is my wife, Lexi."

I smile sweetly at the striking female on his arm. She is tall, slim, has olive skin and inky-black wavy hair. Her eyes are wide and an unusual shade of silver, her cheekbones are perfect, and she is wearing a short white dress, which compliments her olive complexion. Her legs seem to go on forever. She smiles a warm, dazzling smile, instantly making me feel at ease.

"Nice to meet you, Peyton."

I smile and shake her hand. "It's really good to meet you too, Lexi."

"It's so nice to meet someone who seems down-to-Earth. I usually feel so out of place. These record company types are such a pain in the arse."

She dramatically rolls her eyes and we both laugh. Alistair kisses her on the cheek.

"Hey! We're not all bad, honey."

She pinches his bottom, and I instantly like both of them.

"I'll catch up with you later. Sam." Alistair slaps him on the back. He nods in my direction, and Lexi winks at me. They both head off towards the bar.

"They seem really nice."

Sam nods. "Yeah, he is a good guy, and we have become really good friends. His fiancée died in a car accident four years ago, they have a six-year-old boy together. I was shocked when he told me. I couldn't imagine losing you ever, and I would totally lose my mind. Just the thought of it tears me up inside."

"I'm not going anywhere, baby, I promise."

I press a kiss to his lips and J.D. interrupts us this time. He is wearing a navy suit with a white shirt open at the collar—he looks a little dishevelled. He smiles a little too brightly at me.

"Peyton, how nice to see you, sweetheart."

He kisses me on both cheeks, and I cringe at his stale alcohol breath.

"J.D., nice to see you too," I say tightly, and Sam senses the tension.

"What's up, J.D?"

He looks me up and down, ignoring Sam's question.

"You're looking ravishing as always tonight, Peyton, darling."

I smile. "Thanks."

Sam taps J.D.'s arm. "What's up?"

J.D looks at Sam and brushes Sam's hand. "I need a word, Sam."

He nods curtly. "I'll be right back."

He kisses me on the cheek and leaves me standing in the middle of the club. I observe him carefully. His energy and sense of silent authority has all the women in the club turning their heads, fawning over him, and hanging on his every word. I am reminded that he is not Sam tonight. Not my shy, loving, adorable Sam. He's Bolt—the cocky, egotistical, arrogant, womanising, and in-demand rock star. They might be the same person, but they couldn't be more different.

As I watch him from across the room, he is smiling his familiar panty-dropping smile, and I can see the change in him. He leans in to whisper in a young attractive woman's ear—she is twirling her hair around her finger and giggling at whatever he has just whispered to her. The green-eyed monster stirs in my consciousness. Danny comes over with two drinks in his hands and snaps me out of my green-eyed reverie.

"Baby girl, the totty in here tonight is to die for!" Danny says in a high pitched, sing-song voice. He hands me a glass of champagne and I down it in one gulp.

"Steady on, girlfriend!"

A waiter with a tray of drinks passes us, and Danny grabs us both two more glasses. He hands me another glass, but I take this one a little steadier.

"It's just seeing all these women all over him," I say through clenched teeth and Danny looks at me.

"As long as he is going to be in your bed tonight, baby girl, fuck them!"

We both laugh and look around the club taking in the crowds of people.

"*Fuck,*" Danny curses, and I look up at him.

"What's wrong, babe?"

I follow his line of sight and see Callum.

"What the fuck is that snake doing here?"

Danny shouts over the music, and I brush his arm to calm him down.

"It's OK, babe, honestly. We kind of had a heart to heart the other day, and we decided to put the past behind us."

Danny's mouth forms a perfect O shape.

"Fuck me you, need your head testing, baby girl, after all he put you through."

Before I can reply, Callum is standing in front of me. His eyes widen, and he smiles brightly.

"Peyton, wow. You look absolutely beautiful. Totally knockout."

He pulls me in for a hug and kisses me on the cheek, the familiar scent of his aftershave filling my nostrils.

"Thank you, don't look so bad yourself, Cal."

We both laugh, and a woman joins us. I recognise her instantly—Savannah Sam's sister and the girl who Callum cheated on me with. I have to admit she is even more stunning in the flesh. She is a tall, large-chested waif with bronzed skin, dark, unfriendly eyes and long, dark hair tied up in a loose chignon. She is wearing an off-the-shoulder, long, red dress that accentuates his slim figure. She looks me up and down. The expression on her face is one of amusement crossed with contempt. I don't meet her eyes and suddenly feel awkward at the situation I am thrust into. Me, my ex, and the woman he cheated on me with.

23

Peyton

"I'm Savannah. I don't think we've met."

Her voice is husky and reminds me of Sam. Her accent is a mixture between English and American. She reaches out her hand, but I don't take it. I know it's rude but why should I be polite? She withdraws her hand.

"I'm Peyton."

I try to sound confident. It is taking everything I have not to reach over and scratch her eyes out. From the corner of my eye, I see Sam dismiss his conversation. He shakes the hand of the man he is conversing with and rushes over, quick to diffuse the situation.

"Sav, I didn't know you were going to be here."

Sam smiles and rests his hand at the small of my back in a gesture of reassurance. His touch instantly relaxes me.

"I couldn't miss my baby brother's big album launch."

She throws her arms around him, and he reluctantly hugs her back.

"It's been so long. Is your phone permanently diverted to voicemail?" she drawls, and he shakes his head.

"No, it must be broken; I'll get a new one and be sure to give you my new number," he dismisses her, and she smiles.

"I've just been introduced to the *lovely*, Peyton."

The way she says that phrase tells me she feels threatened by my presence. Ha. *Bitch*. One nil to me, I think! She puts her arm around Callum, and Sam gives Callum a death stare. He takes a long pull on his drink, and I can tell Sam is silently seething at Callum's presence. Savannah pulls Callum to her, and she kisses him on the cheek—the public display of affection looks forced and rather pathetic. I see Danny from the corner of my eye taking in the situation unfolding in front of him. He looks bemused. Callum looks to me for support, and I shake my head slowly in warning.

"Do you want a drink, babe?" Callum breaks the silence and Savannah nods.

"Yeah, actually, I would love one, sweetie. Catch you in a while little, bro."

They both stride off, and I let out the breath I didn't realise I was holding.

"I'm so sorry about that, I didn't know they were going to be here, I swear."

I shake my head. "It's OK, honey, honestly. I'm fine."

Danny looks at me and rolls his eyes dramatically. "What the actual fuck was that? If looks could kill, I think we'd all be dead by now!"

We both laugh awkwardly, and Sam wraps his arm around my shoulder protectively.

"You shouldn't have had to endure that, babe. I can't apologise enough."

I squeeze him before saying, "I'm fine as long as I have you, baby."

I smile, and Danny makes a vomiting motion.

"I'm so sorry you two haven't been properly introduced. Sam, this is one of my best friends and neighbour, Danny. Danny, this is Sam."

Danny curtseys in front of Sam. "It's so nice to finally meet you, Mr. Rock Star."

Danny winks, and I can see him blush. I know he is having the same effect on Danny as he has on me, and Sam chuckles.

"Nice to meet you too, mate, but you can call me Sam."

Sam bows dramatically and they both laugh. The tension from a few minutes ago has soon dissipated. I look around, and I think by the growing crowd, the party is getting into full swing. Sam looks up, and his face breaks out into a grin.

"All these people are here for you, son, who would have thought it?"

An older man joins us; he is rather handsome for his age. He is tall, thin and his salt and pepper hair compliments his features. I look at him; he has the same bright green eyes as Sam, framed by thick, black-rimmed glasses and he has the same dimpled smile as Sam. He's wearing a black suit and white shirt, minus a tie. He pulls Sam in for a hug. Danny and I look at each other, seeing the situation unfolding in front of us.

"You came? It's so good to see you, Dad." Sam's face lights up as he grins.

"Of course, I wouldn't have missed it for the world, son."

Danny raises his eyebrows, and he brushes my arm. "I'm going to mingle, sweetie, catch up in a little while."

He winks and kisses me on the forehead, leaving me with Sam and his dad.

"Dad, this is my girlfriend, Peyton."

His dad nods and smiles warmly. "Ah, the famous, Peyton. I've heard a lot about you, you're even more beautiful in the flesh. It's so nice to finally meet you. I'm Marlowe Newbolt."

He takes my hand and plants a soft kiss on the back. I smile shyly, and I can definitely see where Sam gets his astonishing good looks.

"Pleased to meet you, Mr. Newbolt."

He rolls his eyes. "Marlowe, please. People only call me Mr. Newbolt if I'm in court!"

Sam and Marlowe laugh.

"Dad, there's a few people I want to introduce you to."

Marlowe nods, and Sam kisses me gently on the lips.

"I'll be right back. I promise."

I nod. "I'm going to the ladies. I'll come and find you."

He smiles, and I go off to find the toilet. I go down a short corridor, and someone grabs my hand. Startled, I jump.

"*Shit*, sorry. I didn't mean to scare you, baby cakes."

I spin around and find myself looking at Callum's amused face.

"Cal, I didn't realise you were coming tonight."

"Me either. Sav kind of sprung this on me last minute. I thought it was a bad idea to begin with, but she insisted, she kind of makes it hard for me to say no."

I shake my head. "It's OK, it was just a shock to be thrust into the presence of the woman you fucked behind my back," I snap, and Callum recoils.

"Ouch! That stings! Right for the jugular, baby cakes."

He puts his hand to his heart mockingly, and he laughs.

"I said I understood why you cheated and I'd forget it, so we could be friends, but I didn't say I forgave you. You fucking destroyed me, Callum, you sent me beyond the pits of hell with what you did and the way you treated me."

He glances to the floor and backs me against the wall. He is so close to me I can feel his breath on my cheek.

"I want to make it right, baby cakes. Tell me how I can make it up to you. I know I don't deserve it, but give me a chance, please," his voice sounds pleading.

"There's no way you can make it up to me, Cal, the damage has already been done. Please just let me be happy with Sam."

He looks me in the eyes and says, "He can never make you happy, not the way I can, baby cakes."

He reaches over and strokes my cheek gently with the back of his hand.

"He's already cheated on you. Why do you think he hasn't been in touch? I know for a fact he has been AWOL for a week. Let me guess, he used the excuse of 'recording in the studio and his oh-so-hectic schedule' and he showed up at yours on ... Wednesday evening? Am I right? He'll go on cheating on you, Peyton, because that's the sort of man he is, the man he has always been. He won't change no matter how hard you try; you deserve so much more than a tosser like him."

How does he know all that? My heart constricts in my chest. *Sam's cheated?* I shake my head and try to quell the tears I can feel stinging my eyes.

"No, you're lying. Sam wouldn't do that."

I try to sound confident, but I hear heels clicking across the floor, abruptly ending our conversation.

"Well, well, well, isn't this cosy?"

Savannah's ice-cold voice cuts through the silence. Callum pulls back from me, and Savannah moves closer.

"It's not what it looks like, babe, we were just chatting," Callum defends himself.

"It didn't look like just a chat to me, Callum. Do you get as close to all the people you talk to as you do to her?"

Callum rolls his eyes but doesn't say anything, and she moves closer to me.

"If you ever hurt my brother, I swear to God I will fucking kill you. Do you understand, you filthy little slut? There's stuff you don't know about Sam, he was a ... drug addict. He's been in rehab, and if you *ever* send him back to that place, your life will not be worth living," she says coldly, and I feel my eyes glaze over. All the things I am told about Sam are overwhelming me, and I don't know if it's the truth or a complete lie. I feel like I have been punched in the gut. I try to steady my erratic breathing and calm my trembling hands.

"Back the fuck away from my girl, Sav," Sam's voice comes out of nowhere. I hear his footsteps getting closer and the tears I am trying to blink back blur my eyesight.

"I'm just filling Peyton in on some of the Newbolt family history, little brother."

She smiles innocently, and Sam's face is like thunder.

"And I thought I told you before to stay the fuck away from her? Didn't I make myself clear enough last time?" He jabs his finger in Callum's direction. "She already broke your nose. What else has she got to do before you get the fucking hint?" he says through clenched teeth, and I know by the look in his eyes that he is angry. By the look on his face, I think he is going to punch him, and Savannah looks wide-eyed.

"You told me that you broke your nose at the boxing gym? You fucking little prick, you lied to me!"

Savannah slaps Callum across the face, and Sam comes closer to me, leaving Savannah and Callum arguing heatedly behind us. He tucks a strand of my hair behind my ear and rests his hand on the wall beside my head.

"Are you OK, angel?"

His voice is filled with concern. I ignore his question, duck under his arm, and run off down the corridor.

"Peyton, wait!" Sam shouts, but I don't respond. I open the door to the toilet and step into the privacy of a cubicle. I lock the door, pull the seat down, and sit down. It is then when I put my head in my hands that the tears start to freely fall. I hear the toilet entrance swing open.

"Peyton, angel," his husky voice sounds pained. "Excuse me for a second, ladies."

I hear the giggles of a few females, and the door clicks shut—I think we are alone.

"Baby, please."

I let out a strangled sob and jump when the door bangs.

"*Fuck*, let me explain. Open the door, please?"

I can't bring myself to speak. *Is everything he's ever said to me been a lie?* My mind is so conflicted right now. After Callum, I vowed I would never allow another man to lie to me ever again. I thought Sam was different.

"Peyton, please talk to me, angel," his voice is barely a whisper and so tender. I unlock the door reluctantly, and he pushes the door open, backing me against the wall. He wraps his arms around me, and I sob into his chest, clinging desperately to his soft t-shirt.

"Shhh, I've got you. *Jesus,* please don't cry, you're tearing me apart."

He runs his hands up and down my back soothingly.

"Everything's going to be all right, angel, but you need to let me explain." His voice is rough and sounds almost desperate. "Sav told me what she said. She had no fucking right, and it wasn't her place to tell you."

I pull away and unravel some toilet paper from the dispenser. I dab my eyes and blow my nose. It is at that particular moment I feel brave enough to speak.

"When were you going to fucking tell me, Sam?"

He hangs his head.

"Not here, baby, the place is crawling with press. Ryan, the owner, is a friend of mine and Alistair's brother; he said we can use his office, we won't be disturbed."

I nod. "I just need a minute to fix my make-up."

"I'll be waiting right outside, angel."

He kisses the top of my head and leaves. I stand in front of the mirror, and my eyes are red. *Great.* I re-apply my makeup in record time and look almost normal again. I run my fingers through my hair, check my reflection one last time, and leave the safety of the ladies' room.

Sam is leaning casually against the wall outside with his hands tucked into his pockets, looking handsome as ever. He is going to make it so difficult to be mad at him being a total distraction and incredibly good looking. Sam gestures for me to step ahead of him, and he directs me into an office further down the corridor, closing the door and locking it behind him.

Sam sits down on the edge of the desk and folds his arms. I stand a few feet away from him; I can't bear to be near him right now, and I don't meet his eyes. I know if I meet his eyes, I will fall under his spell.

"So when were you going to fucking tell me you were in rehab, Sam?" I spit out, and he hangs his head.

"I thought it was common knowledge, it was all over the news, the internet, and the papers when it happened. But when I found out that you had no idea, I kept putting it off. It was refreshing that you seemed to know virtually nothing about me. I was terrified you were going to run again. You have to believe me; I was going to tell you, babe, I promise."

"Don't you think it was important? You could have told me the night we went out for dinner, we were being honest with each other laying our cards on the table, and you've had plenty of opportunities since then. How do you think it felt for me to hear it from her? Isn't it enough that I have to endure being in the same room as her? She's the woman who Callum fucking cheated on me with!"

Sam gets up and stalks towards me. "Callum this, Callum that. I'm sick of hearing his fucking name. He's the third person in our relationship; you always bring it back down to him. You're with me now, isn't it enough that I love you and worship the ground you walk on? I understand he hurt you beyond belief and he broke your heart, I can't imagine what you must have gone through, but it's in the past now. You need to get the fuck over it!" Sam shouts, and my eyes widen. I can't believe he just said that. I am trembling with anger as I slap him hard across the face. The slap echoes around the room.

"How fucking dare you! You've got no right to bring it back around to me when this is all your fault!" I scream at him, and Sam nods.

"Yeah, and what good would it have done you knowing I'd been in rehab? Would it have made a difference? Would it have changed the way you feel about me?"

I pause, and I actually can't answer that question.

"I deserved to know. We're meant to be a couple. Being in rehab is a big fucking deal, Sam, don't you get that?"

He moves closer to me. "I was in rehab because I was a fucking drug addict; I was a total fuck up. I was an absolute mess. I turned to drugs because I was barely an adult with the added pressure of our growing fame, because of J.D., because I was so God damn weak. I couldn't resist the temptation, and I couldn't say no. Is that what you want to hear? Do you really want to drag the past up? Because the past is fucking irrelevant, what matters is the here and now. Us, in this room, right now. When I saw you walk in earlier, you took my breath away, and I felt so proud to say you were mine. You are the most beautiful woman in this club tonight by far." He reaches over to stroke my face. "Look at me."

His voice is commanding, and I meet his eyes. *Oh, shit, I'm in trouble.*

"I've never felt like this ever it's all new to me and hearing you constantly go on about Callum, I actually felt violent, and I wanted to smash his fucking face in as soon as I saw him near you," he says through clenched teeth. "You've got no idea how vulnerable and fragile you are, baby. Being in this industry, there are people who'll want to steal you away from me, and I'm not going to let them, I'd fucking die for you, Peyton."

I melt at his words, and Sam's voice is pained yet determined. There is something in the way he says those words that makes me believe him one hundred percent. I lean into his hand, which hasn't moved from my face.

"I'm so sorry, that was like a different life back then, and I'm not that person anymore."

I am silent, and Callum's words begin to echo in my ears. *He has cheated on you, and he'll go on cheating on you because that's the sort of man he is.* I recoil from his touch and back away from him. His face drops, and he moves closer to me. I take a step back; I can't be near him right now. Every time I am near him, I lose all sense of coherent and logical thought.

"Baby." He frowns, and I shake my head.

"Is there someone else? Have you cheated on me?" My voice comes out desperate and barely a whisper. His eyes widen, and he shakes his head.

"What the fuck! *No,* of course I haven't, I swear to you. I love you, you're all I want." I look to the floor. "Who told you that?"

I am silent, reluctant to mention Callum's name again.

"It's not important."

"Yes, it is fucking important. Someone told you I cheated on you, and it's quite obviously upset you. Do you remember what I said to you before? Anyone upsets you ever again, and I swear I'll hurt them."

"Callum," my voice is small as a sob escapes from my mouth.

"I might have known, he's not going to be fucking happy until he has split us up, is he? You said it yourself, he's a born liar, Peyton. You don't honestly believe him, do you? He fucking cheated on you, and he has the cheek to rat me out for the same thing?" Sam spits out sarcastically. "I'd never hurt you intentionally, I haven't been with any other women, *just you,*" he whispers the last two words and his voice sounds sincere. I shake my head.

"Why would he say it if it wasn't true?"

Sam sighs.

"*Jesus Christ*, he's done such a fucking number on you that you're completely stupid, naïve, and oblivious that he's trying to manipulate you and get back between your legs!"

I slap him hard across the face again, and he growls. He moves closer to me and backs me into the desk. I feel the back of my legs collide with the smooth wood. He places his hands on the desk either side of me, trapping me.

"I haven't been inside you for a whole week, baby; I can tell you're just as frustrated as I am," he whispers huskily in my ear, and I shiver at the intensity in his voice. He runs his finger down my arm, and my body instantly responds, goose bumping under his touch.

"See how your body responds to me, you shiver every time I'm near you. You're not really mad just ... *sexually frustrated*"

He is so close I can feel his warm breath on my cheek.

"Lie back on the desk for me, baby."

It is as if our argument has been forgotten. He is trying to satiate me with sex, and boy, is it working! I do as he says and lie back on the desk.

"Look how easily you submit to me, angel."

He smiles cockily and runs his nose down the middle of my chest. He trails down my stomach and stops at my sex.

"I can tell how ready you are for me, baby; I can smell your arousal."

He has a mischievous glint in his eyes. He pushes the material of my dress up, so I am exposed to him. He slides his hand up my inner thigh, and I shiver with anticipation.

"This is going to be purely for my pleasure, not yours, do you understand?"

I whimper as his finger brushes my slick folds.

"You need to understand that it's just you, Peyton, no one else. *Just you.*"

He runs his finger down my slit.

"Under any circumstances, do not come."

I gasp at the enormity of what he has just said. How can I not come? *Stupid, stupid man!* He plays me like an instrument. He knows which buttons to press with me sexually. He only has to touch me, and I'm putty in his hands. Very wet putty!

"Look at me, baby."

I look at him, and I melt into those sparkling green eyes. He rubs my pussy in desperate, deliberate, slow circles. I am writhing under him, and he is smiling that familiar smile.

"*Just you,* Peyton," he whispers. He unzips his trousers and releases his already rock hard cock. He strokes himself.

"Look what you do to me, baby."

He yanks my knickers down my thighs roughly and brushes the tip against my clit. I moan with pleasure.

"Do you like that?"

I nod and bite my lip.

"Say it, tell me you like it, baby. I need to hear the words."

I let out another moan.

"Yes! Yes! I like it, Sam, please, just fuck me!" I plead desperately. He smiles and plunges his cock deep into my waiting pussy. I let out a strangled cry, and he puts his hand over my mouth.

"Shhh, quiet, angel, I'll take care of you."

He starts to quicken his pace, and I know by the look on his face he is holding back. He removes his hand from my mouth and rolls my nipple between his fingers. I mewl softly and writhe beneath him as he is pumping in and out of me in frantic strokes. I am so close I can feel my orgasm cresting to the surface.

"Oh, God, Sam, please don't stop."

I pant, and suddenly he pulls out, leaving me wanting and fraught sprawled over the desk. He chuckles softly, tucks himself in, and zips up his trousers.

"I told you I wouldn't let you come. You were throbbing around my cock; I could feel how close you were, angel," he whispers. I am shocked, and he grabs my hand as if nothing has happened. He pulls me to my feet, pulls my knickers up, and straightens my dress. I perch on the edge of the desk when the door handle rattles, and there is a loud knock.

"Sam, are you in there? Get your fucking arse out here, you're needed."

J.D. shouts impatiently from outside the door, and Sam kisses me gently on the lips.

"Maybe now you'll believe it's just you, baby."

He winks, and I get to my feet, still speechless at what just happened.

"Duty calls, angel." Sam opens the door. "J.D."

Sam nods, and I leave the office behind him. He saunters off down the corridor and J.D. hangs back. He grabs my arm roughly.

"I thought I told you to back the fuck off, little girl, he doesn't need you. Was it your bright idea to run off to Brighton and make him practically unreachable?"

"Get the fuck off me J.D., Sam's got his own mind. He knows what you're like."

J.D moves closer to me and backs me into the wall.

"He doesn't need you in his life. I know he's stupidly fallen in love with you, I've seen the way he looks at you. But I'm not going to stand by and watch him get his heart ripped out again. Just walk away, you fucking little whore."

I struggle with J.D., and he tightens his steel grip on my arm. He is so close I can feel his warm alcohol breath on my cheek.

"I know about you and Sam, J.D, I know you manipulated him into having sex with you," I whisper, and his eyes widen in shock. It takes him a few seconds to process, and then he straightens, rolling his shoulders.

"I wasn't the one who did the manipulating, sweetheart; he was more than a willing participant if my memory serves me right."

He smiles maniacally, and I pull my arm away from him.

"Get the fuck away from me. How could you do that to him?" I spit out.

"You don't know what you're talking about; you're just a naïve and pathetic little girl who happens to be flavour of the month. He'll find someone else soon, and he'll move on when he is bored."

I look up defiantly at him. "You don't fucking scare me."

He laughs bitterly. He grips me around my throat and pins me to the wall.

"Well, you should be fucking scared, you little slut."

I hear a voice come out of nowhere and J.D loosens his grip.

"Hey, get the fuck away from her, J.D.," Lucas shouts in his thick American accent, and my heart is pounding so hard. I feel like it might jump out of my chest, and I begin to think I am *way* out of my depth.

24

Peyton

"What the fuck is going on? Are you OK, Peyton?"

I look at Lucas and nod. He is looking extremely handsome tonight; his dark brown hair is spiked into a faux hawk, which sets off his flawless bronzed skin. He is wearing dark-blue jeans, a black vest, and a black suit jacket, which emphasises his broad muscular shoulders. I can't say I have ever noticed him before because he is the quietest member of the band, but tonight he is certainly excelling himself.

"Lucas, I'm fine, honestly," I say quietly. I start to shake, and Lucas puts his arm around me.

"*Jesus Christ*, what the fuck have you done to her, J.D.?"

"I haven't got time for this shit now, Lucas," J.D. says intolerantly and storms off down the corridor, ignoring Lucas' question.

"Hey, it's all right. I've got you, honey. Do you want to tell me what happened?"

Lucas' warm, concerned, blue eyes regard me intently, and his voice is soft and soothing.

"He-he threatened me. He's been doing it for weeks," I manage to choke out, and he stands in front of me gripping both of my arms, as if he is checking me over.

"Did he hurt you?"

I shake my head. "No, I'm fine, thank you so much for riding to my rescue."

He laughs. "Just call me ... What is it people in England say? A knight in shining armour?" I laugh genuinely. "If he threatens you again, come and find me, honey. He can't get away with this."

I nod, grateful that he believes me, and he witnessed it first-hand.

"Lucas, please don't tell Sam," I plead. He is about to protest but stops himself; he makes a cross over his heart and blows me a kiss. I smile shyly.

"Come on, honey, let me get you a drink. You look like you could use one."

I go back into the club with Lucas, and the party is in full swing. There is a sea of people dancing on the dance floor and people standing in groups chatting. I spot Danny talking to a tall guy with highlighted hair, and I decide to leave him to it. I go to the bar with Lucas, and Ruby bounces over to me.

"There you are! I've been looking for you everywhere, babe!"

Lucas gets me a large glass of white wine, and I take a big gulp, relishing the warm fuzzy feeling the alcohol creates in my stomach.

"Thanks, Lucas."

Lucas smiles and brushes my arm. "Remember what I said, honey?"

His concern is welcome, and I appreciate that at least one member of Sam's band actually believes what J.D. is capable of. Ruby looks at me and narrows her eyes.

"What was that all about?"

I shake my head. "It's nothing, I'll tell you later, babe."

Ruby and I chat for a while, catching up on the night so far, leaving out the part where J.D threatened me. We go onto the dance floor and dance to our favourite club tunes. I get a few more drinks in me and feel comfortably tipsy.

I go off down the corridor and into the toilets. I hear raucous laughter from the office that Sam and I were in earlier. I walk to the office and curiously listen at the door.

"So she knows you've been in rehab, so fucking what? Lighten up; she doesn't need to know that you still do the occasional bit of Charlie, dude."

I recognise the voice as Brody. Brody laughs, and my eyes widen, I cannot believe what I'm hearing.

"You know, you and I were close before she came along. It's like she has your balls in a vice or something, slowly squeezing the fucking life out of you," Brody slurs.

"I love her so fucking much, Brody. She's changed me for the better, I gave up all this shit for her. This is the last fucking time; I can't carry on lying to her, she's going to find out that I was in there for more than drug addiction and it's going to fucking crush her, it will destroy us for good this time."

Sam's voice is barely audible. Destroy us? *What could he possibly mean by that?*

"Come on, Sammy, you can't honestly believe that. Live a little. Some of the best night's we've had have been while we're off our faces. Why end the party now? Just because of the old ball and chain? It was never like that with Lyla."

Who's Lyla? I can't bring myself to listen to anymore. I fling open the door to the office and see at least a dozen white powder lines all over the desk. Brody and Sam are leaning over sniffing line after line of cocaine through rolled up twenty-pound notes. Brody looks up.

"Oops! Caught red-handed by the missus!"

He giggles, and Sam looks wide-eyed in my direction. My eyes are glazed over.

"This is fucking awkward!" Brody laughs again, and his eyes are glossy.

"Baby, please, wait I can explain."

I look at Sam in disgust and raise my voice. "No, you don't get to call me baby."

He steps towards me, and I shake my head.

"Don't fucking bother, just stay away from me, Sam," I shout, turn around, and storm off down the corridor. I hear Sam shouting after me, but I don't turn around, and I don't bother going back into the club or saying goodbye to Danny and Ruby. I go straight out into the street, and the cool air hits me. I suddenly feel a little more drunk than I realised.

"Do you need a taxi, Peyton?"

Skip smiles, and I nod, not meeting his gaze. He flags down a black cab, and it pulls up at the kerb.

"Thanks, Skip."

He salutes and smiles. My feet are screaming in my heels; I knew I should never have listened to Danny's style advice. I take off my shoes and step into the taxi. As I close the door of the taxi, I see Sam standing in the entrance of the club running his hands frantically through his hair. I can see his deeply wounded expression and what looks like a heated exchange between Skip and him as the taxi drives away with me sat in the back.

"Where to, love?" the driver's voice cuts through my whirling thoughts.

"Give me a sec, please just drive."

The driver nods. I get out my phone and dial the first number I think of.

"Hey, honey bunny," Seb's soft, soothing voice fills my ear, and I let out a sob. "Honey, talk to me, is everything OK?"

I clear my throat. "Can I come over please, Seb?"

He doesn't hesitate. "Of course you can, darlin', you know that you're welcome anytime day or night."

Relief washes over me.

"I'm in a taxi now."

"OK, I'll see you in a little while, honey."

I sniff. "Thank you so much, Seb."

"You're very welcome, sweetheart. See you soon, bye."

I hang up the phone and lean back heavily in the seat.

"Canonbury Street, Islington, please, mate."

The driver smiles. I let the tears flow freely, and my phone starts ringing. I see Sam's name flash up, and I quickly disconnect the call. I don't want to speak to him; at this moment, I'm not sure if I ever want to see him again. He lied to me, he told me he was in rehab for drug addiction, and then I find him sniffing cocaine. My head is all over the place. My phone starts ringing again—it's Sam again. I disconnect the call again and switch off my phone.

Soon, we are pulling up outside Seb's apartment. I pay the taxi driver, pick up my bag and shoes, and exit the taxi. I press the buzzer, and I am buzzed in straight away. I go up one flight of stairs and Seb is waiting on the bright open landing for me with bare feet. As soon as I see him, I break down in tears in his strong, safe arms.

"Hey, shhh, it's going to be all right. Come on inside, honey." He takes me inside and closes the door behind him. "Sit down; make yourself comfortable, I'll get you a drink."

I sit down on his large corner sofa. Seb's place is a plush, spacious, light, and airy four-bedroom apartment. It has made a feature of the modern brickwork, teaming it with clean white walls and wooden flooring throughout.

"Tea, coffee, water, wine, whiskey, or vodka?" Seb leans in the kitchen doorway.

"Vodka, please, babe, I need it."

He nods and pours us both large glasses. He brings the drinks out and puts them down on the table in front of the sofa before he sits down next to me.

"Do you want to tell me what's happened, honey?"

I take a long pull on my vodka and enjoy the burn in my throat.

"Where do I start?"

Seb smirks. "The beginning usually helps!"

I smile.

"First of all, Callum turned up with Savannah, Sam's sister, and the woman he cheated on me with. She started spreading her poison and generally being a complete bitch. She told me that Sam had been in rehab."

Seb lowers his gaze, avoiding eye contact.

"You fucking knew, didn't you?" I snap.

"I thought you knew already, babe."

"Apparently, I'm the only one that didn't."

I drain what is left in my glass and Seb raises his eyebrows.

"I'm assuming there's more?"

I nod. "We had a massive row; he turned it around on me basically telling me that he thinks Callum's the third person in our relationship."

I look at Seb, trying to decipher his reaction.

"Maybe he's right, babe. You have been seeing a lot of him lately. He's your ex for a reason, because he cheated on you."

I shake my head.

"We had a heart to heart a few days ago. He explained everything, and about why he freaked out when he found out I was pregnant. He was actually honest with me for once."

Seb takes a sip of his drink before admitting, "I didn't think that boy knew how to be fucking honest." His voice is dripping with sarcasm, and I narrow my eyes at him.

"I came here because I needed to talk, not to be judged, Seb."

He puts his glass down and holds his hands up.

"I'm not judging, babe. I'd never judge you, I'm just being honest. Would you prefer it if I lied to you?"

I shake my head and get to my feet. I need another drink to finish relaying the rest of the night to Seb.

"Where do you keep your vodka, babe?"

He laughs throatily and shakes his head. "In the kitchen, honey."

I walk barefoot across the floor and into the kitchen. I can feel Seb's eyes burning into me as I am walking. I grab the bottle and go back into the living room, sit down on the sofa, and tuck my legs underneath me, making myself comfortable. I pour myself another large glass of vodka.

"Don't you think you should slow down?"

I shake my head. "I'm nowhere near drunk enough to deal with all of this shit, Seb."

I take a long gulp of my drink, and Seb regards me intently.

"I can't stand seeing you this way, Peyton, *fucking rock stars.*"

His jaw tenses and he frowns. I turn to look at him. I take in his strong masculine jawline, sharp, rugged features, and his deep-blue eyes. It feels as if I am just seeing him for the first time.

"Why can't all men be like you, Seb?"

He laughs, and he leans back on the sofa.

"Because the world would be a very boring place, honey."

I put my glass down and stroke his rough, stubbled cheek.

"You're kind, sweet, caring, and honest, and the gentlest soul I know."

He cocks his eyebrow. "If you want to carry on stroking my ego, I'll gladly sit back and let you, but you won't remember any of this in the morning."

He smiles. I scoot closer to him and rest my head on his shoulder. He puts his muscular corded arm around me and kisses the top of my head.

"Everyone said that we were perfect for each other, why didn't I listen?"

A tear escapes from my eye, and I wipe it away.

"Please don't say stuff like that, babe."

I look up at him. "It's true; I've been ignoring someone who's been under my nose for years."

"I've wanted to hear you say that for years. I guess I just stopped hoping, but when you called earlier, I literally had to stop myself from coming to get you and riding to your rescue."

I run my finger down his chest; he leans down and kisses me passionately on the lips. His lips are so warm and soft; I instantly lose myself in the kiss. He lays me down gently on the sofa, and I find myself kissing him back, enjoying the feel of his lips on mine. I grip his t-shirt and pull him closer to me. I can feel his erection straining against me, and he pulls away quickly. He wipes his mouth with the back of his hand. We are both breathless and flustered.

"*Fuck*! *Shit!* I'm so sorry. That shouldn't have happened, honey," he curses, and I drop my gaze. He pulls me upright and gets to his feet.

"I'll call you a taxi."

He leaves the room, leaving me on the sofa speechless and in complete shock at what just happened. Seb and me, me and Seb, *we kissed*. An actual full-on snog, I kissed him back and actually enjoyed it. *What the fuck?*

25

Peyton

I wake the next morning with a banging headache and a mouth that feels drier than Gandhi's flip-flop. I don't remember getting home last night and the after-effects of drinking last night are setting in. I wake to the phone ringing constantly and the buzzer of the flat ringing. I don't have time to dwell on my hangover; I go out into the living room to investigate. As I open my bedroom door, I hear Ruby pick up the phone and shout in frustration.

"Just fuck the fuck off!"

She looks at me and narrows her eyes.

"That fucking phone and that buzzer haven't stopped ringing since half past seven this morning. That shit should be illegal on a Saturday morning."

I put my hand to my head.

"I'm so sorry, babe," she says on a sigh. I know Ruby doesn't function unless she has at least a full eight or nine hours sleep.

"Are you going to tell me what the fuck happened last night? I was so worried about you; you just left without a word. I was calling you for ages."

The phone starts ringing again and even I am getting sick of hearing it. We both leave it to ring, and Ruby goes into the kitchen to make us some coffee. The answering machine picks up a message.

"Hey, honey, it's Seb. I wanted to apologise for last night. I didn't mean for that to happen. Anyway, there's press camped out outside the shop. I know it's your day off, but I just thought I'd warn you. Call me please, darlin', let me know that you're OK. Bye."

Ruby leans over the breakfast bar and raises her eyebrows.

"You're going to tell me what happened, Harper, even if I have to fucking force it out of you."

I groan. She is calling me by my surname, so I know she is serious.

"My head hurts."

Ruby smirks. "Too much to drink? Yeah, me too, I was sipping strong black coffee and in the shower for a while before I even started to feel normal again. It was a pretty crazy night."

I flop down on the sofa and groan. "You're telling me."

Ruby brings in the coffees and puts the cups down on the table.

"Come on then, spill the tea, babe."

Just like that, it all comes tumbling out: Sam being in rehab, Savannah's presence, J.D threats, catching Sam and Brody doing drugs, and the kiss with Seb. The morning goes by in a haze of tears and confessions. By lunchtime, I have got it all off my chest, showered, and have started to feel a little more like my usual self.

The phone and the buzzer stopped ringing a while ago, so I assume I'm safe, for now at least. I dread to think of the headlines when I finally bring myself to look at the papers and the Internet. I am in the kitchen making more coffee when the door knocks.

"I'll get it." Ruby jumps up and goes to answer the door.

"Hey, Ruby, is Peyton here? I really need to see her."

It's Sam. *Oh, shit.* She looks him up and down with a look of disgust on her face. I quietly rush into my bedroom but watch through the crack in the doorway. His muscular body fills the doorframe, and he leans into the flat. I can't face him, not after last night. I saw a completely different side of Sam and found out things about him that I didn't like one bit.

"She doesn't want to see you or speak to you, Sam, she's really upset."

He hangs his head. "I know, but I need to see her. It's important. I fucked up so bad, and I need to apologise."

His voice sounds desperate and pleading. I start to soften towards him, and my heart constricts at hearing the hurt in his voice. Ruby steps out of the doorway and lets him into the flat. She closes the door, and he still looks awkward standing in our small compact flat. He tucks his hands into his pockets, and Ruby stands with her hands on her hips. She frowns and narrows her eyes at him. By the look on her face, I know she is about to lay into him good and proper. *Christ,* this isn't going to be pretty.

"You know, we made a pact after Callum cheated on her. She shed so many fucking tears over him, we promised each other that day that we would never shed any more tears over guys ever again. It's not worth it. Ever since you breezed into her life with your leather and your tattoos, all she does is cry and doubt herself. She thinks I don't know, but I hear her sobbing, and she can't know that I know. She hates burdening other people with her problems, and she hates making people worry. But you've caused all this, Sam, *you.*"

She moves closer to him, so they are toe to toe, her frame slight compared to his muscular one. She looks up at him and jabs her finger in his chest.

"Now, you make it fucking right, or I swear to God, I will kill you if you ever hurt her again. Are we clear?"

Sam doesn't defend himself, and he nods, hanging his head to the floor. *Boy*, does that girl know how to intimidate a man! I am suitably impressed!

"I'll go and get her. Don't blame me if she doesn't want to talk to you."

He doesn't say anything, and I hear Ruby's footsteps across the flat. I quickly lie down on my bed not trying to make it too obvious that I was at the door all along listening. She taps the door softly.

"Babe, Sam's here. Can I come in?"

I clear my throat to say, "Yeah."

She comes in and sits down on the edge of my bed.

"If you don't want to talk to him, I can tell him to leave."

I look at her.

"He looks like shit if it's any consolation!" she says with a laugh, and I smile.

"I'll see him. I need to hear him out."

Ruby takes my hand in hers. "If you're absolutely sure, babe?"

Nodding, I relent, "Yeah, I'm sure."

Ruby smiles sympathetically, and she pulls me to my feet. She fixes my hair and smoothes out my clothes.

"If you need me, I'll be in my room. I need to call Jax."

She hugs me tightly, kisses me gently on the forehead, and we leave my bedroom. I see him standing in the living room, and Ruby was right—he does look like shit. His hair is flat and un-styled, he has black bags underneath his eyes, he looks deathly pale, and he still hasn't shaved. He looks up from the floor and into my eyes. His eyes don't have their usual sparkle, and my heart constricts. Ruby sees the silent gesture between us, and she goes into her room shutting the door behind her.

"I'm so fucking sorry, babe, I had to see you," he says, his voice barely a whisper and pained. It takes everything I have not to break down in front of him.

"I need you to know I never meant for any of that to happen."

"First, your sister turns up and makes me feel about two feet tall, then I find out you were in rehab. What happened to honesty, Sam? It's like everyone else knew but me. I feel so fucking humiliated, naïve, and stupid for trusting a word you've ever said."

He walks towards me, and I take a step back.

"No, Sam, don't. I can't be near you right now."

He stops.

"I love you so much, angel, you need to know that."

A tear rolls down my cheek, and I hate my emotions for betraying me. Even mad at him I just want to run up to him and wrap my arms around him. I know I have to stop being so soft where men are concerned, and I take a deep breath. *Grow some balls, Harper.*

"I'm not sure I can be with you, Sam, not after last night. I saw a completely different side of you, a side that I really didn't like."

My heart is breaking inside, but I know this is the only option. He shakes his head.

"Please, Peyton, don't leave me, you can't leave me. I'm nothing without you. Having you in my life has completely changed my perspective on everything. You've shown me how to love and be loved in return. Last night was just a blip, I never meant for it to happen. I just needed ... I needed something to take the edge off." His voice is pleading, and his eyes glaze over. I hold my finger up.

"You could have talked to me! You didn't have to do that. How do you think I felt walking in on you and Brody?"

He hangs his head, and I can see him trembling.

"I know it must have been hard for you, but in this industry, you have to accept the darker side of fame. I know it's not an excuse, but you have to believe that it won't ever happen again, you have my word."

He steps closer to me, and his tall frame towers over me. He tips my chin up, and I look at him. I see the anguish and pain in his eyes, and it's more than I can bear. A tear rolls down my cheek.

"Please don't cry, angel, you're fucking shredding me," he whispers and kisses my tears away. I close my eyes, relishing his touch and the effect it has on me.

"Look how good we are together, Peyton; I'm so in love with you. How many times do I have to prove myself to you?"

I suddenly come to my senses, and the voice in my head takes over. *He lied to you, and you kissed Seb.* My eyes fly open and I back away from him.

"You need to leave now."

His eyes widen. "Peyton, I understand that you're mad, but please, *please* don't do this. I'm willing to die trying for you. I'm *nothing* without you; you make me a better person."

I shake my head. "Please, just go," I choke out.

"Not until you've fucking heard me out."

I know I promised I would hear him out, but even being in the same room as him right now is too much for me to handle. Every time he is near me I lose my mind. I know I have to stand my ground or I'll cave, and I'll be a slave to him just from him being near me.

"I just want you to fucking leave!" I scream, and Ruby rushes out into the living room.

"What the fuck is going on? What have you said to her? You said you'd make it right, you prick," she shouts, and Sam doesn't say anything. "I think you should leave right now and don't come back."

I am sobbing uncontrollably, and the tears won't stop. Sam looks at me and a tear rolls down his cheek. He leans in to kiss me on the cheek.

"*Just you*, Peyton, I love you. I'll always love you, please don't ever forget that."

He strokes my cheek. With those words, he turns, walks out of the flat, and out of my life for good this time.

A few hours later, the dramas of the day seem to have calmed down. My tears have finally subsided, now I just feel numb after saying goodbye to the one good thing to happen in my life for a long time. Ruby and I are on the sofa with a tub of Ben and Jerry's, a Channing Tatum DVD fest, and a bottle of wine. I haven't heard from Sam since he left the flat earlier and I'm nursing a shattered heart. I think I'm in the pits of hell; he was the first man since Callum that I let into my heart and into my bed. I didn't think it was possible to hurt this badly; the pain I felt after Callum pales in comparison to how I feel now. I fell head over heels in love with Sam, but it could never have worked. I never really knew him at all—our lives are total poles apart. He is a famous rock star who lives his life in the public eye and within the glare of the paparazzi's lens. I can't live like that; I like the quiet life, surrounded by my family, my friends and the people who mean the most to me.

It is late evening, and the door taps softly. Ruby and I look at each other.

"Do you want me to go? If it's Sam, I'll get rid of him."

I shake my head. "I'll go."

I get to my feet and go to answer the door. Danny is on our doorstep waving a bottle of Lambrini and newspaper in the air.

"Oh, my God, baby girl, what the actual *fuck* happened to you last night? Thank God you're all right." He throws his arms around me and squeezes me tightly.

"I'm fine, Danny, honestly."

He pulls away and looks at me. "I was so worried about you, I called you a thousand times, but your phone was off."

He barges into the flat. Ruby and I laugh as he sits down on the sofa.

"I bought cheap plonk, it's always good in a crisis!" He puts the newspaper down on the table. "Listen to this!"

I look at the headline 'Is Bolt heading back to rehab?', and I inwardly cringe at the invasion of Sam's privacy. How does he deal with living his life under the scrutiny of the press? It can't be easy on him, and I suddenly feel like I may have been a little too hard on him. Danny begins to read the newspaper article aloud.

"We can exclusively reveal the dark truth of Samson Newbolt. Newbolt, lead singer and frontman of rock band Rancid Vengeance, is at the centre of an all-night booze and cocaine binge. Samson, or Bolt as he is known to his diehard fans, dubbed as rock's bad boy, could be heading back to rehab because of a drug-and-booze-filled album launch. Rancid Vengeance, whose line up also includes Jackson 'Flash' Chase, wild man Brody 'Snake' Hart and Lucas 'Axeman' Landon, celebrated the band's tenth-anniversary album launch last night at premiere night spot *Neon Nights*, owned by playboy Ryan Holmes. Newbolt, who has recently hit the headlines for dating the daughter of 1970's pin-up model Sophia Bailey, was spotted snorting cocaine and guzzling vodka after an alleged spat with Harper and manager John *Johnnie Diamond'* Dalton. In the past, it is widely known of Newbolt's battle with drugs, severe manic depression, and a previous stint in rehab." Danny tuts and rolls his eyes. "Where the fuck do they get all this shit from, baby girl?"

I put my hand to my head and flop down on the sofa in-between Ruby and Danny. They both put their arms around me, and I'm glad to have the support of my two best friends.

I spend all day on Sunday hiding out in the flat, vegging out on the sofa, staying away from the newspapers, Internet, and the gossip columns, avoiding my phone like the plague, nursing a broken heart, and catching up on missed sleep. I also spend some well-needed girl time with Ruby. I don't hear from Sam all day, not until I am ready to crawl into bed that night. I am lying in bed staring at the ceiling, my thoughts racing through my head at a thousand miles per hour, trying to get to sleep and my phone vibrates. I grab it from my bedside table and look at the screen. Sam's name and a picture I took of him while we were in bed one morning with him looking gorgeous and sleep mussed flashes up. It feels like my heart skips a beat. I open the message.

I miss you so God damn much

S xx

I consider not replying, but he deserves a chance, a chance to explain.

I miss you too

P xx

I do miss him. I miss waking up to him in the mornings. I miss the way his arms feel around me. He completes me—he is the other half of my heart, and I'm willing to let it go all because he decided to keep a secret to himself. I start to think of his previous words, that everyone is entitled to a past, and everyone should be entitled to secrets too. Suddenly, I find myself feeling bad for judging him so harshly. I am about to reply, as my phone vibrates again.

Then come to me, I just want one more night, please.

I want to sleep next to you one more time; I want to feel your heartbeat.

I want your head on my chest and my arms around you. I want to feel your skin against mine.

I want to pretend, just for one night that we didn't fuck

it all up. That you're still mine...

S xx

Before I have even finished reading the text, I'm pulling on my clothes. I have to go to him; I can't stand one more minute without him. I hate myself for being so weak where Sam is concerned, but I can't deny my feelings for him. Despite all our faults, we are good for each other. I throw some things into my overnight bag and go out into the living room. Ruby is already in bed, so I try to be as quiet as I can. I grab my coat and leave Ruby a neon pink post-it note stuck to the fridge.

Gone to Sam's

Please don't worry about me

I promise I'll call you tomorrow

P xx

I leave the flat quietly and make my way to the parking garage. I start my car and begin the journey to Sam's place. Before I know it, I'm pulling into Sam's parking garage and heading up to his place in the waiting lift. My heart is pounding in my chest as the lift ascends and I'm wondering if he will be pleased to see me. The lift slowly stops, and I step out into the familiar foyer. I walk over to the door and knock gently. Sam answers the door bare-chested, in loose jeans and bare feet—he looks so much better than he did yesterday. He is clean-shaven, and his hair is back to its familiar spiky style. His eyes are back to the same sparkling green as he looks at me, taking me in as if he can't believe I am actually standing in front of him.

"Angel."

He wraps me up in his strong, muscular arms, and I wrap my legs around his waist. I can't get close enough to this gorgeous man. He takes me inside, kicking the door shut behind him, and sets me down on my feet.

"I spent the whole of yesterday in the pits of hell because I thought I'd never see you again."

I'm glad I wasn't the only one.

"I'm so sorry. I overreacted, and I didn't give you a chance to explain properly. Please forgive me."

He reaches out and strokes my face.

"There's nothing to forgive, angel, I'm the one who should be on my knees begging you for forgiveness. I lied, and I kept things from you."

"It's OK; I just need you to be honest with me. Make me understand, Sam."

His eyes glaze over, and he nods. "I promise I'll tell you everything, baby."

Sam makes us both large mugs of hot chocolate and marshmallows. I smile at his sweet, simple gesture, and we snuggle up on the sofa.

"I still see the papers, the pictures on the Internet, and the news reports today from the day I went into rehab; they still come back and haunt me after all these years. All I want to do is to give that pale, ill, withdrawn, scared, and fucked up kid a hug. Looking back, I think I was actually scared how successful we were becoming—we were invincible, no one would say no to us, whatever we wanted we got it, no questions asked. When I told you that Jax saved me, you have no idea what that boy did for me. Brody and I went on a seventy-two-hour bender, we stumbled from one club to another, they wouldn't refuse us because we were spending ridiculous amounts of money and they could say that they had celebrities in their club. We were doing speed bombs, popping pills, snorting coke, and drinking, all to excess. Everywhere we went, the press were there, following us, they wouldn't leave us alone. We were still new to the music industry, we already had an album out, which was doing quite badly at the time and we were about to release a second. We were hot property, so any press coverage was good for our profile.

We ended up randomly wandering into some guy's student house party just to get away from them. This guy was so happy that Bolt and Snake from Rancid Vengeance were at his party. They welcomed us, we did shots, took a lot of drugs, and we were completely off our faces. Brody won't touch heroin because that's what killed his mum, but I thought why not. I wanted to forget who I was for a while. I injected heroin that night, and I blacked out. The next thing I remember is coming around in the hospital with J.D. and the rest of the band at my bedside. Apparently, I overdosed that night. Jax scoured the streets looking for us, and we were followed as per usual. There was a photographer parked not too far away, and he led Jax to us—he found me just in time. I had my stomach pumped, and J.D gave me an ultimatum: go to rehab, or he was going to kick me out of the band. I chose rehab. I owed it to myself, my band, my family, and everyone around me who I had let down. The next day, I was flown to a rehab centre in Connecticut, I was twenty-two years old and going into rehab. I was fucking terrified. I was there for thirty days, and it changed my life around completely. It stopped me from spiralling further into that world. I owe Jax *everything* for finding me that night."

I listen to his story intently and am shocked at the revelations Sam has revealed to me. I am relieved and glad that he is finally being totally honest with me. I snuggle closer to him, and he squeezes me tightly.

"I've wanted to tell you all this for a long time, but I was scared you'd run from me again. I kept putting it off. The more we got to know each other, the deeper I was falling in love with you. I know it's selfish, but I didn't want to ruin what we had by dragging up the past unnecessarily. I'm not a drug addict anymore, I swear, but Brody brings out the worst in me. It was stupid and careless of me to let you just walk in on us like that. I wasn't thinking straight."

I shake my head and put my finger to his lips to stop him from talking.

"Shhh, just take me to bed, baby, I need to feel your arms around me," I whisper, and he smiles that familiar dazzling smile that I love so much. He takes me to bed, no other words needed.

The next morning, I wake before my alarm and surprisingly, before Sam, even though I don't have to be at work until twelve. I pull on a white shirt of Sam's and go out into the kitchen. I want to surprise Sam by cooking him breakfast. I turn on the iPod dock and listen to soft music, the distinctive sound of Hinder coming through the surround sound system, while I set about finding the ingredients for breakfast. I make bacon, scrambled eggs, and toast—I am not the best cook in the world, but I can make a mean breakfast! I am dancing around, singing, and playing air guitar in Sam's kitchen when I hear his soft chuckle.

"Someone's in a good mood this morning!"

I look up, embarrassed at being caught singing and dancing like a total loon.

"Good morning, angel, something smells good."

He strides towards me and pulls me into his arms, kissing me gently on the lips.

"Good morning, handsome, I thought I'd surprise you."

He smiles—even in the mornings he looks delicious. He is shirtless giving me a glimpse of his perfectly-sculpted muscles and tattoos. He is barefoot, and his hair is perfectly sleep mussed. He is wearing a loose-fitting pair of grey jogging bottoms that hang off his hips, revealing a perfect V on his lower abdomen.

"You didn't have to."

"I wanted to."

He perches himself on the worktop. "Is there anything I can do to help, angel?" he asks gruffly.

I take the warming plates out of the oven and place them on the worktop. I shake my head and plate up the food as Sam's observes me carefully moving around his kitchen. I didn't realise how hungry I was until my stomach growls in protest. I take the plates over to the table, and we sit opposite each other. Sam smirks as he takes a mouthful of food. I look at him expectantly, waiting for his reaction.

"Mmm, it's really good." Sam smiles.

"Whatever flips your pancake, babe." I smirk, and he regards me intently.

"Do I flip your pancake then, angel?"

He sounds amused. I bite my lip seductively. I am sat in his kitchen, wearing my lacy black bra, a pair of sexy black French knickers, with Sam's white shirt open, barefoot and comfortable.

"Don't bite your lip please, baby, because I haven't had you since Saturday night. I've been *aching* for you."

He knows how much his voice affects me; he is doing this on purpose! I run my foot up the inside of his leg, teasing him. He gives me a knowing look, and I feign innocence. *Two can play that game, Newbolt.*

We finish our breakfast in a comfortable silence. After breakfast, we make slow, leisurely, sensual love on Sam's silk sheets. Satiated and relaxed, we take an unhurried shower, and I dress for work. I am checking my reflection when Sam comes behind me, wraps his strong arms around my waist, and rests his head on my shoulder.

"You look gorgeous, baby," he says as he kisses my neck.

"So do you, rock star."

I wink and cuddle him tightly before grabbing my coat and bag ready to start my first week as shop manager at work. I kiss Sam goodbye, promising to meet him for lunch. Sam leaves with me, and we make our way to the parking garage. Sam blows me a kiss goodbye, jumps in his Porsche, and speeds out into the London traffic. I smile to myself, unlock my beloved car, jump in the driver's seat, and crank up the stereo to get my morning shot of rock music. I am in the mood for a bit of Stone Sour and Corey Taylor's dulcet tones blast through the stereo, and I sing along and begin my journey to work with a stupid grin plastered across my face. I'm in the best mood I have been in in a few days.

I drive to the exit, and the security gate automatically lifts up. Cole must have recognised my car on the CCTV. I am about to pull out of Sam's parking garage, and a bus is coming in the opposite direction. I go to pump the brake, panicking when I realise that the car isn't slowing down. I pump the brake more furiously.

"Come on," I plead. My voice sounds hysterical, and I realise the car isn't stopping. That's when everything went black.